NOBLE BEGINNINGS

Also by Christine Marion Fraser

RHANNA
RHANNA AT WAR
CHILDREN OF RHANNA
RETURN TO RHANNA
SONG OF RHANNA
STORM OVER RHANNA
STRANGER ON RHANNA

KING'S CROFT
KING'S ACRE
KING'S EXILE
KING'S CLOSE
KING'S FAREWELL

Autobiography

BLUE ABOVE THE CHIMNEYS
ROSES ROUND THE DOOR
GREEN ARE MY MOUNTAINS

CHRISTINE MARION FRASER

NOBLE
BEGINNINGS

HarperCollins*Publishers*

The characters and events in this book are entirely
fictional. No reference to any person, living or dead,
is intended or should be inferred.

HarperCollins*Publishers*
77–85 Fulham Palace Road,
Hammersmith, London W6 8JB

Published by HarperCollins*Publishers* 1994

1 3 5 7 9 10 8 6 4 2

Copyright © Christine Marion Fraser 1994

The Author asserts the moral right to
be identified as the author of this work

A catalogue record for this book is
available from the British Library

ISBN 0 00 224101 3

Set in Linotron Galliard by
Rowland Phototypesetting Ltd
Bury St Edmunds, Suffolk

Printed in Great Britain by
HarperCollinsManufacturing, Glasgow

TO KEN,

For keeping me fed and watered
when the muse is upon me.

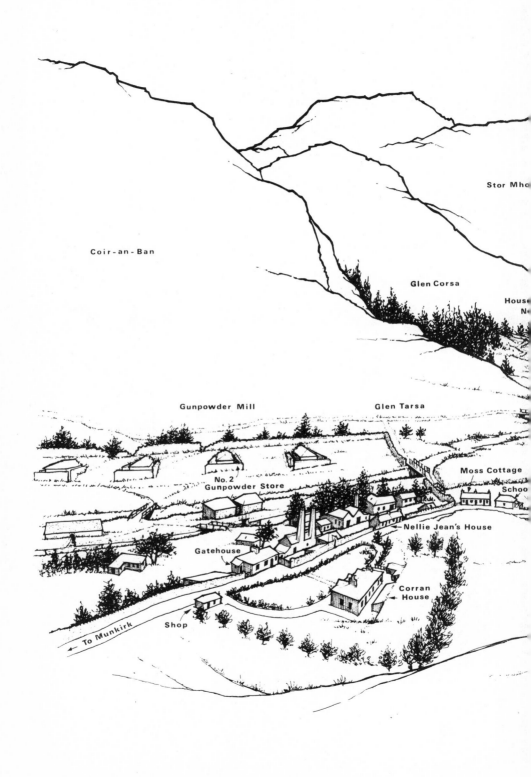

Coir-an-Ban

Stor Mho

Glen Corsa

House
N

Gunpowder Mill

Glen Tarsa

No. 2
Gunpowder Store

Moss Cottage

Schoo

Nellie Jean's House

Gatehouse

Corran
House

To Munkirk

Shop

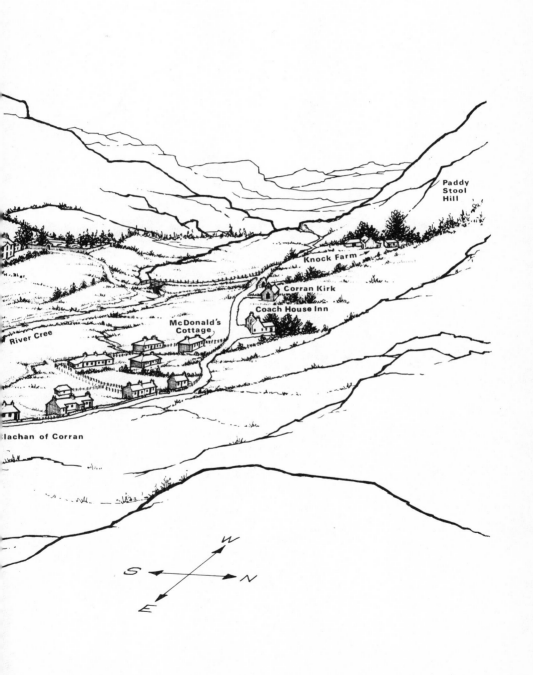

PART ONE

1889

Anna

ANNA LAY IN BED, listening to the wind sighing and whining through the corries of the hills, before it came gusting down to moan amongst the trees on the banks of the River Cree, stripping the crackling leaves from the branches, tossing them helter-skelter against the rooftops of the mill buildings.

It was like the lamenting wail of a human voice, sad, lonely, lost, a tormented soul of the night, strong and forceful in its persistence. Eerie too, out there in the darkness . . . as if it was a flesh and blood creature who stalked the sleeping countryside . . . hiding in the trees, creeping round the house, waiting, just waiting – to pounce!

Anna's heart missed a beat, in a burst of terror she pulled the sheet over her head and lay as still as her shivering limbs would allow. Half suffocating, she strained her ears – listening – listening – for what? The wind sucked in its breath, in the stillness the mournful hoot of an owl echoed amongst the trees, far in the wooded glen another owl answered the call, then there was silence.

But still she listened – for other things that were far more frightening than anything made by nature and the elements – house sounds, creaking timbers, groaning walls, mice scampering behind the skirting, bits of plaster falling down . . . the sound of feet that went creeping and shuffling through the rooms – ghostly feet – or something else . . . ?

Gasping for air she threw the sheet back from her face. An oblong of light had lanced the darkness of the room. The pale face of the September moon was shining through a cloak of purple-grey clouds. The misty shreds clung on to it for quite some time then suddenly it was riding the heavens, high and clear, a huge silvery sphere that shone like a brilliant lantern above the hills.

Seen from the girl's cold little room it was like a picture, framed by the window, and she stared and stared at it, praying for the clouds to disperse so that the shaft of light lying across her bed would remain there till she fell asleep.

A smattering of dry leaves rasped against the window pane, like the fingers of someone scrabbling to get in, and Anna snuggled deeper into her sparse blankets as the wind rushed through the sash which, summer and winter alike, lay open to the elements.

'You must learn to be tough! Bairns are pampered nowdays! When I was a lad I often had to break the ice in the tub before bathing in the cold water.' She shuddered as her father's voice broke into her thoughts like a stinging whiplash. He had preached such things so often they were imprinted into her brain, just like the cruel brand burns on the beasts who grazed the slopes of the Corran Estates.

The boom of the river rose above the sound of the rain now lashing down outside. It had been a wet September, and the frothing burns on the hills had swollen the River Cree into a spate that roared into the deep bowl of The Cauldron, a peaty brown pool that swirled restlessly twenty feet below the overhanging rocks of the riverbank.

Anna loved the river. When it was calm it brought her a sense of peace, when it was a raging torrent she made herself stand on the Overhanging Rocks so that she could look directly into the gaping black mouth of The Cauldron.

With the rocks trembling and beating beneath her feet she would feel terror and heart-sinking apprehension, but above all, the knowledge that here was power, timeless, indestructible, awe-inspiring.

And Anna liked things that had their own order in the world – her small world – so often insecure – so powerless and helpless . . .

The rain stopped, the wind abated, the even breathing of her brothers sounded very peaceful in the sudden hush of the night.

They were huddled together in the double iron bedstead in the corner, close in the harmony of their dream-world as they never were in their waking hours.

It was a sleepy sound. Anna listened and felt her eyes closing. Her limbs were heavy with fatigue yet she knew she wouldn't rest till she heard her father come home.

He never bothered to quieten his movements for the benefit of the sleeping household. Every night it was the same. She would hear him going through his nightly preamble of roughly stirring the fire with the heavy brass poker before settling down to smoke his pipe.

Back and forth, back and forth, creak, creak, creak the rocking chair would go before there was a pause in which he would tap his pipe against the bars of the grate. It was a very fancy pipe with a hinged silver hood and a transferable mouthpiece, but nothing was too good for Roderick McIntyre, under-manager of the gunpowder mill.

Creak! Creak! Creak! Tap! Tap! Tap! The sounds would go on for perhaps half an hour before he would get up to blunder along to his room which was situated at the front of the house through connecting doors from kitchen and parlour.

If the mood took him, he never hesitated to call Anna from her bed to make him a hot supper of brose and thick tea. If he came home with Nellie Jean, supper was the last thing on his mind. Anna knew she could rest easier – except for the hoarse giggles and moans that filtered through the dividing wall of his room.

But Anna had learned to accept such things as part of the night, they had been a regular feature of her life at The Gatehouse ever since her mother had 'gone away to the asylum' when Anna was just six years old.

Anna couldn't remember things before that too clearly, she only knew that her mother had been a gentle person who had loved her dearly.

'She was a quiet woman, your mother,' people told Anna. 'She always kept herself to herself and none of us knew her very well. After your brother Adam was born, it seems she withdrew into herself even more. Some say it was a difficult birth and she was never right afterwards. At times she seemed fine, then she would start shaking and crying and no one could get her to stop. She was never violent though, and never harmed anyone, but she couldn't take care of herself, never mind look after her family. In the end the doctor decided she would be better locked away for her own and her family's good.'

That had been almost seven years ago now, though sometimes it seemed only yesterday that her gentle, bewildered mother had stood trembling at the door of the cottage, tears in her eyes while she waited for the waggon to 'take her away.'

The cruel chants of the village children echoed in Anna's mind, words that she would never forget. 'Set a trap to catch a moose! Your mammy's in the loony hoose!'

'No, no,' Anna whispered, 'please don't say these things about *her*.'

The calm, hazel eyes of her mother smiled into her thoughts and the warm, firm hands of the past seemed to reach into the present to reassure her.

'You're not mad, Mother, I know you're not!'

Over the years she had longed to see her mother again but Roderick wouldn't hear of it. 'She isn't fit to see anyone, she's become violent and would tear you to pieces as soon as look at you,' he had said firmly. 'She's got worse as the years have gone by and thinks everyone's against her. Demented, the doctor called it. A deterioration of the brain. I asked if I could bring you all to visit but he advised me against it, they don't encourage children to go to these places and that's an end to the matter.'

Anna licked the salty tears from her cheeks and buried her face into her pillow. She turned her head again, straining her ears as she listened.

Because her bedroom lay at the back of the house it was difficult to make out the comings and goings on the quiet country road at the front.

It was easy enough to hear the clatterings of horses' hooves and the rumbling of cart wheels on the stony ground but footsteps of people weren't so easy to distinguish, especially the stealthy paddings of anyone not wishing to be heard.

But all was quiet, except for the wind keening round corners and moaning down the chimneys.

The clouds were scudding along and now the sky was clear, with the stars winking in the dark reaches outwith the bright halo of the moon. A ray of brilliant light lay over the rough, woollen coverlet on Anna's bed. Extricating a hand from the blankets she touched the moonbeam with a sense of wonder. So transient a thing, so cold a light, yet so welcome in the darkness.

Objects in the room stood out from the shadows. Adam and Magnus, humped shapes under a jumble of patchworks; the sturdy outline of the mahogany tallboy; the dull glint of pewter on the scratched surface of the dresser; the bulky oblong of the crofter's kist over by the window.

Everything that the room contained was purely functional. Roderick McIntyre maintained that there was neither need nor space for anything that induced 'vulgar primping'.

His one concession to anything that could be called embellishment took the form of drab samplers that hung on the walls throughout the house. Enclosed behind oblong pieces of glass each one bore a motto of a religious nature. The one above Anna's bed spelled out a gloomy message. 'A flighty spirit may soar high but never reach heaven.' Above the boys' bed, male superiority was conveyed with the words, 'Man is all things to all people, humbler creatures be glad to serve him and allow him to further his purpose.'

From experience Anna knew only too well what the samplers meant. Women were the humble creatures, put on the earth for man's use. It was wrong for females in her position to seek life's pleasures and if she allowed herself to laugh or sing too exuberantly she would pay for it later on because her spirit would somehow miss the path to heaven.

The thought worried her a good deal. Despite the restrictions imposed on her she was prone to light-heartedness and out in the open fields she often sang aloud with the sheer joy of living. Then there were those other times, when euphoria bubbled inside of her, and there was simply no way she could stop that happening. Times like now, when the Highland moon lit the dark night with silvery beams and the wind played with the rustling autumn leaves.

As the moments passed her spirit was soaring higher. No matter how much she tried to push it down, it kept on rising till her heart bumped in her throat.

'Please, God, I'm sorry about this but I can't help it,' she whispered before reaching for her shawl at the foot of her bed. It was a beautiful garment, crocheted for her by old Grace, a widow woman who lived in tiny Moss Cottage in the Clachan of Corran.

The moonlight sparkled on the shawl's rainbow colours and lovingly Anna wrapped herself into the soft folds. Gingerly she put her feet on the cold floorboards. Despite the warmth of the shawl she shivered as the keen night air swept over her.

But the moon was beckoning, and resolutely she skipped to the window to stare with delight at the black mass of Coir an Ban etched against the sky. Coir an Ban, the fair mountain, misty green in spring-time, golden in summer sunlight, tawny in fiery autumn, cold and forbidding in November when the sun disappeared behind its craggy shoulder. In winter Coir an Ban was dark and bare with mist skulking in the corries and great gleaming icicles hanging from the rocks like gigantic teeth. But winter and summer alike Anna loved it and always found solace whenever she gazed up at its glowering bulk.

Tonight she could see everything quite plainly: the sparkling gleam of a burn; the glint of the rushing river; the sturdy outlines of the stone sheds; the winding water courses, black and snakelike in the shadows; the waggon rails twisting through the mill workings; the wooden bridge leading over the river to the store buildings with their thick protective baffle walls.

Huddling into her shawl, Anna murmured softly, 'River Cree, speak to me, speak before you reach the sea.'

The river swished angrily into The Cauldron and a chuckle escaped the girl's lips. She was a thin little sprite with an oval face and deep set blue-grey eyes fringed by abundant dark lashes. Her skin was fair, with a pure milk and honey complexion of an alabastrine quality. The fairness of her was doubly enhanced by eyebrows that were almost white and a long mane of flaxen hair that hung round her shoulders like a silken mantle.

She was known to everyone as Anna Ban, the fair one, the child who had been obliged from an early age to take a woman's place in the home.

When it had become apparent that Lillian McIntyre's stay in the mental asylum was to be more than a temporary one, the villagers had waxed eloquent on the subject.

Moira O'Brady, who ran the post office, had not minced words over her opinion. 'A disgrace! A child of that age cooking and cleaning for the likes o' Roderick McIntyre! Poor, poor, Lily, no wonder she went off her head wi' a man like that to contend with!'

Janet McCrae, proprietress of the local general store, had nodded in agreement, even though she knew that Moira didn't give a hoot about Anna or her welfare. Moira O'Brady didn't like children and took no pains to hide the fact. Her attitude brought out the worst in the village youngsters who simply delighted in dreaming up deeds of mischief that never failed to incite her to fury. It was quite a common sight to see a red-faced boy or girl being decanted from her premises, helped on their way by a wildly thrashing broom or anything else that came to hand.

But more than anything, Moira hated Roderick McIntyre. Very few people liked him, but Moira's aversion to him was extreme and no one, not even the most inquisitive in the community, had managed to find out why this was the case, though it certainly wasn't for the want of trying.

Moira's solicitous words about Anna didn't fool the kindly Janet but since the postmistress had very neatly voiced her own sentiments on the subject she couldn't help but say, 'Ay, you're right there, Moira, I know fine he could well afford to get someone in to see to the house but no! He has Anna! A poor mite who looks as though a puff o' wind might blow her away at any minute.'

Anna hadn't blown away. Over the years she had developed a strength of character that more than made up for any physical frailties. She had found her own ways of escaping the harsh realities of her home environment.

'A dreamer!' her father was always saying that, making it sound like an accusation. 'One o' these fine days you'll find out there's more to life than roses and rainbows!'

Sitting at the window, bathed in the white rays of the moon, Anna was certainly not dreaming of roses and rainbows. She was preoccupied with much more immediate things, matters that were of great importance to her, though they might not mean much to anyone else.

She wasn't aware of the cold seeping through her threadbare cotton nightdress. Old Grace had offered to make her one of cosy flannelette but Roderick had sneered when Anna had mentioned it to him.

'Flannelette! Whatever next will you think of? Look to yourself smartly, madam, or you'll go naked to bed, and that's a promise.'

Anna shivered, her breath came out in frosty puffs. Next month was her birthday and, after that, she would never be twelve again as long as she lived. The realization made her clasp her hands to her lips. The enormity of the coming occasion had the effect of making her feel still and silent inside of herself.

Being thirteen meant being grown up. It also meant she was on the brink of becoming a witch! All through her childhood her father had told her she had all the makings of a witch because she liked to braid flowers in her hair and brighten her drab clothing with little pieces of lace and simple ornaments.

But to be a real witch you had to stop being a child and become grown up. Next month, on the ancient festival of Samain, the festival

17

of Hallowe'en, she would be thirteen and, according to her father's prophesies, she would turn into a creature that nobody liked and everybody feared.

The thought was very sobering. Time was galloping away, she had only a few weeks left to hold onto her childhood.

A muffled sob broke from her lips and her eyes filled up. The moon blobbed and wavered above the crags of Coir an Ban, the stars swam together till the whole sky looked like the glistening waters of Loch Longart on a sun-bright day.

CHAPTER TWO

Magnus and Adam

BED SPRINGS CREAKED AND Anna's brother Adam emerged in tousled indignation from his mound of patchworks. 'What are you crying for?' he hissed unsympathetically, the edge of his voice dulled by the dregs of sleep.

He was a year younger than Anna, a rude, confident, blundering bully of a boy. His brown hair was tightly curled, his dark eyes snappishly alive in a face that was crudely hewn yet oddly attractive.

Sleep had left him and he sat bolt upright in bed, flapping his arms, making moaning noises in his throat, his face protruding moon-like from the folds of his voluminous nightshirt.

'Wooo! Wheee! I'm coming to get you cos I'm a *banshee!*' He thought this to be very clever and went on mockingly. 'Why aren't you laughing, Anna? Is it because you're afraid o' me? Afraid I might do dirty things to you?'

She didn't answer which only encouraged him to expand further. 'If Father catches you out o' bed he'll give you the *belt!*'

The emphasis on the last word was gleefully vindictive but Anna was not to be brow-beaten. 'Father isn't in yet,' she said evenly.

'He soon will be – if you lift up your nightdress and let me see you naked I won't tell him I caught you at the window talking to the witches.'

The sudden change of subject was no surprise to Anna. He was forever trying to goad her into anger with his spicy tongue.

'I'll let you see me,' he wheedled. The bed springs creaked louder and in seconds he was beside her, looming above her, a head taller than her.

'I'll let you see me piddling,' he sniggered, darting away to reach under the bed for the chamber pot. 'Watch me,' he urged as he lifted his nightshirt. 'Look at my willy . . . look at it, Anna.'

19

He began urinating into the china pot, thin, spurting jets that deliberately prolonged the function, all the while snorting with laughter at his own audacity.

Anna shut her eyes and averted her face, an action which maddened him. 'If you don't look at me you'll be sorry.' He spoke in an eerie, threatening whisper. 'I know about the things that creep about in the night. I know about the Nuckelavee and how it likes girls with fair hair. It saw you at the window, waiting for it, it heard you crying, tonight it will come and get you in your sleep.'

Anna felt her skin crawl. The Nuckelavee was the most horrible creature to spring from the superstitious minds of the Dark Ages. It was reputed to have a rotund body and a hideously lolling head; with no legs to aid its travels it dragged itself about on long arms, its muscles contracting and expanding and its blood visibly coursing through its skinless body.

The idea of such a gruesome monster, carrying her off in its transparent arms to some nameless den in the black night hills, provoked her to anger at last. Turning, she faced her brother, but before she could speak he stuck out his pelvis and jeered, 'I made you see my willy! I made you see my willy! Come on, Anna, touch it, you'll like it, it grows big and hard when you play wi' it. I could come into your bed and we could play wi' each other. Sheena McCrae lets me do it to her in the shed at playtime, so does Bunty Walters, all fat and fanny and giggling her head off when I take her knickers down . . .'

His proud boasting was interrupted by the sudden appearance of Magnus who grabbed his young brother by the scruff of the neck and bulldozed him back to bed.

For a few surprised moments Adam was speechless but it wasn't long before he found his voice: 'Don't you dare touch me again, Magnus,' he growled warningly, 'or I'll tell Father you were hitting me.'

'The day I start hitting you I promise I won't ever stop,' Magnus spat the words out contemptuously. 'You were tormenting Anna again, weren't you? You dirty wee upstart!'

Adam sniffed loudly and scuttled under the blankets while Magnus took Anna by the arm to lead her back to her bed.

'You shouldn't be up,' he said quietly. 'You're freezing.'

'I was waiting for Father to come in. I couldn't sleep for fear he would call me up to make his supper.'

'I know, I know,' he said soothingly, pushing her into bed and tucking the blankets round her. 'But you needn't worry tonight, Anna. He's gone down to the inn at Munkirk and he won't be coming home alone. Go to sleep and don't worry anymore.'

'Ay, Magnus . . .' She paused. 'It wasn't just Father – it's – next month – my birthday. I'll be thirteen years old.'

'It just means you'll be a year older,' he said placatingly, though inside of himself he felt an anger that Anna's birthday would be just another day for her, no different from any of her other chore-filled days.

Their father could easily have paid someone to see to the running of the house. He seemed to have plenty of money to spend on his doubtful pleasures but his only concession to helping his daughter was to give blankets and quilts twice yearly to old Grace who 'took in washing'. He also paid Janet McCrae to bake fresh bread and scones for him because Anna was, as yet, too inexperienced to make bread to his liking and he couldn't stand the 'bought stuff.'

Magnus suspected the gestures weren't for Anna's benefit. Roderick was jealous of his standing in the community. He prided himself as a man of charitable inclinations whose kindly actions to those less fortunate than himself spoke louder than words; a man who conducted himself and his affairs in a dignified manner despite having the burdens of a sick wife and a daughter who was too lazy and too vain for her own or anyone else's good. 'As proud as a pea-hen is our Anna,' he would say with an indulgent shrug of his shoulder and a smile of patient resignation. 'Always too busy day-dreaming and decorating herself with ornaments to be of much help in the home.'

Magnus thought of these things and his fists bunched. He was too young yet to face up to the bull-like strength of his father – but the day was coming! And when it did he would be only too ready to meet it!

'Father says I'll become a witch when I'm grown up.' Anna's words were muffled by the bedclothes.

'Och, come on!' Magnus's voice was gruffly teasing. 'When your birthday comes you'll still be the same wee lassie you are tonight – after all . . .' He gave a soft chuckle. '. . . some people never grow up. I don't think Adam ever will and Father hasn't though he must be forty past.'

Anna didn't fully understand all of this but she felt better, Magnus always had that effect on her. 'Will you coorie in beside me, Magnus, just for a little while. I'm so cold.'

He climbed into bed beside her and put his strong young arms around her, as he had done ever since he was a toddler and she was just a baby.

She was warm and soft against him. 'Wheesht, my babby,' he crooned into her hair. 'No harm will come to you while I'm here.'

'Tell me a story,' she requested, her lips brushing his ear.

His spine tingled, it was a strange sensation, that warm little mouth of hers innocently touching him as it had done on countless occasions . . . only this time it awakened in him something that made him feel hot and restless . . . and uneasy.

Guiltily, he moved away from her but she was having none of that. She snuggled into him, closer than ever and to cover his feelings he said abruptly, 'Alright, I'll tell you a story, but only a short one, I'm getting sleepy.'

Without further ado he proceeded to weave an imaginary tale around the Norse Earl, St Magnus, rich in adventurous deeds.

'You won't be killed by an axe the way St Magnus was killed by his cousin, Haakon, will you?' she asked urgently.

'I don't have a cousin,' he answered lightly, 'At least, not that I know of.'

A stealthy scuffling of sound came from the kitchen. Brother and sister held each other tighter. In the corner Adam snored in the oblivion of sleep, unaware of the creaking of doors, the padding of feet.

Their father's room was just through the wall from theirs, a wall that was more than two feet thick but which couldn't entirely shut out Nellie Jean Anderson's muffled giggles or the hoarse, deep mutterings of Roderick McIntyre.

'He's brought *her* again,' Anna hissed tearfully. 'Why does he bring Nellie Jean to sleep in Mother's bed, Magnus?'

'I don't know. Go to sleep. It's none o' our business.'

'It is our business, it's our mother's bed. Do you remember, Magnus, how good it was when we were little and Mother used to chap messages through the wall? The one I liked best was the four knocks that meant, "Goodnight, bairns, sleep well." Sometimes I think I can still hear her tapping that out to us.'

'I remember, Anna, I miss her too and hope someday she'll come back to us.'

'Do you really think she will, Magnus? It would be wonderful to have her home again.'

'Hope, Anna,' he said gently. 'Always hope for the best.'

Anna sighed, she curled up against him and put her arms round his waist and he held her close till her even breathing told him she was asleep.

The animal-like grunts and moans from the next room were growing louder, interspersed every so often by an excited giggle. Then came an obscenity from Roderick's throat, followed by a quivering wail that was eerily primitive and very disquieting.

Not a man, thought Magnus, a creature, a lusting wolf that lifts its nose to bay at the moon; a wailing warlock that wanders the wilderness of darkness, seeking release from its ungodly urges; a being of dark and primeval forces unleashing its unholy desires for all the world to hear . . .

The wailing was reaching a pitch, growing thicker, coarser, to be followed by a shuddering groan, a long, drawn-out sigh, a few sleepy mutterings and . . . silence.

The hot flush of shame burned through Magnus's being, almost as if it was he who was lying in his mother's bed, betraying her memory by his lusting and craving, mounting a woman who had no right to be there, riding her like a stag in rut . . .

His heart pounded, he felt strange and sad and lonely – very, very lonely – and bewildered. These things that had happened to him in the embrace of his very own sister . . . how could he feel like that . . . think like that?

Gently he extricated himself from Anna's trusting arms and crept over to the bed in the corner, his half of which was uncomfortably cold.

His very bones were leaden with weariness but for a long time he lay awake in the moonlit room, thinking of his father and Nellie Jean through the wall, lying so shamelessly together, smug in the knowledge that not a hint of their indiscretions would ever filter outside The Gatehouse.

Adam was too frightened to utter a word, Anna was too hurt and too proud, while he – Magnus – was so filled with bitter shame and humiliation it was as if he was personally responsible for his father's depravity.

Never, never, would he breathe anything to anybody, far less to the coterie of village crones who were only too ready to seize upon any spicy titbit of gossip that came their way.

23

Magnus buried his head deep into his pillow, the contempt he felt for his father twisting his mouth. He was fifteen now and no longer did he look at the world through the innocent eyes of a child.

CHAPTER THREE

Birthday Morning

ANNA AWOKE STILL FEELING tired. It was five o'clock. There was no alarm clock at her bedside to stir her awake, nothing but the habit of years, even at the weekends when she didn't have to go to school.

The room was dark in those hours before dawn. Adam still snored, there was no sound from Magnus. The biting chill of the October morning swept in through the window, the smell of winter was in the clean hill air.

Anna wasted no time in dressing herself, first slipping her legs into her brown woollen frock and pulling her arms and head out of her nightdress. Hastily, she fastened the bodice of her dress before completing her attire with long-legged bloomers, brown lisle stockings and finally, a pair of stout boots.

The stockings and boots were a luxury, one that was denied many of the village children who went about barefoot in all but the worst months of winter. But in Roderick's book the McIntyres were 'a cut above the rest' and the boots were a status symbol that was not to be treated carelessly. Anna could have given lectures about them herself, so well did she know every warning word. She must never kick stones with them, nor walk in puddles; scuffing was a crime worthy of a clipped ear and a hole in the sole guaranteed a belting.

If Adam did any of these things that was different. There was a separate set of rules for him altogether.

Very aware of every step she took, Anna was almost afraid to wear her boots, but if she hadn't she would have got a clipped ear anyway so she couldn't win, whichever way she might handle the situation.

Splashing her face and hands with cold water from the pewter basin on the dresser she dried herself hastily then went to kneel by her bed.

But not to pray. She had seldom asked for Higher Help since her mother's departure from the house. God, she reckoned, had deserted her when she most needed Him in her life, she only addressed herself to Him when it was strictly necessary, be it to apologize for small, unimportant misdemeanours or the trivial untruths she so often had to invent to make her life bearable.

Magnus was her god, one who was there when she needed him, a warm and wonderful being who provided her with love, who worried about her and protected her with all his young strength.

Magnus was real, God wasn't. In her bruised thinking it was as simple as that, even though she went to kirk on the Sabbath and pretended to pray and ponder with everyone else.

Her treasures weren't of the soul but of the heart, and they were kept under her bed in a small writing case. Here was stored all her small possessions, things that her father would most certainly destroy should he ever lay hands on them. Only Magnus was aware of 'the secrets of the writing case' and she knew he would never tell.

Old Grace had given her the case some years before. It was made of fine wood with a hinged, leather-covered writing top which, when lifted, revealed a row of small drawers. Most exciting of all was the tiny secret compartment at one side which could only be opened by releasing a securing pin on the carrying handle.

Eagerly she felt for the pin and the drawer sprung open. In the darkness her fingers curled round the heavy silver necklet that had been given to her on her sixth birthday by Lillian McIntyre before her departure to hospital a few weeks later.

Sometimes Anna wondered if her mother had known she was going away and had given her the piece of jewellery as a token of her love.

At the time she had said sadly, 'Keep this always, my baby, it will protect you from evil.'

'Where did you get it, Mother?' Anna had asked.

'From someone who loved you.'

'Who, Mother. Who was it?'

'Don't ask, Anna, just remember it's yours by right. Don't let *him* see it though. He would know . . .' Abruptly she had checked herself and Anna would always remember her face, pale and frightened, and those words 'He would know . . .'

What would her father know? She had asked herself the same question a hundred times but could never find the answer.

26

Magnus didn't understand either. When she told him about the strange conversation he had shaken his head in puzzlement.

'Maybe she was trying to say he isn't what he seems,' he had once hazarded and they had gazed at one another, wondering what it all meant – if indeed it meant anything. Their mother's mind was unbalanced, so their father reminded them often enough, she might say anything without really knowing what it was she was trying to convey.

Anna had never worn the ornament; it was enough just to look at it and to trace the outlines of the raised silver hearts surmounted by a crown set with two sparkling stones. A solid silver backing, in the shape of one big heart, encompassed the design, giving it a rather clumsy appearance. But Anna treasured it and was always reassured by its solidity. Unlike more fragile structures, this one looked as if it might last forever, and things of that nature always pleased Anna.

She wondered if she ought to wear it. But what would her father say, do, if she displayed such an elaborate decoration? Reverently she traced the hearts with loving fingers, agonizing over her decision, then, with a resolute toss of her flaxen head she clasped the chain round her neck and tucked the silver hearts inside her dress.

It was her birthday! She had every right to wear the precious gift, even if she was the only one who knew it was there. From another one of the tiny drawers she extricated a delicate piece of snow-white tatting and pinned it under her collar, spreading it out till it resembled a fanned dove's tail.

There, she told herself, now you're a real birthday girl and Father will just have to put up with it.

She pushed the writing case back under the bed, making a scraping sound on the floorboards. Adam stirred, muttered in his sleep. She held her breath, but in moments all was silent again and, tiptoeing to the door, she opened it and slipped through to the kitchen.

The room was cold, a penetrating cold that seeped into the marrow. Last night Roderick had come home late again and he hadn't bothered to damp the fire with wet dross. He forgot about such domestic matters when Nellie Jean came home with him. They always went straight to the bedroom – to the bed – Mother's bed.

'Happy Birthday, Anna,' the girl murmured with a rueful smile and went to fetch her apron from its hook on the door. The kindling was

27

kept in a box on one side of the hearth, another of paper twists was stored in a small cupboard near the fireplace.

Raking in the box she grabbed a handful of the expertly rolled twists and knelt down by the grate. Only then did she see that the fire was already set and the tiles clean and tidy. The door opened and Magnus came in laden with logs, bringing with him the sharp tang of morning.

'Magnus!' she gasped. 'Why are you up so early?'

He grinned. 'Wheesht! I knew the fire would need re-kindling and decided to get up a bittie earlier than usual. Farm workers can't afford to laze about in bed, even on darker mornings. Anyway, it isn't fitting for a birthday princess to tackle such chores.'

'Och, Magnus, you shouldn't,' she said quietly even while her heart sang at being called a princess. He hadn't forgotten it was her birthday; she ought to have known he never did and always tried to make the day special for her.

In minutes a cheery blaze was leaping up the chimney. Anna swung the big black kettle over the flames to heat the water for her father's wash and shave. She had already set the table the night before so that all her morning jobs would be accomplished before she left for school.

Even so she was sometimes late. There was so much to do, both in and out of the house, and she was never allowed to leave until she had completed each task.

But it was worth it, to get away, to mix with other children, to sit in the classroom and be a part of it all, and to learn about things that went on in the world – the big world that existed outside the Clachan of Corran – big, wide, and unreal, but interesting and exciting for all that.

Worth rushing about for, even though she was often so tired it took her all her strength not to nod off in the classroom. Miss Priscilla McLeod was very disapproving of that sort of behaviour, taking it as a personal insult, or a disruptive influence, even as a sign of dumb insolence, or perhaps a mixture of them all, depending on the mood she happened to be in at the time.

Anna didn't mind Miss Priscilla's moods, she understood them, she liked her teacher very much indeed and she loved the way she explained things, clearly, precisely and patiently. Yes, Miss Priscilla was very precise, an uncluttered woman with an uncluttered mind – and strong – despite an unhappy past – strong, and bold and unafraid.

Perhaps that was why Anna liked and understood her and hoped one day to have that same kind of strength herself.

Clover lowed in some annoyance from her stall when Anna at last opened the door of the little hayshed above the manger to throw in a bundle of hay.

Clover had been house cow to The Gatehouse for nearly seven years and she knew its routine well. She liked to be fed and milked with the utmost allegiance to her inner clock and she rolled her eyes in disapproval when Anna came flying down the mossy steps to the byre, ten minutes later than usual, swinging the milk pail in a most frivolous fashion.

Anna patted the cow's nose, it was wet, warm, and woolly. Clover was that kind of cow, rough, hairy, soft in places, tough in others. She also had a mind of her own and kicked the pail away twice before condescending to stand still and allow herself to be milked.

'Moody old besom!' giggled Anna. Pulling up her little stool she laid her brow on Clover's shaggy flank and began working the soft teats in a rhythmic movement. The milk squirted out in steady spurts, the creamy foam rose higher in the pail.

'It's my birthday today, Clover,' Anna imparted conversationally, 'I'm thirteen years old and I'm grown up. You and Fern are just babies compared to me.'

From the adjoining stall Clover's summer calf snorted impatiently and the girl laughed, 'Alright, Fern, I'm coming with your milk, then I must get Father's breakfast. I wish he was as easy to please as you but all he ever does is grumble and complain.'

Leaving the byre she went to look at a cloth of crowdie cheese that was dripping on its hook outside the larder window. The air was cool and sweet and forgetting the cheese, she stood there, breathing deeply. Trails of frosty vapour lay over the shadowy fields; dawn was just a streak of silver in the eastern sky above the hills of tiny Munkirk village, nestling in a hollow two miles distant.

The wind had died completely away, and the tall trees that bordered the high wall surrounding the mill stood silent with just an occasional puff of air stirring the brittle leaves.

Coir an Ban was swathed in gossamer scarves of mist. Only its dour, dark shoulder rose clear against the sky while down below some tiny roe deer were making their way out of the trees.

Anna hesitated, wondering if she had time to feed the graceful little animals, then, making a swift decision she ran to the hayshed to seize a small bale which she carried to the field to scatter near the trees. The deer had disappeared but no sooner was she back at the house than they reappeared to eat the unexpected treat.

Footsteps at her back startled her and she swung round with a little gasp but it was only Magnus, his tanned skin glowing from a recent douse in ice-cold water.

'Father's up,' he told her. 'You'd better hurry wi' the cheese.'

'I haven't started the porridge yet!' she cried in panic. 'I was feeding the deer.'

Magnus smiled at her. 'Your birthday's gone to your head, Princess, but don't worry, it's already made and bubbling away merrily on the stove . . . I've got something for you – only a wee thing,' he ended with a touch of embarrassment.

He held up the lamp he was carrying and she gazed at the object he had pushed into her hand. It was a lovely book, filled with pictures of famous paintings by the old masters. It was also an expensive book and her heart twisted with emotion as she thought about all the extra work he had been putting in lately at the farm.

He had been saving up to buy her a present and she bit her lip to keep back the tears.

'It's beautiful, Magnus, I can't believe it. I never get anything on my birthday.'

'Then it's high time you did. Don't worry, I can manage, I'm getting a shilling a week extra now that I'm fifteen.'

She looked at him, his face was alight, and she loved him more than ever for his thoughtfulness. He had none of the brash good looks of his younger brother; his beauty was of the heart, a shining quality that radiated out of him like a light.

He was tall for his age, with muscles on him that were rock hard from days of sweated labour in the fields; his hazel eyes reflected inner strength; a firm, strong jaw made him look mature beyond his years; his mouth was wide and sensitive and his thick wavy hair was the colour of autumn leaves.

More than anything Anna treasured the way he cared for her and protected her and made her existence bearable.

He knew her so well, her moods, her wants, her desires, and gazing down at the book she said simply, 'Thank you, Magnus, I'll look at it over and over again.'

'Ach well, I know how much you enjoy all that art stuff, but we've blethered too long, we'd better get in, the old man might throw a tantrum if breakfast is late.'

Slipping the book into her apron pocket she went to collect bread and oatcakes from the cool, stone-flagged larder, before following her brother indoors where the fire was stealing away the chill of morning.

Adam was seated at the table, fidgeting restlessly, his hair rumpled, his shirt creased.

'Go and wash and tidy yourself,' ordered Magnus firmly, 'I've been clouted for less.'

'Father won't clout *me*,' came the cocksure answer. Nevertheless he got up and went back through to the bedroom while Anna lifted the heavy black kettle from the swee above the fire.

Her thin young arms ached with the effort, sweat broke on her brow. Now came the time of day that she dreaded; peace was about to depart, in its place would come blackness and unrest.

But somehow the thought didn't disturb her nearly as much as usual. It was her birthday and she was happy. Magnus had been right, she still looked and felt the same as before. She hadn't turned into a witch and she never would. She felt good about herself, she was wearing her mother's necklet, the white lace at her throat made her feel special, Magnus's book nestled in her pocket.

It was a lovely morning to be thirteen years old, and no matter what her father might say and do in the coming hours, he could never ever take away those first precious minutes of her birthday.

CHAPTER FOUR

Roderick McIntyre

RODERICK WAS IMPATIENTLY WAITING for his hot water, but he said nothing as Anna poured it into a china basin set into the middle of an elaborate washstand.

Roderick's bedroom contained so much evidence of luxury it was wholly out of keeping with the rest of the house. The marble-topped washstand was fitted with towel rails, a mirrored splashback, and a neat little cupboard. Behind the china jug and basin stood a conical container that held rings and other pieces of jewellery. Some of it belonged to Anna's mother though a few items were missing, having found their way into Nellie Jean's possession.

Anna looked at the crumpled sheets on the roomy double bed and she couldn't suppress a shudder. Later she would have to tidy the room and clear away soiled linen carelessly left under the sheets or below the bed.

Nellie Jean had already departed to her own cottage which was situated a short distance away. Anna was quite fond of the widow woman. She was carefree and sunny natured, good with children though she'd never had any of her own. She had often pressed little gifts on Anna but lately the girl had refused them and Nellie Jean now looked at her with wary eyes.

Although she had left The Gatehouse in the early hours her heavy perfume still hung in the air, cloying into Anna's nostrils, making her shut her eyes so that she wouldn't have to look at the bed.

But she couldn't shut out the sickly-sweet smell of Nellie Jean nor could she forget her hoarse curses and giggles of the night before.

'Will that be all, Father?'

Anna spoke the words automatically. Every day she asked the same question and this day, as on every other, all she received in reply was a rude grunt of dismissal. She crept out quietly.

Roderick was too taken up with his reflection in the mirror to bother his head with much else. Bleary eyes peered back at him and he experienced a pang of unease. He looked older than his forty years this morning. The pale halo of light from the lamp cast his eyes into deep sockets and seemed to find grey hairs everywhere, even in his nose and ears.

He had drunk too much last night. The aftereffects throbbed in his head, the taste in his mouth was thick and sour. He stuck out his tongue and stared with distaste at the furring of yellow that reached right back to his tonsils.

In some annoyance he grabbed his toothbrush and scrubbed at the offending coating till his tongue tingled.

'Moderation, my lad,' he told his reflection indulgently. 'Next time, moderation.'

He could limit the drink, but how could he take Nellie Jean in small doses? Last night she'd extracted every ounce of his strength with the enticement of her smooth, big-breasted body. Every part of him had throbbed with his need of her and in the night she had awakened him again. Exhausted, he had pushed her away but she had soon roused him once more and, locked together, they had writhed in the bed like two animals.

God! The woman was insatiable! At times he felt he could take no more of her but, afraid that she might desert him for someone else, he occasionally managed to fob her off with gifts of money and trinkets.

She was discreet about their relationship, he had to admit that, if she had been anything else he would have sent her packing long ago.

Sometimes, when his tongue was loosened by drink, he told her things he would never dare tell anyone else though he doubted if she ever took any of it in. She was so intent in pursuing the pleasures of her flamboyant life she never seemed to be serious about anything. Still, he would have to learn to be more careful, one never knew with a woman – any woman.

Vigorously he stropped his razor before applying it to his soap-lathered face. The blade rasped over his skin.

Hot-blooded bitch! His thoughts were still on Nellie Jean. He watched himself in the mirror and stuck out his chin. Hot blooded, lovely bitch! He would show her who was boss man in her life. He wasn't known as Iron Rod for nothing! The perpetrator of his nickname, whoever it was, had invented it to portray his authoritarian ways, but Nellie Jean had soon discovered its other meaning. She had told him often enough that no one satisfied her the way he did. And that took some doing!

Before her there had been others but none of them could hold a candle to Nellie Jean. They were all so insipid in comparison, he could hardly remember what any of them had been like in bed. At times he thought he must be losing his memory, but he reckoned his affair with Nellie Jean was so overpowering it overshadowed all else.

The children were seated at the table, waiting for their father, while the porridge grew thicker in the pan, its ebullient bubbles gradually slowing to dismal sluggish plops.

Roderick strode into the room and, taking out his pocket watch, he glanced at it meaningfully. 'Five forty-five! We're late this morning, my girl! You'll have to be quicker with my hot water in future!' He was himself again, strong as a bull, confident. The wash and shave had restored his ruddy complexion, his skin shone in his coarse-featured, heavy-jawed face. He was crudely good looking with his neatly clipped moustache, thick greying hair, brown eyes and immaculate clothing.

He stood with his back to the fire, a thick-set, sturdy figure, muscular arms folded behind him in characteristic fashion, legs apart as he rocked on his heels, charging the atmosphere with tension as he began his morning catalogue of fault finding.

For fully ten minutes he rambled on while the ever-thickening porridge adhered to the pan and the tea grew cold on the table.

When he eventually seated himself he glanced at each face briefly and accusingly. The children bowed their heads, waiting for him to say Grace in his gruff deep voice.

'Lord,' he intoned with just the right note of meekness, 'We ask you to forgive us our sins and to help us lead humble and useful lives. Look mercifully upon the weak in our midst and show them the error of their ways. Let us always be thankful for the food and drink on our table. Amen.'

Anna rose to fetch the porridge. Its texture and appearance resembled cement and she had to coax it to leave first the pan and then the wooden spoon.

He eyed the contents of his plate in disgust and said scathingly, 'Your cooking grows worse by the minute, my girl!'

'We were waiting for you, Father.'

Anna's voice held a note of defiance and he looked at her sharply. 'Were you indeed, madam? Is our little witch criticizing her betters again? Speak when you're spoken to or you'll find my hand across your ears.'

She stood beside him, saying nothing, her head held high, her face pale above the white tatting at her throat.

'All dressed up in silly bits o' lace,' he sneered, his leering face so close to hers she could smell the staleness of his breath. 'You've got fancy ideas for a lass o' your standing, ay, very fancy, blood will out, eh? If you'd been reared in a cave in the hills it would still be the same story. I wonder if it's blue!' he sniggered.

Anna stared at him, wondering what on earth he meant. Surely he was speaking in riddles, last night's drink still fermenting inside his head.

'But I nearly forgot,' he continued, 'today is your birthday, isn't it? How does it feel to be a witch, madam? You are indeed a strange one. A fair witch! There can't be many like you around. I wonder if you'll be accepted by the other witches.'

'I don't feel like a witch, Father.' Her chin trembled but her voice was steady. 'I feel much the same as I did yesterday.'

'Oh do you now? Will you still feel the same when I tell you that next week you'll be leaving school? You can tell that to old Miss – whatshername! The house is neglected, my girl. There is no time to spare for all this silly schooling when you're needed at home. Go to your place now and let the rest o' us sup our food in peace – if food is the correct word for pigswill!'

'Can I leave school too, Father? I want to start work at the mill.' Adam cried so eagerly he choked on a spoonful of porridge.

Roderick threw back his bull head and laughed, 'A boy after my own heart. Not afraid o' hard work! But stay wi' your school books awhile yet, my son. Come spring we'll talk about it again.'

Adam grinned and dug into his porridge with a triumphant flourish. Anna tried to swallow some food but found it sticking in a throat that was tight and dry with unshed tears.

Leave school! Forsake the one thing that meant so much to her. Her happiest hours were spent in the cosy little classroom with Miss Priscilla McLeod of Knock Farm, whose wisdom made Anna forget for a while the daily drudgery of her existence.

Magnus's hand crept under the table to squeeze Anna's. His face was taut with anger but he knew it would be useless to say anything. It would only cause a scene and put Anna in a worse position than ever.

'This table isn't set properly!' cried Roderick, pushing aside his half-eaten porridge with a disdainful grimace. 'Oatcakes and bread, ay, but nothing to put on them! Where is the crowdie?'

Anna scraped back her chair but Magnus was up first, 'I'll get it.'

'Sit down, boy!' thundered Roderick. 'It's a woman's place to do such tasks.'

Magnus clenched his fists. 'There is no woman in this house now that Mother's away.'

Roderick's eyes darkened with rage, 'Be quiet! How dare you interfere! Your sister is woman enough to do the work around here. Why can't you be like Adam and accept that?'

Magnus's lip curled. 'I'll never be like him.'

'Ay, you're right!' snarled Roderick. 'You'll never be like Adam. You're like her, neither o' you belong here and never will – now – sup your food, boy, and get along to the farm! There's plenty o' work waiting for you there.'

Magnus pushed oatcakes and cheese into his lunch box and went quickly outside, followed by Anna who had dared to leave the kitchen without Roderick's permission.

'I'm sorry you got into trouble because o' me,' she said quietly.

'Och, don't worry about that, he's in a foul mood, probably suffering from a hangover . . .' He frowned. 'In his temper he said some strange things, though.'

She shivered. 'Sometimes I think he doesn't really know what he's saying, rage gets the better o' him and he just enjoys hurting us. You'd better get along, I'll bring you some broth when school is over.'

He took her small hand and held it briefly. 'It doesn't matter, you've enough to do here. I'm – sorry about school. I couldn't leave it soon enough but I know how much it means to you.'

'Ach well, it's the way o' things,' she said with a weary philosophy that made her sound old beyond her years. 'I often wondered how long it would last – now I know.'

At six twenty-five precisely Roderick let himself out of his front door to walk to another door at the far end of the building. This was the entrance to his office where, as timekeeper and under-manager of the gunpowder mill, he spent his working hours, though certain periods were taken up in leisurely strolls through the mill workings, his over-vigilant eye and continual interference being a constant source of irritation to the employees.

The entire gunpowder estate was like a fortress: at the main entrance, outside Roderick's office, massive stone pillars supported heavy wooden gates; a high wall ran to the edge of the village, continuing round to enclose acres of woodland that successfully camouflaged anything that was man made.

Other entrances were used mainly for horse-drawn supplies of empty barrels from the Munkirk cooperage. The filled barrels were then stored in the sheds to await delivery to Munkirk where they would be loaded onto cargo vessels when the tides were right on Loch Longart.

Looking at the wooded glades inside the mill acres, seeing the sun gilding the sylvan fields, hearing the river meandering peacefully along, it was difficult to believe that anything else but beauty and tranquillity reigned there. In reality however, it was a potentially dangerous place, everyone who worked there knew of the hazards but were never over-shadowed by them. After all, it had been in existence for a long time and so far only two men had been slightly injured, one of them being Angus McLeod whose facial hair had been badly singed but only because he'd been drunk at the time and had dropped a forbidden cigarette into a minute amount of gunpowder.

Roderick unlocked the gates and swung them apart. He glanced at the clock set into the window of the men's changing room which was on the walled side of the grassy track. Fumbling for his pocket watch he checked it against the time clock. Both were exactly right and he smiled with satisfaction. Hooking his thumbs into his waistcoat he spread his thick legs and took a deep breath of air. The morning was still sharply cold but the blue sky held the promise of a fine day ahead.

His head was clearer now. He felt much better. Rocking on his heels he chuckled and thought. Twice last night, my lad, and ready for it again. Watch out, Nellie Jean, tonight I'll show you what I'm made of.

Tonight? But it was Hallowe'en! The night of the Samain Ball held annually by Lady Pandora at The House of Noble on the Leanachorran Estates. He wouldn't be seeing Nellie Jean tonight.

Lady Pandora's husband, Sir Malaroy Leonard Noble, owned the land for miles around. The mill and the Clachan of Corran were part of it all. He was a wealthy and much-loved landowner whose gentleness endeared him to everyone.

Lady Pandora was altogether different and it was because of her that the doors of the big house were regularly thrown open. Tonight there would be a Hallowe'en party for the children followed by a ball for the estate workers.

Roderick frowned. Since coming to the mill eight years ago he had never been to any of Lady Pandora's social occasions. Lillian had become a near-recluse by then and wouldn't go anywhere, then the poor, silly bitch had very inconveniently gone off her head which meant that he didn't have anyone to partner him anywhere.

She might have been mousy and dowdy but she would have been better than nothing and he could have enjoyed himself a bit more.

Still, he chuckled, in many ways she had done him a favour; he was free of her now even though he was still married which meant he could satisfy himself with other women yet remain unfettered. None of them could very well argue with a marriage certificate!

But at times like this it was damned difficult. To go to the ball he had to have a partner. Sir Malaroy had issued him with the invitation a week ago. It had only been done out of politeness and he had been somewhat taken aback when Roderick had accepted.

Because, partner or no, he had decided he *would* go to the ball, mainly because he was sick to the teeth of listening to William Jordan rabbiting on about his social standing with The House of Noble.

Jordan was manager of the mill, a position that had earned him a fine eight-roomed house set in two acres of walled and wooded ground that was well cared for by a gardener and two jobbing men. Corran House was almost directly across from The Gatehouse and was a constant reminder to Roderick of his lesser managerial status.

He had been determined to show Jordan that he wasn't the only one who could hob-nob with the gentry, but now that the time had come his pride made him rebel at the idea of going to a dance alone.

He couldn't take Nellie Jean; she was alright for the bedroom but that was all. Roderick stood there, deep in thought, in his mind going through all the single women of his acquaintance. One by one he discounted them as being unsuitable. Then he remembered Rachel Simpson, the wife of the Reverend Alistair Simpson. She had mentioned her disappointment at not being able to attend the ball this year. Her husband was in bed with influenza and was likely to remain there for a day or two at least.

What could be better? And so respectable. Rachel was a fine woman, hardly glamorous but that didn't matter. All she wanted was an escort. She was the gregarious sort and would be quite happy mixing with all those other cackling jays who had too much to say for themselves, while he found his own amusement.

His eyes gleamed. There would be plenty of attractive women for him to pass the night with. If she agreed it would be a perfect arrangement and as soon as clocking-in was over with, he would take the gig and go down to Munkirk to see her.

The mill was beginning to stir. At the far end of the lane, Jeemie McGregor and his son, Calum, were leading the Clydesdales out of the stables. Voices and laughter grew steadily louder outside the wall as the workers came drifting along from the village. Cartwheels rumbled on the road, bringing mill employees from Munkirk.

Roderick looked at the clock again. Six-thirty! He would have to talk to the lazy buggers! They were supposed to start work by six-thirty and here they were, chattering their heads off, seemingly without a care in the world as they clattered in through the gates to the changing rooms, men in at one end, women at the other, the women giggling like fools in response to the male banter on the other side of the wooden partition.

'Get a move on,' growled Roderick, 'And leave matches and other inflammables in the shed.'

He gave the same order at the beginning of every day and behind his back the men mouthed the words as he spoke them.

'One o' these days I'll light a bonfire in the storehouse and blow him and the whole shooting match to hell!' muttered a big, burly Munkirk man known as Boxer Sam.

The men shouted with laughter and Roderick glowered at Boxer Sam. Their tolerance of one another was built on flimsy foundations. In Roderick's book Sam was just a labourer unworthy of any standing in the community while he, Roderick McIntyre, was a figure of authority who had the right to be treated with respect.

Boxer Sam however, viewed matters from a different angle. In Roderick he saw a man whose inflated ego very badly needed deflating and he took great pleasure sticking the pins in where they would hurt most. He also knew that he was highly regarded by William Jordan, and Roderick could not dismiss him.

Roderick enjoyed socializing but kept away from the Coach House Inn, it being too near home for his own good. Because of his role in the church, he had to be very careful of his public image and whenever he could he took himself off to the inn at Munkirk where he would be less likely to bump into his immediate neighbours.

Even so, there were a few flies in the ointment, one of these being Boxer Sam who was a regular customer at the inn, so much so he might have been one of the props holding the place up! He even had his own particular seat, kept vacant for him by his cronies should he be absent for any reason! To make matters worse, the proprietor of the Munkirk Inn condoned all this and was altogether indulgent of Boxer Sam and his loud, loathsome ways. Roderick knew the reasons for this. Boxer Sam was a good draw. Everybody liked him, the coarser the jokes and stories he told, the better. He could also play any musical instrument he chose and whenever he was present the place fairly bounced with music, laughter and song.

Roderick didn't really mind any of that. In fact, if truth be told, he thoroughly enjoyed the ribaldry though never would he admit that to anyone. Sam's music, his stories, the fun and the banter, were all part of the carefree atmosphere, and if that had been all there was to contend with, Roderick would have been happy.

But that wasn't all. Boxer Sam took a positive delight in flirting openly with Nellie Jean and he, Roderick, could do nothing about it since his contrived meetings with that particular lady must be made to appear as purely chance affairs.

In these respects Boxer Sam had Roderick over a barrel but never, by word or action, would Roderick give him the satisfaction of seeing how much it rankled.

Nellie Jean came breathlessly through the gates, a handsome, full-busted woman in her mid-thirties, tossing the black hair out of her eyes, all smiles and dimples and flashing dark eyes. 'Sorry I'm late, Mr McIntyre, I had an awful job risin' this morning.'

Her meaningful tone, her confidence, annoyed Roderick. 'Don't make a habit of it, Mrs Anderson!' he said sharply.

The look she threw at him was one of pained surprise before she flounced away to the changing shed.

The men were dispersing to various parts of the mill. Boxer Sam brushed past Roderick and with a meaningful glance at Nellie Jean's disappearing back he murmured, 'Your bed would be well warmed last night, eh, McIntyre?'

He swaggered unhurriedly away leaving Roderick to look after him with rage-blackened eyes. If Boxer Sam didn't watch out, his days at the mill were numbered, Jordan or no Jordan.

CHAPTER FIVE

Elizabeth Jordan

ANNA LET HERSELF OUT of The Gatehouse to meet Elizabeth Jordan who was waiting impatiently at the end of Corran House driveway.

'Anna! I've been here for ages!' she cried in annoyance. 'We'll be late for the bell. What kept you?'

'Sorry, Beth,' Anna apologized breathlessly, 'I had to see to Clover and Fern and then I had to feed the hens.'

'Never mind all that, let's go.' Beth linked her arm through Anna's and as they hurried along, she continued importantly, 'I've got something for your birthday but I've got no time to rummage in my satchel for it just now. I'll let you have it at playtime.'

Beth had been Anna's close friend for as long as she could remember. She was a tall girl for her twelve years with a freckled complexion, pale blue eyes and long, sandy hair which was invariably tied back with an expensive satin ribbon.

Everything that Beth wore was of the very best. Everyday dresses of finest wool were offset by pinafores of starched white linen. Visiting clothes and Sunday best were made from such grand fabrics as velvet, muslin or silk, according to the season of the year. Her shoes and boots were of quality leather and it didn't seem to matter if she scuffed them or damaged them in any way. Her father scolded her mildly, her mother fussed for a time then took her into town to see the shoemaker.

Beth was an only child and Anna often wondered if that was why her parents treated her with such lenience. Violet Patterson of Dundarroch Hill Farm had no brothers or sisters either and *her* mother also spent a great deal of time and money dressing her up, while Mr Patterson smirked with pride when he led her into kirk on Sundays.

Anna knew it was the mothers who were behind the clothes and the pretty ribbons. Fathers might indulge their children but it was the mothers who took care of their appearance.

Anna had never been spoiled nor indulged. Her father only ever thought about himself, and her mother . . . her mother had been gone from her life so long now she was beginning to forget what it had been like when she was at home.

Anna looked at tall, self-assured Beth, with her disconsolate mouth and confident air. Anna thought she was beautiful with her sandy hair shining in the morning light. Everything about Beth was lovely, elegant and expensive but Anna felt no jealousy, only gratitude that Beth had remained her best friend for so long when she could have had the pick of the more affluent children in the glen.

'A present, Beth?' Anna said, trying to sound calm but unable to resist saying in the next breath, 'I wish it was playtime now so that I could see it. Magnus gave me a present too – a book.'

'That was good of him – I don't suppose that horrible little Adam gave you anything – or your father?'

'N-no . . .' Anna slowed to a halt and continued in a whisper, 'Beth, do I – do I look any different to you today?'

Beth gave her friend a long, considering look, her gaze travelling from the stout, well-polished boots to the drab little frock with the lace at the neck. The fresh air had stung Anna's face to a glowing pink which enhanced her eyes and her tumble of flaxen hair. Beth felt a pang of envy at the sight and wondered how her friend always managed to look exquisite despite her lack of finery.

'You look the same as ever, Anna – why do you ask?'

'Father always said I had the makings of a witch because I was born on Hallowe'en. He said I would become one when I was thirteen years old and grown up – that's today, Beth.'

Beth laughed derisively. 'Ach, your father's a silly man! How could anyone as fair as you are be a witch. And you're not grown up yet – I mean, you don't have . . .' She lowered her voice and with her eyes indicated Anna's chest, '. . . big bosoms or any of the other things that the *real* grown-ups have – do you?'

'No,' Anna's voice trembled with relief, then she remembered something else. 'I'm grown up enough to leave school. Father said I've to tell Miss Priscilla that I won't be coming back after next week.'

Beth stared, aghast at what she had just heard. 'After next week!

Anna! You can't leave school just like that! Miss Priscilla would never allow it! And what will I do for a best friend?'

'We'll still be best friends, at weekends and everything.' Anna, unable to bear the thought of losing Beth, spoke swiftly and anxiously.

'It won't be the same!' cried Beth furiously. 'He's a hard man that father of yours!'

She stomped along moodily and Anna felt sick with misery. Her brooding was interrupted by the sight of a figure coming along from the Clachan of Corran. Long before it reached them they heard the familiar cry, 'Nearly nine and everything's fine!'

It was Donal McDonald, better known to the village children as Daft Donal.

He was a fair-haired youth of twenty with a forward-leaning gait that made him seem as if he was about to trip himself up at any given moment. His boyish features were finely hewn but for a loose mouth that was always twisted into a leering grin.

He was one of a family of three mentally handicapped children whose first-cousin parents were dead, leaving the trio to fend for themselves as best they could.

Daft Donal's father had 'worked to Leanachorran' and so now did Deaf Davie, the eldest son, a dour, quick tempered creature who wasn't as hard of hearing as he liked to make out. Because he had more wits than his brother and sister he was 'head of the house' and exploited his position by regularly thrashing his young brother and brow-beating his sister Sally.

Daft Donal spent his days striding purposefully through the glen, calling out the time gleaned from a single-handed pocket watch which he jealously guarded from his bully of a brother. He could neither read nor write but had somehow learned to count.

He was also a human magpie and would pick up anything that gleamed, whether it was a worthless piece of metal or otherwise. Whenever anybody lost anything Donal got the blame, a fact which was much to the advantage of the neighbourhood children who simply pointed the finger at Donal if they had been careless with money or trinkets.

His disposition was sunny, his temper sweet, and he was well liked. The broken watch could keep him happy for hours, at regular intervals he would put it to his ear, smile, shake it, then go on his way, chanting out his strangely apt little rhymes.

'Listen to my watch!' he cried as he approached the two girls, 'Nearly nine and everything's fine!'

Beth pushed his hand roughly away. 'Och, go away, daftie, your stupid old watch is as simple as you! What is Silly Sally today, then? A duck, or a cow, or a baa baa black sheep?'

He considered the question seriously. Quite often his sister took it into her head to jump out at the village children from behind walls and hedges, realistic animal noises issuing from her frothing lips. It was her unsophisticated way of getting back at them for mocking her.

'Sally's no anything today. Nothing at all.' Donal intoned with a grin.

'Is she ever?' snapped Beth. 'Away you go, Daft Donal! We're late for school as it is.'

'Nearly nine and . . .'

'Shut up!' Beth stamped an enraged foot and Daft Donal took himself off with a pleasant nod, his cries echoing along the road to Munkirk.

Anna looked after him. 'You didn't have to take your temper out on Donal, Beth.'

'You shut up too – or – or I might not give you your birthday present after all!'

Anna's head went up and she disengaged her arm. 'If that's how you feel.'

Beth's lips folded into a grim line. '*That's* how I feel. Anyway, what do I want with a friend whose mother's in the madhouse?'

Anna's face drained of colour, she stopped to lean against a dyke, and immediately Beth's eyes filled with tears of remorse.

Putting her arms round her friend she cried, 'I'm sorry, Anna Ban! I'm sorry! I don't know what gets into me sometimes. I'm just so depressed because you're leaving school. I don't know what I'll do without you. Forgive me, Anna Ban. Say you'll forgive me.'

The only time Beth called her friend Anna Ban was when she was desperately repentant for the unthinking words of her quick tongue. Usually Anna forgave readily but this time she couldn't find it in her to utter a single word and she wondered, as she had so often wondered before, if she would ever be allowed to forget her mother's dreadful illness that had taken her out of Anna's life.

CHAPTER SIX

Lady Pandora

ANNA AND BETH STOOD leaning against the dyke, neither of them looking up as coach wheels rumbled on the road. The clatter of the horses' hooves slowed, stones crunched as Neil Black, the driver, drew the carriage to a halt.

Lady Pandora looked out and said laughingly, 'What have we here? Two little maidens in the doldrums. And the school bell ringing for all the glen to hear.'

Both girls gave a start of dismay, suddenly hearing the clanging of Miss Priscilla's silver hand bell clearly on the breeze. Anna looked up at the smiling face framed in the carriage window and she couldn't help smiling back. Her path seldom crossed that of her ladyship since Roderick had forbidden her to go near The House of Noble. Such a dwelling was 'no place for the likes of witches.'

She often saw the coach passing on the road and once or twice she had glimpsed Lady Pandora riding in the meadows of Leanachorran. Not until now, however, had she been so close to 'the gentry lady' and she couldn't help staring at her.

At thirty-seven Lady Pandora still had the looks of a girl. Her skin was fair and dewy fresh, her honey-gold hair was pinned into elaborate swirls that showed her slender neck and delicate shoulders to advantage. But it was her eyes that were her most striking feature. The irises were a deep violet, circled by purple, with an expression in them so mysterious that to gaze into them was to feel tantalized beyond measure.

The radiance of her smile dazzled the girls but Beth composed herself quickly and said politely, 'Good morning, Lady Pandora.'

'Good morning, Beth,' she responded, though her gaze was fixed on Anna who was regarding her in some awe.

46

'What is your name, child? I don't believe we've met though I'm sure I've seen you around. I thought I knew all the village children.'

'Anna McIntyre . . . Mistress – Mistress . . .' faltered Anna till a quick poke in the ribs from Beth made her finish uncertainly, 'Mistress Noble.'

Lady Pandora smiled. 'What a charming, unspoiled girl – and Roderick McIntyre's daughter too. I believe he has mentioned your name once or twice though he has more dealings with my husband so we seldom get a chance to talk. You have a brother who works on the estate farm – Magnus, I believe?'

'Ay, that's right,' Anna agreed shyly. 'I have another brother called Adam but he's still at school.'

Lady Pandora frowned. 'Strange, I've never noticed any of Mr McIntyre's children at the parties I give.'

'Her father won't allow them to go to parties,' volunteered the bold Beth. 'He makes Anna do all the work in the house because they don't have servants like we do at Corran House. And – because . . .' Beth glanced at Anna's red face before rushing on, '. . . her mother's been in hospital for years now with her head.'

Lady Pandora looked compassionately at Anna's sensitive little face and she felt her anger rising against Roderick McIntyre. She had always found him to be ill-mannered and over-confident but put up with his visits since her husband seemed to have developed an odd sort of liaison with him over the years.

This puzzled her. She felt there was a mystery here, but couldn't work it out. The two men were so vastly different from one another. Sir Malaroy was the reserved type, trusting his friendship only to a chosen few whom he had known most of his life. She wondered what he saw in Roderick McIntyre though she had to admit that the man had a certain unsophisticated charm . . . But no! That was not an apt description of him as he was in no way artless or simple. Crude was the word for him. Boorish. One sensed it there behind the genial veneer.

She knew he took an active part in church affairs, he gave generously to the various fund-raising events for the parish poor – too generously. As if to show himself to be above others of his level.

His character appeared to be without blemish but then she missed a lot owing to the restrictions her position imposed upon her. Even so, unless one was deaf and blind, it was impossible not to miss the whispers and giggles of the servants over the doings of Roderick McIntyre.

She looked again at Anna. The child was well enough dressed, drab but better and warmer than the majority of village children with their poor unshod feet and ill-fitting clothes. But though Anna seemed fairly well nourished she was too thin, her small face was pinched and much too solemn for a girl of her years. Her heart went out to the young girl.

'You must come to my Hallowe'en party tonight, Anna.' Lady Pandora's voice was full of warmth. 'There's enough fruit to feed the entire village and so much of everything else I need as many mouths as possible to eat it all. Tomorrow you'll all be waddling to school like fat little ducks and what will Miss Priscilla have to say if she can't squeeze everyone behind their desks?'

Her laugh rang out, Beth smiled coyly, Anna lowered her head to stare at the ground when all the time she wanted to join in Lady Pandora's laughter and to accept her invitation to the party.

But she knew that she couldn't and so she said nothing, even though she was aware that Lady Pandora was watching her and waiting for her reply.

The horses were growing impatient and Neil Black was hunched on the box, annoyed at the idea of having to wait while 'her leddyship' passed the time of day with two 'bairnies' when he had a whole load of work waiting for him back at the stables.

At that moment old Grace hove into view and he gave vent to an audible groan because she never paid court to time.

She sprachled up to the coach, a kenspeckle figure, dressed in an ancient black cloak, brown leather boots which had burst at the toes, and a tweed deerstalker hat held in place by bits of tape tied under her whiskery chin. Her smooth skin was a rosy pink, her eyes a startling blue, a cloud of snowy hair framed a face that was as artless as that of a child.

But that was only an illusion. Grace had led a long and full life and knew all there was to know about human nature. She was as inquisitive as a bird, as bright as a new button, as wise in the ways of the world as it was possible for someone of her restricted life to be.

Originally from the Hebrides her marriage had brought her to the glen fifty years ago and she had never left it since. 'God's country' was how she referred to her surroundings and woe betide anyone who demeaned it in her hearing.

'A good mornin' to you, my leddy,' she greeted Lady Pandora in her lilting voice, her manner neither awed nor disrespectful.

'And to you, Grace,' Lady Pandora returned with admirable enthusiasm, for a meeting with Grace demanded much patience. She was prone to lengthy meanderings about the past, interspersed with minute details of her adored cat's latest exploits, running into tearful lamentations about her late husband's untimely demise.

Lady Pandora tried never to hurt the old lady by cutting her short but today it was Grace who was in a hurry, much to the relief of Neil Black.

'There you are, Anna,' she began plaintively, 'I've been waiting at my gate for you and myself busy with a tub of washing. I wanted to give you your birthday present since I'll be over at Knock Farm come dinnertime.'

'Your birthday!' Lady Pandora stared at Anna. 'On Hallowe'en?'

'Ay indeed,' said old Grace softly. 'Our Anna Ban is thirteen today. She hasn't her own mother to see to her wee fancies so she has to make do wi' an old wifie like me.' Taking Anna's hand she pressed a small parcel into it. 'Don't be using it to blow your nose in. Keep it for special occasions, then you can show people what a grand wee lady you are. I'm away now, my water's getting cold, I have no time to stand here blethering.'

She hurried away on spindly legs and Neil raised his whip in readiness for a quick departure to Munkirk. Her leddyship wanted more supplies for the Hallowe'en party, as if there weren't enough already. Still, he smiled indulgently, she was a kind one and no mistake. Last year she had given him such a good Christmas box he'd been able to buy boots for his five children with enough left over for some festive treats.

She could twist people round her finger like bits of cotton but no one minded being manipulated by her. She had a way with her that brought out the best in everybody, no matter their station in life. She would likely want to go from Munkirk to Dunmor seven miles away because she liked the shops there. That was why she had ordered the coach instead of the gig, but she was the mistress and had a right to go where she wanted – and he could always pass the time in his favourite hostelry.

The leading horses jibbed friskily, the coach wheels began to turn. Lady Pandora looked back and cried. 'A birthday deserves a party. I'll expect you tonight, Anna Ban!'

CHAPTER SEVEN

Miss Priscilla

ANNA WATCHED THE ELEGANT coach rumbling away over the rough road and slowly she said, 'She's a lovely lady, isn't she, Beth?'

'She's not bad,' Beth grudgingly admitted, annoyed because Anna, despite her lack of sophistication, had attracted all the attention for the last ten minutes. 'She's made us late for school!' she added crossly. 'And that old Grace! She would stop you and talk to you even if you were invisible! No wonder Mother calls her a blether.'

'Don't speak ill of Grace,' Anna's tones held a warning. She was angry for two reasons: one, she loved the old woman who had cared for her in a hundred little ways over the years, two, she was still smarting at Beth's cruel comments about her mother.

'*Your* mother's a blether,' she went on with unusual pique. 'So are you when it comes to the bit. In fact we're *all* blethers when we get the chance so don't pass judgements so hastily, Beth Jordan.'

Beth was a little taken aback by this. She was about to open her mouth in protest when a quick glance at her friend's flushed face warned her against it.

Linking her arm through Anna's, she said persuasively, 'Och, come on now, there's no need to get angry over such a tiny thing. Let's stop grumping at one another and be friends again. Best friends.'

'Alright, best friends – only don't you ever say nasty things about my mother again.'

'I promise, I promise.'

Anna's thoughts were still on the encounter with Lady Pandora and she and Beth chatted about her as they hurried along.

'Pandora, it's a wonderful name – but strange,' Anna said dreamily.

'I know what it means,' Beth said triumphantly. 'I read it in a book of Father's. Pandora was the Greek Eve and her name means "all gifts" though I don't know why. She was created by Hepha – Hepha –something. It's a big word but he was the Greek god of fire. Zeus was the Greek father of gods *and* men and he ordered Hepha-something to make Pandora. Well, he did, and she was so tempting a creature men could never resist her, but all she ever did was punish them. She kept a box full of evil to afflict all mankind.'

'Lady Pandora isn't like *that!* She's sweet and kind and beautiful. She wouldn't hurt anybody!'

Beth nodded knowingly. 'The Greek Eve was beautiful too, all the men fell in love with her because she cast her charm over them only to smite them with evil when they got too carried away. Lady Pandora has power over men. I heard Mother telling Father she's a temptress and a shameless flirt.'

'Well, I don't believe it,' Anna's tone was resolute. 'And even if it is true, if I was a boy I'd fall in love with her too.'

Beth giggled. 'You say funny things sometimes, Anna, but I do think Lady Pandora is kind. Her parties are always special, even better than the ones Mother gives for me. People say she *adores* children but could have none of her own and makes up for it by having other people's children around her, like Lucas and Peter.'

'Who are Lucas and Peter then?' Anna had never met the twins from the big house, but had occasionally seen them going past in the coach with their tutor.

'Their mother was Lady Pandora's sister but she died a few years ago and their father got killed in some sort of accident last year. He was a Noble too, a cousin of the family, so the boys are also Nobles. They'll come into loads of money when they're older but for now they have Mr Mallard who is a fresh air fanatic and he makes them swim and run and climb whenever he can. They're both very wild. Perhaps that's why old Quack Quack makes them do things to get rid of their energy.'

Beth had obviously done her homework well. She paused for breath, eyes shining as she waited for her friend's reaction.

'Quack Quack?' Anna queried, a puzzled frown on her brow.

'Och, Anna! Is *that* all you can say! Oh, never mind, Quack Quack is what the boys call Mr Mallard though he's not really an old duck. In fact, he's actually quite good looking and young too and very, very, fit.'

She gave an impatient shrug. 'All this is beside the point. We were talking about parties. Oh, why don't you come tonight, Anna? You'd love it. Please, please, say yes. It's your birthday and birthdays ought to have parties. If you do I'll still be your best friend even though you're leaving school.' They were almost at the sturdy square little building that was the village school. From the squat chimney a welcoming banner of smoke drifted into the sky.

Although they were late Beth had pulled Anna to a halt to look at her with pleading in her eyes. It was never Beth's way to show excessive emotion and Anna realized how badly her friend wanted her company that evening.

Nevertheless, she shook her flaxen head and said, 'Beth, why do you torment me like this? You know I can't and it only makes me feel bad to say no. I would fair love to go but Father would never let me. He doesn't even allow Adam to go to the big house though he lets him do a lot of things I'm never allowed.'

'Damn your father!' Beth cried passionately. 'Listen, Anna, he doesn't have to know about it. He lets you go to the bonfire on Paddy Stool Hill, doesn't he?'

'Indeed, but I have to be home by nine, never any later.'

As she spoke, Anna felt a strange quiver in her belly at the very idea of going to the Hallowe'en party at The House of Noble.

Beth clasped her hands to her mouth and stared at her friend, the pupils of her pale eyes big and dark with excitement. 'Don't you see? That's just perfect. Your father's going to the ball tonight. He came over to our house this morning and told Father he was going to ask Mrs Simpson if he could escort her and could he take an hour off to go down to Munkirk to talk to her about it. I know for a fact she's bursting to go and will likely accept even if it *is* your old Iron Rod. Don't you see, Anna, he won't be home tonight so you can do anything you want . . . The party's at seven-thirty, so he'll have to leave soon after that to pick up Mrs Simpson and get to the ball by nine-thirty.' She frowned. 'Didn't you *know* he was going to the ball?'

'He never tells us anything but it makes no difference anyway. Every-one would see me and tell him I was there.'

'Really, Anna, sometimes you're sillier than Donal and Sally put together! You can sneak away from the bonfire halfway through. I'll meet you and dress you up as a ghost or something. No one will know you so no one can tell. I've got *two* turnip lanterns that Willie the jobbing man made me. You can have one. Say yes, Anna. I get fed up with you never being allowed to go anywhere with me.'

Beth's enthusiasm was infectious. Anna gazed at her for a long moment before her answer came out in an odd little squeak. 'Alright, Beth – oh yes! There's nothing I want more in the whole world.'

Beth gave a shriek of pure glee and hand in hand they sped up the path to school, slowing to a sedate walk as they reached the door.

The class was chanting monotonously from its reading books, but the volume diminished when the two latecomers opened the door a peep before sidling discreetly round it. Beth tried shutting it with as little disturbance as possible but the hinges needed oiling and gave out a loud 'sque-e-e-e-k' that sounded like an explosion in the suddenly silent room.

Miss Priscilla McLeod was seated at her desk, seemingly engrossed in the lesson. But the class knew better. Even though some of them might falter over the written word they could read *her* better than any book. For the last fifteen minutes Miss Priscilla had been waiting, Miss Priscilla had been watching, Miss Priscilla was getting ready.

But still she pretended not to be concerned. It added to the drama, it did no harm to make children feel uncomfortable for a few moments. Let them squirm like little worms and shuffle their feet as they glanced uneasily at one another, wondering what punishment was about to befall them.

So she didn't look up at the noisy closing of the door. She allowed a few minutes to elapse, minutes in which she feigned great interest in the open book on her desk, the state of her pencil point, the contents of her inkwell.

Then, quite suddenly, her head jerked up as if pulled by a string. The element of surprise had its desired effect. Not only did the recipients of her tactics quail in their boots, the entire class sat ramrod straight, waiting in hushed anticipation for act one to' unfold.

Miss Priscilla glowered long and hard at the two girls standing meekly before her, their hands folded submissively behind their backs. For what seemed a very long time she behaved like a cobra hypnotizing its prey. A pin could have been heard to drop in the utter silence of the room.

Miss Priscilla's strength came not from her physical appearance. She was a wiry haired woman, thin as a matchstick in her long tweed skirt and shapeless blouse. Her steel-green eyes looked enormous behind her thick-lensed glasses. She had a habit of raising her eyebrows and tilting back her head to peer down her long, sharp nose, as if she was viewing everything and everybody from a great height.

She made children feel smaller than they were, an illusion which kept her charges just where she wanted them, very firmly under her thumb.

The older inhabitants of the village said she had been pretty at one time but great tragedy had come into her life when her youthful sweetheart had been killed in the Crimean War.

She had been a mere slip of a girl when the news of her young soldier's death had reached her. She had never looked at another man after that but had buried herself in books and had dedicated her life to teaching.

The little girls in her class thought the tale to be so sadly beautiful they sometimes cried over discussions of it during playtime breaks. The boys scoffed at the girls and their romantic notions and told them that no one 'right in the head' would ever have looked at 'old Prissy McLeod.'

Yet all the children respected and loved her because she made each one of them feel special, even the poor ones whose parents couldn't afford to buy them shoes and who, by unspoken law, sat on one side of the classroom, segregated from the 'snotty snobs' with their wool stockings and leather boots.

To Miss Priscilla, each child that came under her bony wing had some good point worthy of attention. If one showed special aptitude she nurtured it like a fragile seedling in the hope that one day it might blossom into full flower.

Disappointments were a part of her life as all too often she had to let a special child slip through her fingers simply because circumstances at home called for another pair of hands.

In more than twenty years of teaching she had only succeeded in setting a few small footsteps on the road to glory but for her that was reward enough and she continued to feel achievement in the work she was doing, alert to change, continually on the look out for the bright sparks in her keeping.

She worked to a rigid regime and enforced strict rules. One of these was punctuality and woe betide anyone who arrived late in school without a very good reason for being so.

Anna and Beth therefore, stood before her with fast-beating hearts as they waited for her to speak.

'Carry on reading!' she ordered the class as one or two of the more daring were starting to snigger at the discomfiture of the latecomers, particularly Adam who stuck his tongue out at his sister from behind his reading book.

But, as every child there very well knew, Miss Priscilla had eyes in the front, back and sides of her head. Very deliberately she got up and walked to Adam's desk to stand looking down her nose at him.

For a few brief seconds he pretended not to know she was there but the hypnosis never failed to work. Slowly his head came up, tough as he liked to think he was. He wriggled, he sweated, the seat of his pants felt as if it was stuck to his chair.

'Let me see your tongue, Adam,' came the ominously calm order.

Adam stuck out his tongue once more and the delighted class held its breath.

'Ah, yes,' the teacher nodded knowingly, 'just as I thought. Very red and angry looking. I can see why you felt the need to give it an airing. Never mind, I have the very solution. Stick it out and keep it out for the next ten minutes. By that time it should feel nice and cool and dry and you will be only too ready to pop it back into your mouth and keep it there until I examine it again.'

The class almost burst with suppressed mirth while Adam, looking as if he would like the ground to open and swallow him up, sat there, feeling very foolish with his tongue sticking awkwardly out of his mouth.

'Now,' Miss Priscilla at last turned her attention to the girls. 'I believe I heard the pair of you coming through that door some minutes ago, a very noisy entrance you made too. Disturbing the rest of the class and wasting my precious time. What exactly have you got to say for yourselves?'

'Please, Miss Priscilla, we met old Grace and couldn't get away from her.' Beth imparted this piece of information very hastily indeed, anxious as she was to exonerate herself.

Miss Priscilla quickly lowered her head, a ghost of a smile lurking at the corners of her large mouth. She knew only too well the truth of Beth's words since she herself was often hard put to avoid the old lady's lengthy ramblings.

She composed herself, her head jerked up, she glared over the top of her spectacles. 'What a very poor excuse, Beth, and most unfair of you to blame Grace for your bad timekeeping when only minutes ago I saw you both from the window, whispering together. I will take an attendance mark from each of you and you will also lose the privilege of making toast at the fire at dinnertime. Put your fuel in the box and go to your seats.'

Anna placed a log on top of the others that were piled up neatly on the hearth where a cosy fire leapt up the chimney, while Beth unwrapped two large lumps of coal and put them in the brass box by the fender.

Every morning it was the same, each child brought items of fuel to school and as there were more than twenty children in the classroom there was always a welcoming fire burning during the colder months.

As Anna seated herself she glanced at Adam who still sat with his tongue protruding dryly between his lips. His face and his ears were red with embarrassment and Anna knew he would curse Miss Priscilla from here to kingdom come for the next few days.

Her lips twitched, he looked so funny sitting there, not daring to move a muscle for fear of further indignities being heaped upon him. If anybody could sort him out Miss Priscilla could – and he knew it.

At playtime Beth and Anna hurried to a corner of the field and snuggled down beside a big mossy boulder among the birch trees.

Although Anna's whole being was trembling with elation she slowly and carefully unwrapped the flat little package Beth had pushed at her. A blue satin ribbon nestled amongst the folds of tissue paper. Wordlessly Anna stared at it.

'Don't you like it?' asked Beth, biting her lip restlessly. 'I bought it myself, with some of my own birthday money. I thought it would look nice – with your hair and everything.'

For answer Anna stroked the ribbon, her eyes misty. 'I'll never ever wear it – it's so beautiful. I'll always just look at it because it's too good to waste.'

'Och, don't be silly! What's the good of just *looking* at something while it rots away in a drawer? Come on, hurry up and open Grace's present.'

It was a dainty linen handkerchief, delicately edged with snow white tatting, the initial 'A' rather shakily embroidered in one corner.

'I'll never ever blow my nose on it,' murmured Anna, overcome at such a day with so many people giving her presents.

'What's the good of giving you things if you never use them?'

'I do – sometimes,' Anna said mysteriously. 'I'm wearing a really special present today . . . do you want to see it?'

'It's not that bit of lace on your dress, is it? I can see that.'

Slowly Anna withdrew the necklet from behind the collar of her dress and was amply rewarded by Beth's gasp of awe.

'Where did you get *that?*' she cried in wonderment, for once forgetting to be cool.

'My mother gave it to me when I was six but I've never worn it until today. She said it would protect me from evil.'

'It's simply beautiful – and valuable looking. But where did she get it? I mean, she wasn't rich or anything – was she?'

'I don't think so. She just gave it to me and told me it was mine by rights.'

'Well, I'd never wear a thing like that *inside* my dress! I would want everyone to see it and admire it.'

Anna shook her head. 'I can't, Father gets angry when I wear nice things. I don't want him to know I've got it because sometimes – when he's really in a rage – he throws my belongings in the fire.'

Beth thought of her own long-suffering father and she looked at her friend with pity. 'I wish God had given you a nicer father.'

'He gave me a good mother.'

'I know, so you always say – but she's not here, is she? She's in the . . .'

Anna lifted her chin. 'I can't talk to you any longer, Beth, I'd better go and tell Miss Priscilla that I'm leaving school.'

They both stood up and looked at one another.

'I wish you were staying on, Anna,' Beth said fretfully. 'I won't have anyone to share secrets with anymore. I used to think it would be horrid having a tutor like Mother suggested. I threw tantrums and screamed at her every time she mentioned it, now it might be the best thing because I shan't like school one bit without you.' She glanced down at the mossy boulder under the slender birch tree. 'Remember in summer, Anna, sitting here in the shade at playtime? Eating pieces of madeira cake that Fat Jane had smuggled into my satchel?'

Anna thought of the dappled, scented days of summer and the music of the little burn tinkling over the stones. Days of lying on the cool river bank to drink the sweet water from the hill; sitting with bare feet in the brown trout pool; whispers and giggles and big rosy apples from Beth's satchel; luscious chunks of fruit cake and slabs of strawberry tart made by Fat Jane, the excellent cook who presided over the Corran House kitchen.

Fat Jane's proper title was Mrs Higgins. She dropped all her 'aitches' and woe betide anyone who called her Fat Jane in her hearing. Out she would puff her majestic bosom, mightily she would boom in her rich, fat voice, 'I'll 'ave you know my name is Mrs 'iggins! The only person that ever called me by my Christian name was my 'usband and 'e's dead and gone long ago – God bless 'im.'

Beth could mimic her to perfection and she would strut about in front of Anna, pushing out her chest, talking in a 'fat' voice till both of them were rolling about in agonies of laughter.

But despite all their fooling they loved Fat Jane with her kindly heart and the thoughtful nature that always made sure there was enough cake for two in Beth's satchel.

Anna's breath caught in a sob. The boulder wavered and blurred, the tiny golden leaves of the birch trees swam together. 'I remember, Beth,' she whispered before she turned and walked away from her best friend, over the leaf-strewn grass to find Miss Priscilla, feeling with every footstep she took that she was leaving the most carefree days of her childhood far behind.

CHAPTER EIGHT

The Visit

AT 12.30 P.M. PRECISELY Miss Priscilla McLeod arrived at The Gatehouse. Because it was dinner time all was quiet in the mill except for the busy hissing and puffing coming from the boilerhouse in the lane.

A few workers drifted by on their way to the Jenny All shop which was situated a few yards along from The Gatehouse on the opposite side of the road.

A Jenny All shop meant one that sold a great variety of goods and as Mrs Janet McCrae also sold lengths of 'good thick material' at a reasonable price, her premises were popular with the womenfolk who considered it worthwhile to make the journey into the glen, either by 'Shanks's pony' or by horse and cart.

The horsedrawn delivery van was making its way up Mill Brae, pulled by a young Clydesdale called Firth and manned by Todd Hunter who had lived in an alcoholic haze for most of his adult life.

Mill Brae was one of the steepest hills in the county and the horses, who pulled all sorts of loads up its winding way, had to be fit and strong to cope with it.

As it was, the delivery man, better known as Tell Tale Todd, was forced to leave half his load at the Rumbling Brig near the foot of the brae and go back for it after he had disgorged the first half at the top. One of his cronies, Shoris Ferguson, lived in a tiny cottage beside the Rumbling Brig and, to make up for all the difficulties in his life, Todd always enjoyed a good dram and a blether with Shoris before making the second trip up Mill Brae.

He spoke about it as if he was ascending Ben Nevis, attaching to it so many hazards, imagined or otherwise, that a newcomer to the area might really have believed there were wild cats lurking in the woods waiting to spring out, or adders slithering about in the roadside grass just longing to spit their venom at passers-by.

Todd even maintained that once he saw a wolf slinking about in the tangle of trees that bordered the road and he had only just escaped 'by a trouser thread' when it had sprung out at him, all glistening fangs and slavering jaws.

Everyone took Todd and his tales with a pinch of salt but that didn't mean they were averse to hearing them, so entertaining was his way of recounting them and embroidering them with each telling.

Firth was a very patient horse, and he had to be, as his master's route through Glen Tarsa was long and arduous and took them both to many out-of-the-way spots in the course of their working day. At every farm, cottage, and bothy, Todd found reason to dally, drinking so many cups of tea and drams he was forced to make further frequent stops to obey the calls of nature.

Firth was always delighted when he had made the second trip up Mill Brae, knowing that rest and sustenance awaited him at the top. Todd's drams with Shoris made him lose all sense of time and he might spend an hour or more going over his deliveries with Janet before having a bite of dinner with her in the back shop.

Today Todd had received a scare as usual, not on the ascent up the brae but at the Rumbling Brig itself, and he was most anxious to impart his experiences to somebody.

That that somebody should be Miss Priscilla herself was most unfortunate for him since she wasn't in the best of moods, as he soon found out to his cost.

'Good day to you, Miss Priscilla,' he greeted her. ''Tis glad I am to get safely here in one piece. I was attacked, Miss Priscilla! At the Rumbling Brig. A man o' my age and experience set upon in broad daylight before I knew what was happening.'

Miss Priscilla looked down her nose at him. Todd was a little man, with thinning sandy hair, broken brown teeth, and a 'boxer's nose' acquired from one fight too many in his younger days.

He was wiry and tough and very, very loquacious, a man not to be intimidated by anybody, especially a woman. The exception to that rule was Miss Priscilla, and he was soon regretting his impulsiveness in choosing her to be the first to hear his latest tale of adventure.

61

'Really, Todd?' Miss Priscilla sounded as if she was addressing a naughty child. 'Attacked? Are you drunk, by any chance?'

'Indeed, no, Miss Priscilla,' Todd felt like a nine year old, 'I haven't touched a drop all day – well – maybe just the wee one that Shoris gave me to steady my nerves after I was set upon.'

'And what was it today, Todd? A wild cat? A snake? Perhaps a bear or a wolf imported all the way from Canada?'

Todd looked crestfallen but stuck to his guns. 'No, Miss Priscilla, it was lads, those daredevils that live up at the big house, Master Lucas and Peter. Swinging in the trees like apes. Making noises like wild animals. It fair gave me the creeps I can tell you and I was just about to hurry away when they came leaping out o' the trees right in front o' my nose, scaring the shat out o' me.'

Miss Priscilla was neither amused nor impressed by all this. 'Really, Todd, these boys would never be allowed to go to the Rumbling Brig on their own, far less leap about in the trees like wild animals.'

'Oh, but they weren't alone, Miss Priscilla, that teacher chap was with them, him that's called Mr Mallard. He was down on the bank o' the river, shouting instructions at them, only he didn't tell them to pounce out on me the way they did.'

Miss Priscilla had heard all about Mr Mallard and his unorthodox methods of teaching. He wouldn't have lasted more than a day at any other establishment, but The House of Noble was different. Lady Pandora had some very strange ideas in her head about lots of things and appeared to give her nephews' tutor a free rein in his handling of them.

Of course, there were those rumours that one heard, her liking for young men, the flirtatious nature that had led to some pretty odd events in her life. All just speculation and gossip of course but one never knew with the gentry, they were able to indulge themselves in ways that would never be tolerated in those of a more menial standing.

Nevertheless, it wasn't her place to judge, even if she didn't approve of Mr Mallard's peculiar ideas of teaching.

She looked again at Todd, only this time she didn't frown down her nose at him. 'Just be thankful, Todd, that it wasn't a wolf or a bear that waylaid you, or you might not be here now. So you have every good reason to be grateful to both Mr Mallard and the Noble boys. You do understand that, don't you, Todd?'

Todd didn't, but he thought it wiser not to pursue the matter further, and he went off rather thankfully to attend to his belated deliveries.

Several womenfolk came strolling by, among them Maggie May, wife of John Greir, the proprietor of the Coach House Inn. She was a quaint figure in her white mutch cap and her dress of rough brown wool, the generous folds of which couldn't quite disguise the magnificent proportions of her figure. Everything about her was wobbly and ponderous. Winter and summer alike, Maggie May's sleeves were rolled to her dimpled elbows and it was generally agreed that her blubber insulated her against the elements.

She and Fat Jane were great friends and it was quite a sight to see the pair of them together, chuckling their plump chuckles and talking in their fat resonant voices. She was an amiable bundle of good nature whose fun-filled anecdotes made the Coach House Inn a popular meeting place for the locals and a haven for weary travellers.

'It's yourself, Miss Priscilla,' she acknowledged the teacher. 'Visiting the McIntyre's I see. Well, you'll be lucky to get *him* in a good mood at any time o' the day.'

'He won't come any snash with me, Maggie May,' came the tart reply.

'Indeed no,' agreed Maggie May with a bubbling kind of chortle. 'He'd be feart you'd take his breeks down and warm his backside for him, Iron Rod or no.' She looked downcast for a moment, ''Tis sad I am to hear that the old devil is making Anna leave school. If it had been that rascal, Adam, well, that would have been different, but Anna – the bairn has a head on her shoulders.'

'News travels fast,' the teacher observed with a sniff.

'Ach well, Mary was hearing it from Bella who was talking to Polly who heard it from our wee madam, Beth Jordan on her way home to dinner.' Maggie May wrinkled her brow in confusion at her own explanation then, shaking her head, she went on up the road to the shop.

Left on her own at last, Miss Priscilla knocked firmly on The Gatehouse door. For several minutes she waited, very straight and dignified, her outward composure giving away nothing of her mounting agitation.

Then came footsteps in the lobby, the door opened with a violent wrench, and Adam stood there, staring dumbly at the visitor.

'I wish to speak to your father, Adam,' imparted Miss Priscilla briskly.

'He's at his dinner, Miss,' Adam said in a voice full of respect and meekness, even though he would have liked nothing better than to have throttled his teacher with his bare hands, still smarting as he was from her earlier treatment of him.

His manner didn't deceive Miss Priscilla in the least. Of all the boys in her class this was the one who caused her the most trouble though he was cunning enough usually never to be seen as the perpetrator of his mischief.

Brushing aside his excuses with an imperious wave of her hand she lifted up her skirts, ascended the step, and walked straight into the kitchen.

Anna was lifting a pan of potatoes from the swee but at the sight of her teacher she almost let the heavy pot fall on the hearth.

'It's alright, Anna,' Miss Priscilla's voice was reassuring though her heart was beating swiftly, 'I've only come to speak to your father.'

Roderick dabbed his mouth with a corner of the tablecloth and scraping back his chair he held out his hand in an affable gesture.

Miss Priscilla ignored it. 'Can we have a word in private, Mr McIntyre?'

'Of course, of course, my dear Miss Pris —'

'McLeod — only my friends and my pupils call me Miss Priscilla.'

'Ah, yes, so many names to remember. Is it any surprise that occasionally we forget the odd one?'

Privately he thought that a woman of her plainness was hardly worth a place in his memory at all and how dare she come barging in on his midday meal like this. But he was forced to concede that she was the schoolteacher and commanded his respect. Pushing down his rage he indicated the parlour door with a show of politeness.

Miss Priscilla followed him into the room to settle her sparse frame on the edge of a hard, leather armchair.

Roderick stood in front of the empty grate, legs straddled, hands folded behind his back, waiting for her to speak.

'I wish to know the reasons for Anna leaving school,' began the teacher with a directness that burrowed into Roderick's facade of geniality. 'And why you suddenly took it upon yourself to make such a decision?'

His ruddy face grew bright with chagrin but he played for time, fiddling in his pocket for his pipe, very deliberately tapping it out on the bars of the grate. A minute elapsed during which he opened his

64

tobacco pouch to poke the shreds around with a stubby finger before stuffing some into his pipe.

Holding it up he leaned forward and addressed the teacher in slightly mocking tones, 'Do you mind – Miss – er – McLeod?'

She glowered disdainfully down her nose. 'Indeed I do, Mr McIntyre. I am allergic to all kinds of tobacco irritants.'

He closed the silver lid of the pipe with a sharp little snap and set it on the mantelpiece.

'Very well, Miss McLeod, I can see this is purely a formal visit. I must say, your questions come as something of a surprise. No doubt you know something of the circumstances o' this family. It is a sad story, Miss McLeod, very sad. Anna's poor dear mother . . .'

'I know all about that, Mr McIntyre, but surely you can't expect a child to take a woman's place in the home.'

'My dear lady, I have no intention of letting my little girl do any such thing. Nevertheless, she must expect to make some sacrifices. It isn't easy for me although God alone knows I do my best to keep my family together. I try to ensure that they are well fed and warmly clothed – you must have noticed that, Miss McLeod? It's a difficult and delicate subject, that o' finance, even with my eldest boy doing his bit to Leana-chorran.

'My children are well educated compared to some, but a man can only do so much.' He twiddled his thumbs behind his back and looked thoughtful. 'You know, Anna's got a lot of fancy ideas for a wee lassie and it's time she shouldered some responsibility, she needs something to bring her down to earth.' He shook his head and looked sad. 'Believe me, dear lady, Anna's lucky to have stayed so long in school. This past year has been more o' a struggle than ever with the boys growing older and needing more attention.'

'I see.' Miss Priscilla's tone suggested she didn't see at all. 'You are just going to allow your daughter's talents to be thrown away, you are quite willing to stand back and watch while she immerses herself in a life of drudgery?'

Roderick looked genuinely surprised. 'Talents? Indeed, I have no idea what you mean.'

'Anna is a gifted child, Mr McIntyre. Not only is she advanced in the field of literature, she is also a talented artist.'

He snorted in utter astonishment. 'Artist? Come now, dear lady, it's just another o' her fads. She's full o' them! Artist indeed! Where does she get her ideas I'd like to know. We are all plain and down to earth in this family. You must see that?'

The teacher glanced round the featureless room, her eyes taking in the dingy walls, empty but for an oblong sampler above the fireplace bearing a dreary quotation from the Old Testament.

'Ay, it's very plain to see, Mr McIntyre,' she agreed with a dour smile. 'Nevertheless, Anna has got her talent from somewhere and I'm very surprised you didn't know about it. She's a child any father would be proud of.'

She leaned forward, her whole being taut with earnestness. 'I ask you – as a gentleman and a respected member of this community – let Anna continue her days at school, let me for once keep a child with such promise. She has the potential for a bright future, but if she leaves school now – think of the waste, Mr McIntyre.'

Very deliberately Roderick took out his pocket watch to give it a cursory glance, his eyebrows shooting up in exaggerated surprise. 'Dear me, duty calls, Miss McLeod, I'm sorry I couldn't be of more help.'

'But you've been no help at all,' the teacher cried angrily, 'and you appear not to have heard one word I've said! Listen to me, I implore you. Let me at least take Anna twice weekly in my own time and in my own home! I have studied the basics of art and I can take her through some of the stages. You know – if you refuse me this, it won't be very good for your reputation. Anna is well liked in this neighbourhood. People are only too well aware of the deprivations she has suffered in a home with no mother to see to her and three men to look after!'

Roderick looked as if he was about to burst. The woman was as good as blackmailing him! How dare such a dried-up crone do that to him?

His eyes bulged, his fists knotted behind his back, desperately he fought to control himself. He daren't let go. The old bitch was right, he did have his reputation to uphold!

Taking out his handkerchief he mopped the sweat from his brow and said with an effort, 'You're right – of course you're right. And how kind of you to make such a proposal. I'm sure my girl will benefit from some further education – even if it is only art. I'm – I'm not sure if I can afford . . .'

Miss Priscilla got rigidly to her feet and held up her hand. 'Please do not insult me, sir! Seeing Anna's talents develop will be reward enough for me. I will see myself out!'

She strode into the kitchen where Adam was wolfing down his dinner and a white-faced Anna was standing motionless by the fire.

'Well, Anna, we won't be parting company after all,' the teacher said triumphantly. 'Your father has kindly agreed to my coaching you two evenings a week – at my home. I will arrange it with you tomorrow. Goodbye for now, dear child.'

She let herself out and stood leaning faintly against the door. She had won! If only a small victory. His reputation to uphold indeed! She knew only too well what a hypocrite he was. It was a wonder the kirk hadn't fallen about his ears a long time ago!

Roderick stood in the kitchen, towering over Anna. 'Well, little witch,' he ground out, 'Are you satisfied? Talent, eh? A fine wee artist? The old bat is as fanciful as you are yourself! One o' these fine days you'll find out what life's really all about, I tell you that! Now, get me my dinner! No doubt it's as dried up as that frump who's just wasted twenty minutes of my precious time!'

Anna lifted the plate from the hob, her face red with a mixture of hurt and happiness. Her days at school were almost over. After next week she would never again sit in the cosy little classroom with magical worlds opening to her. How happy had been those short hours from nine in the morning till midday. She had crammed so much into them, reading, writing, drawing . . . and best of all . . . studying the beautiful art books Miss Priscilla brought to school specially for her.

Everyone wondered how a schoolmistress could afford such books but Anna knew that her every spare penny had gone towards their purchase. And not just art books, every kind of book imaginable.

Schooldays would soon be no more for her but she had something else to look forward to, something perhaps even better. Evenings at Knock Farm, quiet, clock-ticking hours, logs crackling in the grate, Miss Priscilla's sister, Kate, snoring peacefully in the rocking chair, Ben McLeod, her brother, reading his newspaper in the lamplight, two or three sheepdogs using his slippered feet for pillows. Also, Old Grace was a regular visitor to Knock Farm and often baked scones on the hot girdle, the steamy smell of them filling the kitchen. And – best of all – Miss Priscilla's tiny study, oak panelled, wonderfully fusty, countless books nestling in the rows of neat shelves that Ben had 'cobbled together'.

Anna's cheeks grew hot with joy. Putting her father's dinner on the table she made an excuse to go outside. The smells of damp earth and wet leaves hung in the air; ecstatically she filled her lungs with the sweetness, loving this hour when the mill was silent save for the hissing from the boilerhouse where old Andy might be having a cat nap after his midday piece.

Wisps of vapour clung to the craggy face of Coir an Ban, looking like trails of gossamer ribbons. Ribbons! She thought about the things she had been given that day and she hugged herself with happiness. She was thirteen now. A child of thirteen not a witch of thirteen! Her father couldn't frighten her anymore with his wicked lies.

She thought of the plans she had made with Beth and shivered in a mixture of joy, anticipation . . . and fear.

CHAPTER NINE

The Festival of Samain

THE FLAMES OF THE bonfire on Paddy Stool Hill leapt high into a sky that was velvet black above the orange glow.

Paddy Stool Hill was part of Ben Ruadh, the red mountain, a towering mass of craggy rock sloping down to softer ground where banks of fern grew in profusion. In the months of May and June, when the ferns were young and tender, the hillside was green, but in the autumn it was a riot of gold and bronze interspersed by the blood red splashes of rowanberries.

By late autumn the ferns were dry and ragged and it was these that the village youngsters gathered for their fire, together with twigs and branches which were heaped on after the bracken was alight.

Now it was blazing like a furnace, sending up plumes of sparks that crackled and burst in the blackness.

The sight delighted the children and, joining hands, they danced round the flames while the older boys, shouting with excitement, grabbed burning faggots and went racing away with them, leaving trails of wavering light in their wake. They began to chant, ghostly rhymes and witching songs that had been passed down through generations. There was something rather primitive about their rhythm, something eerie about the fire and the dancers up there on the slopes of Paddy Stool Hill.

Anna held onto Magnus's hand and shivered. Strange emotions churned in her belly, the blood flowed swiftly in her veins, her cheeks burned with elation, and her hair streamed out behind her as she spun round with the others.

Her brother's hand was warm in hers. She felt attuned to him, his face bronze in the firelight. There was something wonderful about his eyes, they were very bright and seemed to send out showers of golden sparks that merged with the flames and the heat and the music of the night.

'You aren't cold, are you?' he suddenly asked. 'I can feel you shaking.'

'Not cold,' The words trembled in her throat. 'Happy, Magnus, just happy.'

'Me too, happiness and excitement all mixed up together.' He laughed. 'Look at our Adam over there, holding hands with Violet Patterson. He won't like that! He'd rather it was Beth Jordan. Where is she by the way? I can't see her anywhere.'

'Around somewhere, I suppose.' Anna was seized with a feeling of guilt. She hadn't told him about her decision to go to the party and wondered if she should. Quickly she decided against it. Beth had stipulated it was to be a secret, and that meant no one must know, not even Magnus.

The circle was breaking up and chestnuts were thrown to roast in the white-hot ash at the edge of the fire. Those children who were going to the party at The House of Noble began to make their way downhill. Anna watched them go, knowing that the time had come for her to make her move also. She had to do it, Beth would never forgive her if she backed out now.

She edged away from the bonfire and sped quickly into the dark shadows fringing the woods, stopping for a moment to look back, seeing Magnus crouched by the fire, poking chestnuts with a long stick.

His profile was outlined clearly against the glow, his hair was ruffling in the breeze blowing over the hill. She knew that soon he would start looking for her to give her a share of the hot chestnuts but he would forget all about her when the leaping competition began.

Consoling herself with that she flew down the hill, past the sprawling outbuildings of Knock Farm, almost colliding with Beth who was hopping about with impatience at the foot of the slope.

'There you are! I thought you were never coming. Quick, get this on, it's an old sheet I got from Frizzy the housemaid. Keep your arms down, silly, and don't worry, you won't smother, I cut holes for your eyes and mouth.'

Roughly she bundled the sheet over Anna's head, arranging the holes to suit, in her haste tweaking Anna's nose and pulling her hair.

'That hurt, Beth! You've got fingers on you like talons!'

'Och, stop moaning! Now, hold up your hand and I'll give you a lantern. You'll just have to grip it through the sheet. Keep still while I light the candles.'

The wind blew out the matches as she struck them but after many frustrated attempts the candles were lit, illuminating the jagged mouths and slitted eyes of the hollow turnip faces.

Anna held her lantern aloft and giggled at the sight of her friend. 'You're a witch! Father was wrong, he said I would be a witch tonight but I'm not, I'm a ghost instead!'

'You can haunt him!' Beth chuckled wickedly. 'Make all his hair and whiskers fall out with fright. Haunt Adam too, scare him so much his teeth will clatter out of his head. Frighten the spunk out of him.'

'Beth Jordan!'

'I don't care! Give him a scare! Hobble-dee-dare! Out come whiskers and Iron Rod's hair!' Beth chanted the words, ending with a convincing witch-like cackle.

Choking with laughter, the two girls ran hand in hand up the winding track to The House of Noble, Beth's long skirts threatening to trip her, Anna's sheet flapping around her in wind-whipped folds.

They stumbled gaily along, holding up the grinning lanterns so that tiny sparkles of light danced on the dry copper leaves of the beech hedges. In front of them flitted strange figures, warlocks, ghouls, gnomes, and other such fabled creatures, unrecognizable as the children who lived in the glen.

Anna had forgotten her fears, she had forgotten her father, her heart bumped with joy, her breath came out in swift, frosty puffs. Although she was dressed as a ghost she felt as if she was riding on a witch's broom, so swift ran the tide of elation within her.

It was a perfect night for the Festival of Samain, the witching moon rode high above Coir an Ban, the orange blob of the bonfire lit the slopes of Paddy Stool Hill, the happy voices of the young party-goers in their outrageous costumes rang loud and clear in the night.

And suddenly, like sunshine at the end of a dark tunnel, appeared the wide, welcoming doors of The House of Noble, spreading light on the dew-drenched lawns, softening the snarling faces of two stone lions guarding the circular carriageway. Turnip lanterns grinned ghoulishly from the trees, spattering little pools of brilliance on the reds and yellows of maples and horse chestnuts.

Anna held tighter to Beth's hand as they mounted the broad steps up to the front door.

Another world awaited them in the big hall, one filled with elegant furniture and plush drapes: exotic rugs were scattered on the tiled floors; crystal chandeliers hung from the peach-coloured ceiling; velvet cushions were piled round the room for the children to sit on; an enormous log fire leapt up the chimney, gleaming on brass coal scuttles, martingales and warming pans.

The marbled fireplace was magnificent, hung on either side with old powder horns that bore gravings of Celtic origin together with names of the various male Nobles who had once possessed them. Arranged alongside the horns were several ancient Scottish pistols. On the hearth, resting on an iron tripod, was a salamander, a thick iron disc brazed onto a long metal handle. Well over a hundred years old it had once been used in the kitchens to brown meat and pastry but was now purely ornamental.

But it was none of these that made Anna draw in her breath, so vigorously the white linen of her ghost sheet was sucked into her mouth to form a damp little hollow. Head tilted, eyes round, she gazed in awe at the life-sized portrait of Lady Pandora hanging above the mantelshelf, set in a heavy frame carved with elaborate gilt roses and leaves.

Lady Pandora wore a dress of claret velvet with white lace at the throat and cuffs, the colour of the dress merging into a background of the same tone. From this rather sombre backcloth the face of Lady Pandora looked out, so lifelike it was as if she had just stepped into the frame to sit and watch proceedings in the big hall. Her expression was vibrant, her lips slightly parted in a faintly provocative smile. Her honey gold hair made a perfect frame for her lovely face, yet despite the uptilted mouth, her violet eyes were secretive and just a little bit sad. The artist had captured everything about her except the innermost thoughts behind those fascinating eyes.

It was a very commanding picture, so overpowering it seemed to dominate the room and put all else in the shadows. This was odd, especially as the face of Lady Pandora was in the softest light of all, yet it glowed so intensely it drugged and mystified Anna's senses.

72

'What are *you* gawping at?' hissed Beth. 'Your eyes are bulging out of your sheet. You look as if you've seen a ghost!'

'It's just the picture,' Anna tried to sound nonchalant. 'It looks so real it isn't like a picture at all. It's as if she had climbed up onto the mantelpiece and walked into the frame.'

Beth gave such a screech of laughter that several children turned to look at her and one chanted 'Silly old witch! Cackling old bitch!'

Beth immediately became engaged in an enjoyable verbal battle before turning her attention back to her friend. 'Really, Anna, you do say some silly things. If that's the real Pandora up there she must be pretty bored because she's been up there a long time. I see that picture whenever I come to the house with Father . . .

'I've been here quite a lot you know,' she continued grandly. 'Sometimes I come to tea with both my parents. Lady Pandora and my mother have quite a lot in common.'

'Ay, you've told me that already,' Anna said quietly, thinking to herself how snobbish Beth could be at times.

'Mother gives Lady Pandora recipes for jam and things. Of course, Fat Jane makes our jam but Lady Pandora has some strange ideas and likes to do things like an ordinary person. Mother was rather shocked and told me I must never do anything that should be left to the servants.'

She gazed consideringly up at the portrait. 'She *is* beautiful – of course, she's a lot younger there. I mean, she must be quite *old* now – though I must admit she still looks young. Mother says it must be powder and rouge but I've been quite close to her – Lady Pandora I mean – and she looks as if she's just washed her face with soap and water. All sort of fresh and shiny.' Lowering her voice she went on, 'Do you know what I think? I think the Greek Eve passed on the secret of everlasting youth to all Pandoras that ever were born so's they can go on punishing mortal men forever. They do this by casting spells on them and tempting them into doing bad things like – like lusting – lustingful practices.'

Her monologue ended on a note of triumph but Anna showed no appreciation for what she had just heard, instead her eyes flashed angrily behind the holes in her sheet. 'No wonder you dressed up as a witch, Beth Jordan! It's because you really are one inside yourself and you can't stop it pouring out like – like snake venom.'

Beth remained unperturbed. Wriggling her long false nose she chanted, 'Yes, I'm a witch! I wiggle my snitch! Ho Hum Fiddle De Doom, picture on wall, come into the room!'

Anna was not impressed. She too had seen Lady Pandora entering the room and knew that Beth had invented the rhyme on the spur of the moment.

The Lady Pandora of today wasn't all that different from the one in the painting. She was wearing a dress of soft green velvet and her golden hair was pinned up into rich coils that emphasized her slender neck and showed her dainty ears to advantage.

Clapping her hands for attention she called out, 'Welcome to Noble House, children. Are we going to enjoy ourselves tonight?'

'*YES!*' came the enthusiastic chorus.

'Come on then, we'll start with the games.'

With a zest that made her seem like a child herself she organized proceedings for the next enchanted hour. So infectious was her gaiety the children soon forgot that she was a titled lady with a fine house and servants to attend her every need. Tonight she was the servant of the children, she danced, sang, and laughed with them till the room rang with merriment.

When the riotous games were over, a tub of apples was brought in by two footmen who set it in the middle of the room. Sir Malaroy, sleeves rolled to his elbows, was the first to 'dook' for an apple. Gamely he dipped his face into the water to come up gasping time after time but eventually he emerged with a rosy apple between his teeth, much to everyone's delight.

'It isn't seemly for a gentleman to be seen in shirtsleeves nor should they dook for apples,' commented Beth with a disapproving sniff, but the rest of the children shrieked with glee at sight of Sir Malaroy's dripping face and soaked shirt front.

He was a tall, handsome man of forty-one whose dark hair was sprinkled with grey. His nose was aquiline, his skin smooth and fair, his blue eyes oddly arresting so filled were they with piercing light. It was an aristocratic face, enhanced by a neat Van Dyck beard which emphasized his individuality, since large drooping whiskers were the fashion of the day. He was of purely Scottish descent but had been educated in England and it was there that his cousin had introduced him to Pandora, a titled lady in her own right.

She had been in the full swing of her coming out season and she had whirled him through a breathless round of social occasions. In her exuberant way she had fallen hopelessly in love with him and with the full approval of her wealthy, widowed mother, they had married.

Soon afterwards, her mother had died and both Lady Pandora and her sister, Lady Penelope, had inherited a considerable fortune and property which included a country mansion in Devon and a town house in London.

Some months after the funeral Sir Malaroy had brought his young bride back to Scotland to become mistress of The House of Noble which had been in his family for generations. So enchanted was she with the place she seldom yearned to go back home, though occasionally she went south to Devon or to the town house in London, depending on her mood.

But her husband was content to spend his days in the lands of Argyll. He was a shy man who disliked the limelight and his wife was wont to tell him she never could understand how he had managed to survive the frivolities she had introduced him to in London.

Though they made such a complete contrast they were a perfectly attuned pair, strikingly attractive when they appeared together at social gatherings – times like now when she laughingly mopped his face with a towel brought to her by a maid while he stood there like a schoolboy, letting her fuss over him.

'He adores her,' Violet Patterson hissed at Beth. 'I wish I looked like she does.'

'Wishing won't get you anywhere,' returned the blunt-spoken Beth who was inclined to envy Violet her clothes. What she didn't admire was Violet's mousy hair and 'buck' teeth and whenever she could she reminded her of these disadvantages.

'Maybe my mother will make me a dress of green velvet,' went on the even-tempered Violet.

'Green won't suit your mousy brown hair,' imparted Beth with satisfaction. 'You might as well wear that peasant's outfit every day! That really suits you, Violet.'

'Jealous old witch,' said Violet with a grin before skipping as quickly as her long skirts would allow over to the tub of apples.

CHAPTER TEN

Lucas and Peter

'BEING A WITCH CERTAINLY suits *you*, Beth Jordan.'

A mocking voice at Beth's elbow made her turn sharply. Master Lucas Noble stood there, only it took her a few moments to recognize him, done up as he was in a pirate's outfit.

'Lucas.' She had been ready with a quick retort but the words died on her lips, her manner underwent an abrupt change. 'Don't you look splendid in your costume? And isn't it a simply marvellous party?'

'It's not bad,' he admitted laconically, his dark eyes flashing with amusement at her eagerness to please him. 'But my costume *is* good, isn't it? I made it myself, every bit of it, even though my brother would tell you otherwise'

'Too right I would!'

A 'Maharajah' made a timely appearance onto the scene, otherwise known as Master Peter Noble, his fine-featured face wearing an expression of indignation under his somewhat untidy turban. 'I made that pirate's outfit, Lucas, and fine you know it. Furthermore it was I who should have worn it tonight. As it was I had to make do with this measly get up.'

Anna found herself staring at the boys, so different to any she had ever known, so posh and proper sounding, so sure of themselves . . . Yet . . . something about the fairer of the two, Peter, touched some chord in her, not as confident as he was trying to make out, not nearly as self-possessed as the other.

They weren't identical twins: Lucas was tall for fourteen, with eyes that were almost black in his smooth, handsome face. But his mouth was cruel, cruel and wide and full. It was one of the first things Anna had noticed about him because it was a feature that was prominent in Roderick and reminded her of him.

76

Peter was slightly shorter and broader; a few curls of fair hair crisped out from under his turban, his face was more open than his brother's; his eyes were a deep, pure blue and though he had just spoken in anger there was a sparkle in them, especially when he suddenly turned his attention to Anna and said with a laugh, 'Who are you under all that bedlinen? Somebody I know or perhaps a real ghost, come to haunt dear old Noble House?'

'There's only one way to find that out,' Lucas butted in, his face shining with devilment. 'Let's de-robe her.'

'Oh, come on, that's going a bit far,' protested Peter. Even so he seemed to find the whole thing amusing enough and reached out to grab Anna while Lucas began pulling at the sheet.

'Don't you dare!' Anna, her heart pounding, tried to struggle out of Peter's grasp and when that didn't work she lashed out at both of them with her feet.

'Hey! she kicks! Just like a silly old mule!' Lucas cried in delight. 'Hold still you little dervish! We're not going to harm you, we only want to find out who you are.'

'Beth, help me!' panted Anna, feeling as if she was about to suffocate under the clinging folds of her ghost sheet. 'Don't let them do this, Beth, please don't let them do this!'

Beth made no move. She stood with the other children as if she was hypnotized, watching while the twins pulled her friend this way and that.

But while Anna's tearful pleas had no effect on Beth, they had a calming influence on Peter. Rather shamefaced, he stood back and said gruffly, 'Let her go, Lucas, a joke's a joke but we've gone far enough.'

Lucas however was enjoying himself too much to heed his brother's warning. 'I'll get you, whoever you are,' he panted, his face red with effort. 'Don't forget, I'm a pirate and I'm out to capture you and carry you off to my cave in yonder mountain. There you will tell me your name and where you come from. So just you be a good little ghost and I promise not to hurt you. Otherwise . . .'

Anna went still and cold with fear. His words had reminded her of Adam and his threats to let the Nuckelavee carry her off to its den in the black night hills. A sob escaped her, she was hardly aware that Lucas had loosed his hold on her till a voice penetrated her senses.

'Stop that at once, both of you.' Mr Mallard had arrived on the scene.

Through the eyeholes in her sheet she saw a towering, tightly-muscled, fair-haired man, eyes flashing angrily, speaking in a controlled voice.

'What on earth do you two think you're doing?' He gritted out, looking from one boy to the other. 'Explanations please, at the double.'

'Nothing, sir,' Lucas spoke boldly. 'At least, we were only having a bit of fun, nothing serious.'

Peter stood with his head slightly bowed, saying nothing, still with that look of shame on his face.

'Nothing, eh? Right, I'll soon give you something to keep you occupied. Go and help Jackson bring in the second tub of apples, and next time you want a bit of fun – pick on somebody your own size.'

'Everything alright here, Andrew?' Lady Pandora was suddenly there, looking into the tutor's face enquiringly, her violet eyes big and beautiful in the perfect cameo of her face.

'Everything's fine, your ladyship,' Mr Mallard's voice had grown softer. 'The boys wanted something to do so I told them to help Jackson.'

She laughed. 'Good. Come on then, boys, all hands on deck tonight, we need all the help we can get.'

They moved off, Peter throwing an apologetic backward glance at Anna before running to join his brother.

'Why did you let them maul me like that?' Anna turned on Beth, speaking in a low, accusing voice.

Beth's pale eyes grew very round. 'Anna! Don't be so dramatic! Maul you indeed! I couldn't help myself. It all happened so quickly. Anyway, Mr Mallard came to your rescue . . . You know, it's strange,' she went on thoughtfully, 'No matter what, you somehow manage to get all the attention . . .'

'Attention!' Anna gripped her friend's arm, 'You always manage to twist everything to suit yourself, don't you, Beth Jordan?'

'You're hurting my arm. Calm down and enjoy yourself. It will soon be our turn to dook for an apple.'

'I can't dook, not with this sheet on – and I can't take it off, as fine you know.'

'Then the water will cool you. Come on, silly, we'll miss all the fun if you go on like this, and you know how much you longed to come to this party. I don't particularly like dooking myself, I hate getting wet, but I'm good at it, you watch and see how I do it.'

78

Anna swallowed hard. She wanted to hit Beth, she wanted very much to hit someone, but instead she took a deep breath and went to join the others round the apple tubs, trying to ignore the fact that Lucas was watching her with undisguised interest.

'Here, I'll get one for you, you'll never manage with that thing on.' It was Peter who was speaking, in a very earnest voice, taking her arm in a reassuring hold.

But she shook him off. 'I can manage,' she returned coldly. 'You get your own apples, cheat if you like, you and your brother seem to be allowed to do anything you want so why not that as well.'

So saying she got down on her knees. Indignation choking her, she buried her face in the water and was forced to come up for air time and again. But eventually she was successful, an apple was in her teeth, held only by the stalk but at least she had done it all on her own.

Half blinded by water she had to blink rapidly to clear her vision. Both boys were watching her with something like admiration and she was very gratified to see that Beth, for all her boasting, had been unsuccessful in her attempts to retrieve an apple.

'Here, take this one.' Lucas fished for an apple and handed it to her. 'It doesn't matter, everyone gets one anyway, whether by fair means or foul.'

Her eyes glittered but she managed to swallow her pride and thank him graciously, even though the expression on his face was one of huge amusement.

When every child at last stood clutching an apple the girls were instructed to peel them, making sure the skin came off in one piece.

'Now throw the peel over your shoulders,' directed Lady Pandora, 'and you will see the initial of your future true love.'

The little girls complied with zest while the boys looked on rather cynically.

'Yours came down as a "W", Anna,' said Beth, 'and mine has made an "A".'

'Mine hasn't come down as anything except a coiled-up apple peel,' said Violet in some disappointment.

Beth tossed her head and spoke loftily. 'Then you will probably never ever get married, Violet. You don't really expect to, do you?'

Lady Pandora was walking round, examining the apple peels on the

79

tiled floor, commiserating with those girls who couldn't see any sort of initial, no matter how much they tried.

'You mustn't worry,' Lady Pandora said soothingly. 'There are other ways of finding out who your future husbands will be. Tonight, when you go home, put a candle on the dresser and when you look in the mirror you could well see the reflection of the man you'll marry. I did this when I was a young girl – and do you know who I saw? Why, Sir Malaroy of course.'

'Really, Lady Pandora?' came the awed chorus.

'Yes, really, *anything* can happen on the night of Hallowe'en.'

The footmen appeared again, gingerly carrying strings of treacle-coated scones which they secured carefully to a pair of sturdy marble lamp-holders, their expressions suggesting that they were far too dignified to carry out such menial and messy tasks.

It was an hilarious game with rows of children, hands clasped behind them, endeavouring to bite the sticky scones.

Anna went into the fray with everyone else, forgetting everything but the fun of the moment.

Lucas appeared beside her. 'I'm glad I didn't find out who you were after all,' he told her. 'Look at you, you're a mess.'

'At least I tried,' she flashed back, 'which is more than I can say for you.'

He didn't take offence but said thoughtfully, 'Yes, you did, I'll give you that. Perhaps you'll come back and see us when you're not a ghost but a real live girl. You are a girl, aren't you? I can tell by your voice and the way you kick.'

She made no answer. The fancy dress lineup was in progress and she went to stand with the others.

Lady Pandora came up and laid a hand on her head. 'Dear me, a little white ghost with a treacly face. Never mind, we'll clean you up before you go home.'

She continued along the line and Anna whispered to Beth, 'What did that mean?'

'Wheesht, Anna,' Beth scolded, 'she's announcing the winners. Would you believe? She's picked that horrible little fatty, Bunty Walters – and Calum the stableboy. That's not fair! Mother was certain I would win this year. I never win!'

Beth's tones were peevish but not even she could help laughing at the sight of Bunty going forward to receive her prize. Bunty was dressed as a turnip and, unknown to her, one of her brothers had pinned a notice on her back which read, 'Take a quick peep. You'll see I'm a neep. I love haggis and tattie. That's why I'm a fatty.'

Already a rotund figure, she was a quaint sight with her legs sticking out of her bulky costume like matchsticks. As she approached Lady Pandora, she tripped and unable to get to her feet, all she could do was roll about helplessly on the floor. The entire company erupted into helpless mirth as Sir Malaroy went forward gallantly to help her upright. Luckily she was a good-natured child and when she was handed her prize her smiles turned into gasps of delight. She had been given a pair of brown leather boots. Inside one was a thick pair of woollen stockings while the other was stuffed with fruit and nuts.

The Walters were one of the poorest families in the district, the children sharing one pair of boots between them which meant that one or other of them had to stay off school or walk there in bare feet. Mrs Walters was a semi-invalid who spent a greater part of her time in bed. Mr Walters was a hard-working farm labourer whose wages went mostly on food for his family.

If her ladyship could have had her way she would have shod all the village children but she was wise enough to know that poverty didn't rob people of pride and she therefore seized upon any excuse to give them a few small necessities. Calum also received a sturdy pair of boots filled to the brim with sweets and other delicacies while William Walters found himself similarly rewarded for being the most horrible ghoul of the evening.

'It's favouritism!' fumed Beth. 'She always does this, gives prizes of footwear to common little beggars who don't deserve them. My costume is much much better than Bunty Walters'.'

'Bunty *did* deserve it,' returned Anna unsympathetically. 'She didn't mind people laughing at her. If it had been you you would have stomped away in a rage.'

The approach of Lady Pandora stifled Beth's retort, though her eyes glittered when her friend was handed a bar of exquisitely perfumed toilet soap wrapped in tissue paper.

'To you goes the prize for the dirtiest little ghost I've ever seen,' Lady Pandora laughed, then, bending low, she whispered, 'Happy Birthday,

Anna . . . Shh, it's alright, I won't tell anyone, no one knows but me. It was your eyes I remembered, they belong unmistakably to the girl I met on the road today. In a few moments you shall come upstairs with me and I'll clean you up.'

She straightened and held up her hand. 'Right, children, inspection time! I want to see all those merry faces that have been hiding from me all evening. Off with the masks and the false noses!'

Anna was so panic-stricken she forgot about Lady Pandora's promise to take her upstairs. 'You didn't tell me about this,' she hissed at Beth.

'I forgot.' Beth looked uncomfortable. 'Make an excuse to go to the lavatory – or something,' she finished lamely.

But Anna was backing away in horror. 'No, I'm going home, I'll see you outside.'

The beautiful elegant room whirled before her eyes; its warmth, its excitement seemed suddenly to close in on her. Hoisting her sheet up to her knees she began to run to the door.

'Wait! Wait, child! Little ghost, please wait!'

Lady Pandora's dismayed cries made all heads turn. Lucas and Peter broke from the crowd. 'We'll bring her back, Aunt Dora,' they said, also starting to run.

Anna paid no heed but kept on going, in seconds reaching the cool entrance hall with its striped Regency chairs and potted plants.

Peter appeared with Lucas fast on his heels. 'Come back, ghostie!' yelled Peter, 'I want to see who you are!'

'Me too!' Lucas shouted, his grins showing how much he was enjoying this unexpected turn of events. 'Come back and be de-frocked! If you don't you're a little cry baby!'

'Her name's Anna, I know that much,' Peter said breathlessly. 'I heard Beth Jordan saying it.'

'Anna who?'

'I don't know, but I'll find out easily enough.'

Desperately Anna turned this way and that, rushing forward she grabbed one of the chairs and hurled it with all her strength at the boys. First Peter, then his brother ran full tilt into it, falling in heaps on top of one another.

Out of the studded oak doors Anna flew, down the wide steps, away from the orange flickers of lamps and lanterns. She was like Cinderella fleeing from the ball, but with no magic horse-drawn pumpkins waiting to whisk her to safety. Heart hammering in her throat, she sped down the long drive, her white sheet making eerie slapping sounds in the playful breeze.

The drive was now petering out into a grass-grown track and she stopped running to sink onto a mossy bank to regain her breath. In her haste she had left her lantern behind but the brilliance of the moon bathed the whole countryside and she could see everything quite plainly. It was very cold. She shivered and wondered what time it was. The ball would start around ten, but her father would be ready long before that. He always made lengthy preparations whenever he was going anywhere special and tonight he would be extra particular. Anna knew all about that. She had spent a good part of the afternoon pressing his suit and an expensive silk handkerchief that smelt of Nellie Jean. Afterwards she had brushed his black top hat and had polished the silver knob of his Malacca walking stick.

Bow ties. Silk-backed waistcoats. Fancy hankies. All the 'silly notions' he abhorred so much in her.

He ought to have left the house by now, taking the horse and trap to collect Mrs Simpson at the manse in Munkirk. Anna breathed a sigh of relief at the thought. She would be safely home before he made the return journey and even if they passed on the road she would look just like another guiser to him.

'Anna!' Beth's voice floated down the driveway. 'Where *are* you?'

'Here, on the bank.'

Beth puffed up, indignant and harassed. 'Really, Anna, I don't know why I bother with you at times.'

'Och, I'm sorry, I just panicked at the idea of them all seeing me and telling Father.'

'It's alright.' Beth put her arm round Anna's shoulder and they trudged along the track and onto the road. 'I most likely would have done the same thing if I had horrible old Iron Rod for a father. Did you enjoy the party?'

'Mostly it was good — except for Lucas and Peter. Even so, if I never have another happy moment in my life I don't care because I had them all tonight.'

'That's silly! You would *die* if you were never happy again. It was very kind of Lady Pandora to give you that soap. Of course, I'm beginning to

83

see how she makes a point of giving things to the needy. She knows I've got nice clothes and shoes. I loved all that nonsense with the apple peel. Fancy yours coming down as a "W". Maybe it means you'll marry snottery William Walters.'

Anna laughed. 'Well, yours came down as an "A". Maybe you'll marry my brother Adam.'

'That horrible little show-off!'

'He is handsome.'

Beth tossed her head. 'He's common, even if he is your brother. Besides, when I grow up I'll be mixing with well-bred young men. Mother will see to that. Adam's like your father, looking at girls' chests and everything. I heard him telling Snotty Watty he likes girls with bosoms that bounce, yet he tried to kiss me in the wee shed at playtime and I don't have any bosoms. He'll grow up to like anything with a skirt on.

'Mother says your father's a bit like that. I heard her telling Father she thought she saw that Nellie Jean coming out of your house early one morning. Is that true?'

Quickly Anna changed the subject. 'Are you going to look in the mirror tonight to see if you can see a candlelit reflection of your future husband? The way Lady Pandora did?'

'Ach, that's daft,' scorned Beth, adding carelessly, 'I might – just for a laugh.'

They were in a quiet part of the glen. On either side of them the hills rose up, aloof and dark against the moonlit sky. Beside them, a grove of oaks rustled dry leaves; moon shadows lay over the fields; a little burn gurgled over the stones. It was a cold, bubbly sort of sound; drips from the bank tinkled into the ditch, others went 'plonk, plunk' as they hit deeper water.

'It's – very quiet,' breathed Anna. 'Where are all the people?'

'At the inn – or just coming along,' Beth said off-handedly, but her spine tingled, the flesh crept on her arms, the glen was very quiet and Anna had a knack of making ordinary words sound spooky.

'There's a holly tree just up the road,' Anna went on fearfully. 'Holly trees can be sort of queer at times, especially on Hallowe'en.'

'Och you! What ails you tonight? Your voice is all quivery and strange.'

'I just feel a bit creepy. Tell Tale Todd told me there's a holly tree at

Loch Fyne that jumps out from the woods and sort of jigs about on the road and no matter which way you turn it doesn't let you get past. It did it to him last Hallowe'en and he's been scared to pass that way ever since.'

'Ach, he'd be drunk at the time! Todd's always drunk.'

'He says he was stone cold sober and he has a witness to prove it. Old Rab Harkness was with him and he doesn't touch a drop. Todd said . . .' Here Anna's voice shook, '. . . the tree got hold of Rab, pulled him out of the delivery van, and did a Highland Fling with him – right there in the middle of the road. His hair turned white overnight and now all Rab ever does is read his Bible and pray that the spirits won't get him.'

It was too much for Beth. She clutched Anna's arm and the pair of them fairly flew up the road, away from the dark whispering woods and the knarled holly tree with its twisted, beckoning branches.

The cheerful lights of the Coach House Inn came into view, voices and laughter drifted outside. A few minutes later the ring of hooves, the rumble of wheels, sounded on the road. Anna's heart leapt in her breast when she recognized her father's stocky figure at the reins.

'It's Iron Rod!' whispered Beth, 'with blethery old Mrs Simpson.'

'Shh!' returned Anna, feeling as if all the breath was being squeezed from her lungs.

'Aha!' Roderick had spotted the quaint figures. He reined in his horse. 'What have we here, eh, Mrs Simpson? A little ghost come out to haunt us and a witch to cast spells on us. Now I wonder, Mrs Simpson, do ghosts and witches like farthings?'

'Indeed, Mr McIntyre, I'm sure they do.'

There was a short pause, followed by the dull chink of coins hitting the stony road. 'There you are, you naughty servants of the devil! You will be so busy searching for my hard-earned coppers you will have no time left to cast your spells on us poor, innocent mortals.'

The whip cracked, the trap trundled on. Mrs Simpson's voice came floating back, 'You know, Mr McIntyre, you really are very good with the wee ones.'

'A man can only try, Mrs Simpson,' came the affable reply, 'A man can only try.'

Beth was grovelling amongst the stones, feeling for the coppers, but a violent tug on her arm made her get up. 'Leave that money be, Beth

Jordan,' ordered Anna tightly, 'or go home by yourself. I'm going, right this very minute.'

'Oh, alright,' snapped Beth, 'but I shall look for it on my way to school tomorrow.'

At the foot of Corran House driveway Beth divested her friend of her ghost sheet, and now the night of fun really was over, she was Anna once more, daughter of Roderick McIntyre of The Gatehouse.

'Soon . . .' murmured Beth reflectively, 'Your last day at school, Anna.'

'Yes, but . . .' Anna's breath caught on a note of happiness. 'Miss Priscilla is taking me for tuition, two evenings a week at Knock Farm. She came to our house today and after an argument with Father he agreed to let me go.'

'But that's no use to me – is it?'

'No, but it is to me,' returned Anna assertively. 'Sometimes I think you're very selfish, Beth. You like everything your way.' The words were out before she could stop them. She had never spoken to her friend like that before and there came a gasp of surprise in the darkness.

'How dare you say that, Anna McIntyre? After me inviting you to Lady Pandora's party!'

'You didn't invite me – she did. You only wanted me to come because – you wanted me to come,' Anna finished lamely, already regretting her hasty words.

'*WELL!*' Beth exploded, '*SOME* people just don't recognize a best friend even when they have one!'

She stomped away, on up the drive to Corran House. For a long moment Anna stood watching the figure of her best friend retreating into the shadows, then she turned and walked slowly over the road to The Gatehouse, praying that her brothers would be in bed. If one or other or both of them were still up, there would be some very awkward questions to answer – and she was too tired to face anyone – even Magnus.

CHAPTER ELEVEN

Walls Have Ears

MAGNUS WAS SITTING BY a well-stoked fire eating a supper of bannocks and cheese washed down with buttermilk. If Roderick had been witness to such a lavish feast he would have had no second thoughts about punishing his eldest son.

The numerous rules he had invented had been to 'create proper values in rebellious young minds.' He firmly believed in disciplining the body to withstand all kinds of hardships and though his bedroom was filled with luxuries he would never admit, either to himself or anyone else, that these concessions were a sign of a self-indulgent nature. He believed himself to be a gentleman of thrift, one who adhered to the belief that 'In the home of a servant of God too much glitter induced improper notions of grandeur, especially in the young.' Of William Jordan he spoke scathingly since his home had all the trappings of a man of 'jumped up affluence' who had neither the taste nor the breeding of his betters.

It wasn't often that Magnus defied the rules of the house because long ago he had learned that if he wanted any peace in his life it was simpler to obey than to defy.

Adam could always be relied upon to 'clipe' but tonight Magnus had packed him off to bed before heaping logs onto the fire.

Roderick had already left the house when the brothers had returned from Paddy Stool Hill. A paltry fire had smouldered sullenly in the grate; a note on the table had given Magnus instructions to damp the cinders with wet dross, which procedure ensured Roderick a cosy glow on his return home.

Magnus moved restlessly. He hadn't seen Anna since the chestnuts had been set to roast in the ashes of the bonfire and he wondered where she had got to. Sometimes he asked himself why he bothered so much about her welfare. It would have been easy just to sit back and let her fetch and carry for him. Adam accepted his sister's role in the home. He expected her to see to his comforts for he had been brought up to the belief that girls were born to be subservient and that it was a masculine right to be waited on.

Magnus couldn't accept such an attitude. He cherished the misty memories of the past, his mother holding a tiny baby girl to her breast, her gentle demonstrations of love. But as well as love she had radiated fear; she lived in dread of that big looming figure of a man who flitted across Magnus's mind in strangely shadowy fragments of recall . . .

Lillian had been an obedient wife to him, yet defiant too when it came to defending her little ones. If Magnus thought very hard he could see her in his mind, bravely facing up to Roderick, warning him away from her children. In those days she had often displayed great strength of character . . . then had come Adam! Bawling and lusty. Charging into the world like a bull . . .

The visions of Roderick were stronger now: puffing up with pride, smiling down at his new son . . . why was it that Adam was so special to Roderick? Why not himself, Magnus, the first-born son? He remembered Lillian, screaming, 'No, no! I can't stand it! I can't! He would be better dead! Better dead!'

Magnus wasn't sure if his memories of that scene were accurate, he had been very young at the time. His mother had never spoken like that before, it wasn't in her nature to wish anyone dead, far less a newborn infant . . . Then came snatches of his mother crying, pleading with Roderick to leave her be. She had never shouted, just that quiet pleading for peace . . . just peace . . . and it had come with the snapping of her mind, the oblivion of not knowing, not caring about anything anymore – not even her children – not even Anna!

Anna! A flaxen-haired mite who had deserved a good chance in life but who had instead been pitched into harsh reality from an early age. No dolls and a mother's lap for her. Drudgery from morning till night, slapped and bullied into doing the kind of tasks many grown women had yet to learn. If Roderick was really upset he would take down his leather shaving strop from its hook in his room and thrash both Anna and Magnus.

Adam had never suffered in this way, Roderick making no excuses

88

for such blatant favouritism. His youngest boy didn't need the strop, he behaved himself without it, it was that simple.

And that was true enough.

Magnus dared to hold his head defiantly high, Anna had the spirit to defend herself . . . but Adam . . . Adam was humble, meek, obedient, a dutiful son whose insides slammed with terror at the sight of the scars on his brother's back, the weals on his sister's shoulder blades.

Adam would do anything to avoid similar punishment so he grovelled and cliped and fought dirty fights so that he could boast about his strength to the terrifying man who was his father. He smiled, he sidled, and there were times he was so ashamed he cried into his pillow and hated himself – but hated his father a thousand times more.

Magnus gazed unseeingly into the fire, remembering the past, wondering if he would ever see his mother again . . . He had often thought of defying Roderick, of making the journey to the asylum to visit his mother but the thought of the consequences were too dreadful to contemplate. Roderick making his life a hell, perhaps throwing him out of the house . . . and he couldn't risk leaving Anna behind, life was bad enough for her as it was . . .

The soft closing of the lobby door brought him out of his reverie. Anna stood there, staring at him, her expression a mixture of challenge and apprehension.

Adam, lying in the dark room, wondered too why Anna was so late. Despite all his teasing and tormenting he liked Anna, he liked the way she moved and talked, he admired her spirit and the way she had of holding up her head, even when Roderick was doing his damnedest to demean her. She reminded Adam of someone else, a woman who had tended and cared for him and who had nursed him through his baby ills. A mother woman, gentle, kind, loving – yet – strange – despite all that she had never seemed as close to him as she had been to Magnus and Anna. The bond she had shared with them had been special and he had sometimes felt shut out – rejected. No one had ever really liked him very much – no one . . . even his father seemed disappointed in him.

Burying his head in his pillow he wept the bitter tears his father would never see.

*   *   *

89

As the door creaked gently open, Magnus swung round, his brown eyes glinting with anger. 'Where have you been, Anna? If *he* was here he would belt you.'

Anna put her cold fingers to her mouth. 'I knew he wouldn't be, he had to leave early to collect Mrs Simpson.'

'That's no excuse! I looked for you everywhere. I roasted a whole pile of chestnuts for you!' In a spurt of temper he turned out his pockets; a hail of shrivelled chestnuts splattered onto the hearth. 'For you, Anna! Only now they're just fit for the fire! Also . . .' He reached into the pocket of his waistcoat to bring out a silver sixpence.

'I won the leaping competition, this is for you – for your birthday. I want you to buy some ribbons, the kind that Beth Jordan wears. She's too plain to do them justice but you're different. If it was more I'd buy you a dress and stockings too, all in pure silk to match the ribbons.'

'Och, Magnus, thank you.' Anna felt herself drowning in a welter of emotions. 'I don't know what to say except sorry for making you worry about me. I never want to hurt you – not you, Magnus.'

Reaching for her hands he pulled her in closer to the fire, standing above her, tall and strong, his boyish face beautiful in the firelight. The lamp on the mantel caught the auburn glints in his hair, his tanned skin was flushed and shiny. He had recently washed, and the scent of soap lingered. She could smell his cleanness, the tiny curls that strayed over his collar were still damp.

His eyes were searching her face and she kept her own averted, unable to face the honest gaze of the brother whose loving nature was so in harmony with hers.

There was a long silence between them, Tibby purred softly from her warm perch atop the oven, sap from the logs hissed and bubbled in the flames, the hoot of an owl filtered into the room.

'Sit down.' Gently Magnus pushed his sister into the wooden inglenook with its sparse padding of worn cushions. 'I'll get your supper, you're freezing.'

In minutes she sat with a bowl of bread and milk on her lap, Magnus at her feet on the rag rug, hugging his knees as he gazed reflectively into the fire.

Anna stared at the steaming bowl of food but she didn't touch it. 'Magnus . . .' she began, then stopped abruptly, unable to go on.

'I know what you're trying to tell me, you were up at the big house, weren't you? Beth Jordan talked you into it. She's nothing but a spoiled bitch who doesn't care who she gets in trouble just as long as she gets her own way.'

'Och, Magnus, she didn't have to coax me, I wanted to go. And it was wonderful. I wish you could have been with me. The house is so fine with velvet cushions and sofas and marble fireplaces . . . and paintings, so many paintings yet I hardly noticed them I was so busy looking at the one of Lady Pandora above the fireplace. It's so real and she's so beautiful. There's a feeling about the house, happy and exciting – just like her – yet – a funny kind of sadness too – a sort of waiting feel. I could have spent the whole night just looking at her, her picture and herself.' Anna's voice was rising with enthusiasm. 'Sir Malaroy is very quiet compared to her yet they – they fit together. He's handsome with blue eyes that look into your heart and a neat little beard like the Van Dyck pictures in Miss Priscilla's books. He's such a gentleman too. Bunty Walters fell on the floor and rolled about like a ball till he picked her up and patted her head. He and Lady Pandora simply *adore* one another . . .'

'You're getting to sound like Beth Jordan,' Magnus's tones were scathing. 'You always sound like her after you've been wi' her for a while – all airs and graces and fancy words.'

Anna looked at him strangely. 'You don't like Beth, do you, Magnus? Why don't you? She likes you – in fact she likes you an awful lot, much better than she does Adam. She says one day you'll be a gentleman even though you might always just work on a farm.' She wrinkled her brow. 'That's a bit daft, isn't it? Gentlemen live in fine houses like Sir Malaroy but I think she means you have the manners of a gentleman.'

'Rubbish!' Magnus said scornfully. 'Beth always talks rubbish! And I'll tell you one thing, for all her fine clothes and fancy airs she'll never be a lady even if she lives to be a hundred. Inside of herself she's common. In fact – in fact I wouldn't be surprised if she grows up to be like Nellie Jean!'

Anna's eyes were round with shock. 'How can you say such things, Magnus? Beth will never be like Nellie Jean. She's beautiful and one day she's going to be a really fine lady.'

Magnus's mouth twisted into a wry smile. 'Ach, I'm sorry I spoke like that, it's just that I get mad at Beth the way she wheedles round you. If Father ever finds out you were up at the big house he would half kill you.'

Anna laid her hand on his shoulder. 'He won't ever find out. I was all dressed up as a ghost. No one knew it was me.'

Her grey eyes searched his face. 'Say you'll forgive me, I'm truly sorry I worried you . . . and say you're glad that I had a party on my birthday for the very first time in my life.'

Kneeling in front of her he took her hands. 'I forgive you, my babby – and I'm glad you enjoyed yourself tonight. Come on, eat your supper, we'll do the chores together then go through to bed.'

'Will you come in beside me and tell me a story?'

He hesitated, remembering the last time he had lain with her, the disturbing stirrings he'd experienced at the feel of her body against his.

'I don't know, Anna,' he hedged, 'It's been an exciting night, I'm tired and so are you.'

'Not too tired for a story.'

'Alright, but five minutes, that's all.'

'I wonder if Lucas and Peter ever get bedtime stories,' she said musingly.

'Lucas and Peter? You mean the Noble boys?'

'Ay, they tried to take my ghost sheet off and I hated them though Peter looked sorry for it.'

'They're a wild pair and you'd best keep away from them. That teacher o' theirs has them jumping and running all over the place. They even come whooping into the farm to see the horses and the one called Lucas thinks it's funny to order me about as if I was one o' the servants.'

'Ay, he would. Beth likes him though, she smiled all the time he was talking, even when he was being rude to her. I'll likely never cross paths with them again, they're far too posh for the likes o' me.'

He smiled and pulled her to her feet. 'You're much too good for the likes o' them, but even little ladies sometimes have to do the dishes and we'd better get ours done or the old man will have something to say.'

Adam took his eye away from the keyhole and, tip-toeing away from the door, he climbed back into bed as silently as the creaking springs would let him. The sheets were freezing cold; he shuddered and glanced malevolently at the open window, wishing he had the courage to shut it.

Curling into a tight ball with his hands between his knees he wallowed in misery for a few minutes but despite his discomfort he smiled to himself in the darkness. Now he knew why Anna had been so late getting home. She had been to the party at The House of Noble. He had often longed to go there himself but had never dared.

Anna was brave, that was another of the things he liked about her. She had defied Roderick in spite of her fear of him.

Adam sighed and wriggled about in the cold bed, wishing Magnus would come through, but he had said he would whisper a story to Anna first.

Adam wished he could get into bed beside his sister, she would be warm and soft and her arms would be comforting – like those other arms in his half-remembered dreamings.

His thoughts moved to Beth Jordan. Anna had said Beth didn't like him yet the last time he had kissed her in the school shed she had put her arms around him and had pressed herself into him before cuffing his ear.

Anna and Beth, Beth and Anna, girls with skinny bodies and bosoms that hadn't grown yet, but they would, one day they would and meantime he would enjoy watching them grow. Warmth invaded his loins, he touched his hardening penis and licked his lips. It didn't matter if Anna hadn't grown her bosoms yet, he could still enjoy himself with her. He couldn't very well get into Beth's bed but he could get into Anna's – and he would! Tomorrow night when Magnus was asleep!

And if Anna wouldn't let him he would threaten to tell their father that she had been to the Hallowe'en party at The House of Noble!

CHAPTER TWELVE

All Gifts

RODERICK WAS VERY SILENT during breakfast. He was thinking about last night's festivities at The House of Noble. It had been a grand occasion. All that luxury! Crystal glasses chinking; china punch bowls with elegant silver and ebony ladles; a cold supper of chicken, ham, venison, duck, and roast beef with all the trimmings.

The dancing had been good. He'd dumped Rachel Simpson quite early on, leaving her with a bunch of chattering frumps like herself, and for the rest of the evening he'd enjoyed himself with other men's wives and sweethearts. Most of them had been happy to partner him because their menfolk had been taken up with other pleasures, mainly the punch table, man talk, and a barely concealed rivalry for the attentions of Lady Pandora.

God! There was a woman for you! Delectable as a rose, gay, beautiful, with that air of elusiveness about her that only made her all the more desirable. Too bad that tutor chap, Mallard, had hung about beside her for much of the time, dancing with her, laughing and talking with her as if he owned her.

Roderick had wondered if the rumours concerning them were true, tales about them carrying on together behind Sir Malaroy's back. They had certainly gazed into one another's eyes a lot and his hands had strayed a bit when they had been dancing.

Still, who could blame him, who could blame any man for wanting a woman like that? For sticking to her like glue and not letting anyone else get a chance to be near her.

Even so, he wasn't her keeper, she had proved that by circulating as much as possible, enchanting everyone with her charisma, even the womenfolk.

Towards the end of the evening Roderick had managed to get her to dance with him. The very smell of her was enough to drive a man mad. Sweet and alluring, as fresh as a mountain stream. She had been aloof and dignified in his arms, head high, that dazzling honey-gold hair of hers swept into a neat chignon, little ringlets of it falling enticingly over her perfect ears.

And her breasts! Creamy white against the blue silk of her dress, small like a young girl's, so sensual and provocative every fibre in him had been aroused. He had wanted to crush their softness in his big hands, squeeze them and play with them and suckle the nipples, kiss the smooth skin, make love to them . . . and all that before sampling the further delights of her slender body now so temptingly close to his own.

So different from Nellie Jean with her rude good looks and her big, bouncing breasts. Nothing restrained about them! Sex with Nellie Jean was fiery and satisfying but it was lacking in grace. She was a hot-arsed wonderful bitch in bed, giggling and coarse-tongued, writhing in a way that brought out the animal in him so that he was unable to wait, ramming into her, hurting her because he was built like a bull, she loving it, crying out in pain and pleasure, primitive noises that made him more frenzied than ever.

Unconsciously he had pulled Lady Pandora hard up against him so that he was aware of every movement of her body. She hadn't moved away from him and for quite a few minutes he had been able to enjoy close contact with her. But it had been too much for him, the hardness in his trousers bringing him out in such a sweat he had been obliged to reach for his hanky in order to mop his brow.

Lady Pandora had raised her brows at him and then she had laughed, a light, teasing laugh, as if she was acknowledging the effect she'd had on him.

He had been somewhat flabbergasted at the look in her eyes, mysterious, tantalizing, beckoning, and he had known then that the ice between them was broken.

On the occasions that he had visited the big house he had only ever seen her briefly and always she had given him the impression that she didn't approve of his presence in her home. Her attitude had annoyed him, after all, he *was* Roderick McIntyre, a man of some importance in his own right, and the sooner she realized that the better.

But she had remained distant towards him and now – here she was, smiling at him in a way that suggested her awareness of his arousal, making him feel that, of all the men in the room, he and he alone had the privilege of sharing such an intimacy with her.

After that she had relaxed and had gone on to tell him about her meeting with Anna. 'You have a charming daughter, Mr McIntyre, a child like that should know more about the big wide world. Why is it, I wonder, that you have never allowed your children to visit my house?'

'Ah well, my lady, it isn't easy for a man to raise a family single-handed – you know – fine clothes and all the falderals that bairnies need for partygoing – especially a lass like Anna with her fancy ideas.' His tone had been apologetic, the words carefully guarded, a wary look had crept over his florid features.

Lady Pandora regarded him for a long moment. 'Of course,' she had said at last, 'your poor wife. Tragic. I don't remember her too well for I don't recall seeing her around the village. What a shame for the children – especially Anna – a girl needs her mother, particularly now when she is beginning to emerge from the cocooned world of childhood.'

'Quite, quite, dear lady,' Roderick had agreed affably while he struggled with the idea of Anna having a cocooned childhood. Perhaps a working childhood might be a more apt description and far better that than idle hands getting into mischief!

'A shy one is our little lass,' he had gone on evenly. 'But I'm sure she'll turn out to be a genteel young woman with the interests of home and family at heart.'

'Miss Priscilla tells me she is a gifted artist. I met the lady coming out of your house and we got talking about Anna. I believe she intends to give the child personal tuition and very pleased I am to hear it. It would be a pity to let such a talent go to waste.'

'Ah, Miss McLeod, a fine woman but a typical spinster, plenty of brains for the classroom but scant knowledge of everyday family life.'

Roderick was becoming tired of the subject and had tried to steer the talk to a more personal level. Lady Pandora, however, was having none of that. Putting her face close to his, she had parted her lips provocatively and had said softly, 'I'd like Anna to come and visit me and hope you can arrange it. The child fascinates me – all that flaxen hair – and those big eyes. You must know how I love children . . . perhaps it's fanciful, but in Anna I see myself . . . or rather, what I imagine my own daughter would have been like – if – if I had had a daughter, of course.'

She had laughed then, too carelessly. 'The whole world must know that I can't have Sir Malaroy's children — because of — well, that's common knowledge too, no doubt.'

Roderick had nodded. It was a well known fact that Sir Malaroy was unable to father children owing to a severe glandular illness that had befallen him at the age of fifteen. His faithful, but loose-tongued old nanny had broadcast the news to her equally garrulous cronies, taking a sad sort of pleasure in announcing, 'Master Malaroy will never plant a fertile seed save for those he puts in the land. The heirs to Noble House will never be o' his making — and that's the gospel truth as sure as I stand here.'

Soon after his illness the young Malaroy had gone to England to be educated, returning some years later with his bride, keeping his secret from her till she was safely his.

Lady Pandora had been devastated when she eventually learned that her husband was sterile. Shock had turned to fury and for a long time there had existed terrible tensions in the marriage. To console herself she had taken to flirting with other men, most of the affairs being of a lighthearted nature, others less so, one in particular almost causing the breakup of her marriage.

It had taken her a long time to get over that episode in her life, and through it all Sir Malaroy had been a sad and lonely man, yet he had never forsaken her, rather he had been a great comfort to her when it had all come to a head and he had faced the consequences with her, nursing her through a mental and physical breakdown that had taken her many months to conquer. After that they had grown closer than they had ever been and she told herself that he was all she needed in her life, all she would ever want.

So she had deceived her mind but not her heart. As she approached forty, the obsession started to grow. She couldn't go on denying her maternal instincts, she wanted children, she longed to hear The House of Noble ring with young voices. It was only natural that she should want to give her husband an heir, she had pleaded with him to let her adopt a child, but for him it had to be his own flesh or nothing and in her grief she once more started to flirt with other men. And now she had met Anna — the very image of the daughter of her dreams . . .

'I want Anna here — Roderick — I can't seem to get her out of my mind so I beg you, let her come to me.'

The pleading in her voice had surprised even Roderick. Looking into

97

her lovely eyes he had found himself glimpsing the sadness of a tragically unfulfilled woman . . . but his sympathy did not last long – immediately he realized how he could profit from such a situation – yet – he hesitated at the idea of Anna hob-nobbing with the gentry. The little brat already had notions of grandeur, there was no knowing where it would lead if she was indulged in this way . . . she was needed at home . . . also, he had some very good reasons of his own for not wanting Anna and her ladyship to get too close . . .

His mind had seethed. From the corner of his eye he had noticed Sir Malaroy watching him and he had wondered how often the poor bastard had stood helplessly by while his wife cast her enchantment over other men.

'My youngest – Adam – is a nice lad,' he had found himself saying. 'Perhaps he could come and keep you company. He'd fetch and carry for you and keep you happy for he has a fine wit and a good brain.'

'Anna,' Lady Pandora had spoken the name softly. 'I want Anna. Another boy would be one too many for me, silly man. I already have my nephews, as wild as the heather but I enjoy having them around. Everyone thinks they should be away at boarding school but they're happier here with me. Mr Mallard is an excellent teacher and keeps them well disciplined.

'No, Roderick, it's a companion I want and no boy could fill that role. Anna would like it here, she could paint and read all day if she wanted – she could paint me . . .' She had laughed gaily. 'If it pleases her she can paint pictures on all the walls in the house.'

'The lass is worth her weight in gold,' he had blustered, annoyed to feel himself trembling.

It had been Lady Pandora's turn to press herself against him, so firmly he had felt the softness of her breasts against his chest. 'You will be well rewarded,' she had whispered. 'I don't expect to take a companion for nothing – and of course – I would be very grateful.' She had ended on a mysterious note and he had stared fascinated at her tongue travelling slowly between her teeth.

'Remember – Pandora means all gifts . . .' had been her parting shot before whirling regally over to her husband, her hands outstretched in a gesture of affection that had made every man in the room feel envious and cheated.

*   *   *

98

Roderick dug into his boiled egg and looked furtively at Anna. She was eating her breakfast slowly, with that air of gentle detachment about her that never failed to infuriate him, simply because he couldn't understand it and knew no way of penetrating it. Bullying and beating only served to make her withdraw more into herself and he hated her, as even in all her vulnerability, she had a strength that made him feel inferior.

'Get me more tea, girl,' he growled.

Obediently she rose to fetch the teapot from the hob and he took the opportunity to watch her, trying to fathom what it was about her that had merited Lady Pandora's interest.

He had seldom taken the time to study the girl whose delicacy of movement always made him feel clumsy and awkward. She was dressed as usual in drab attire and as usual the little bit of white lace at her throat so attracted the eye everything else faded into unimportance. Those tiny bits of finery were her stamp, a shout of defiance in the face of grey domesticity. She moved like a young deer, gracefully, easily, yet alert and wary at the same time. Her hair was unbelievable, hanging around her shoulders like a silken curtain, with a chain of late daisies woven into the shining strands.

He forgot to be careful and stared openly. She was exquisite, silently, purely lovely, like a creamy rosebud struggling to assert its beauty in a neglected flowerbed. How could such a girl be his daughter?

Turning with the teapot Anna saw his look and caught thus, he could do nothing but hold her gaze. For the first time he noticed the depth of her eyes, blue-grey, so dark in her fair face, so filled with expression he couldn't bear to look into them and was the first to turn away. He knew now why she was able to move so quietly through her days, everything that was life was in those eyes, they mirrored a soul that burned with the eagerness and joy of living, compelling all who looked into them to take notice of her and to remember her.

'Can't you do something with your hair, girl?' he snarled. 'Look at it, hanging about your face. Makes you look like a little hoor!'

'Can I tie it back, Father – with a ribbon?' She seized on the opportunity, hardly daring to breathe while she waited for the answer.

His eyes glittered, a quick refusal sprung to his lips, then Lady Pandora's hinted promises flashed into his mind and with forced jollity he said, 'Ribbons! Of course! Our little girl must have pretty ribbons. After all, you never know where a lass o' your breeding could end up. Better to be prepared. Next week we might go into Dunmor and get you some nice material, I'm sure old Grace will be only too willing to run you up a frock or two. Ay, it's time you had some better clothes.' He had exhausted his benevolence, turning his attention back to his breakfast he dipped bread into his egg yolk and scooped it up to his lips with sounds of rude enjoyment.

Anna was so surprised she could do nothing but gape at the top of his iron-grey head. Magnus and Adam were also taken aback and all three stared at the big bull figure of their father, sucking up egg yolk, gulping down hot tea, cramming buttered bannocks into his mouth, giving every appearance of guileless contentment.

Magnus glowered at him suspiciously. Something was afoot, something was behind it all, something out of which Roderick McIntyre stood to gain. A tyrant didn't change into a caring father overnight.

Magnus picked up his lunch box and motioned Anna to go to the door with him. 'You take care,' he murmured warningly, 'The old man's up to no good.'

She nodded, she knew Magnus was right, but she couldn't help feeling a surge of excitement at the idea of owning some nice clothes at last. Wait till she told Beth about *that*.

Shoris Ferguson was at his window, peering through his field glasses when Tell Tale Todd arrived for his usual dram.

'Well, well, would you look at that now,' Shoris muttered with obvious enjoyment. 'Those rascals are at it again, swinging about in the trees like monkeys. They're good at it too, that Mr Mallard has taught them well,' he ended on an admiring note.

'Taught them how to kill themselves,' Todd said dourly, taking the glasses from Shoris so that he could view the action for himself.

'Just look at them,' he breathed. 'One o' these fine days there will be an accident in yonder trees. You mark my words. All it needs is for a branch to snap and crash! They'll break their necks as they come down on those big boulders in the river.'

'Or maybe the bridge parapet,' Shoris chortled fiendishly, his round, red face beaming from ear to ear.

'Or maybe the teacher chappie will get it,' went on Todd, screwing up one eye against the glasses. 'He shows them how to do everything first.'

Shoris grabbed the glasses for another look. 'Ay, and that might no' be all he's showing them. Here he comes wi' her ladyship, the pair o' them strolling along the bank without a care in the world.'

'Let me see!' clamoured Todd, annoyed when Shoris elbowed him away. 'Och, come on now, man, it's my turn. Are they kissin' or cuddlin' or are they doing both?'

'Nothing o' that sort,' Shoris sounded disappointed, 'Just laughing and talking. Of course, they *could* be holding hands, I canna see too well for the branches.'

'That wouldn't surprise me.' Todd sounded self-righteous. 'There's a lot o' talk about that two – though of course,' he added hastily, 'it's all just rumour, and wi' her being gentry and a Noble into the bargain, who are we to judge.'

Shoris turned a watery eye on his friend and closed it in a rather painful wink. 'Ay, who are we to judge right enough, Todd my lad? Gossip can get a lot o' folk into trouble, even a man like yourself that no one in their right mind would associate wi' a woman – a *married* woman at that,' he finished heavily.

Todd's face went red, mouth agape he stared at Shoris. 'And just what are you implying, Shoris Ferguson?'

'Oh, it wasna me, it was rumour, just some nonsense about you and Janet McCrae in the back shop together at dinnertime.'

'Me and Janet McCrae!' exploded Todd. 'What in the name o' God will they think o' next! Janet? Janet McCrae? She's a married woman I'll have you . . .' He stopped, he stared at his friend who was slowly nodding his head in the fashion of a marionette, his ear-splitting grin revealing two ancient brown incisors.

'Ay, ay, Todd, that's what I've just been saying. It just goes to show how gossip can get out o' hand. I mean to say, man, Janet's a respectable woman, she would never dream o' associating herself wi' a drinkin' body like yourself.'

Todd glowered long and hard. He couldn't make up his mind which was the most insulting, to be labelled as a wife stealer or to be branded as a man that no woman would look at.

Shoris threw back his head and roared with laughter, then, putting his arm round his friend's shoulder, he said comfortingly, 'I have just the thing for you. A wee drop o' the malt that Bob the Post gave me for snaring him a few rabbits. Och, don't look so down, man, for all I know you might be hob-nobbing wi' Janet, and even if you aren't, think what fun you can have swingin' the gossips along. Right now a good dram is what you need before you face the menagerie going up Mill Brae.'

Todd gazed reverently at the amber liquid in his glass. 'Here's to the bonny malt, better than any woman any day,' he intoned huskily, and downed his drink in one gulp.

CHAPTER THIRTEEN

Tantrums

A NNA HADN'T SEEN BETH for a week. She had been ill in bed with a cold which Mrs Jordan had attributed to 'All the damp and smoke she had inhaled up on that dreadful hill at Hallowe'en.'

But Beth was better now; last night Fat Jane had puffed down to The Gatehouse to let Anna know that her friend would be fit for school in the morning. Morning had arrived but there was no sign of Beth at the foot of Corran House driveway when Anna and Adam made their appearance.

Normally Adam set off on his own as Anna was invariably busy with last minute chores but today he had some very good reasons for accompanying her.

It was a damp, dewy morning; nebulous webs clung to the dead roadside grasses; smoke from the chimneys drifted in blue banners amongst the trees; the scent of the pines was sweet and heavy in the calm air.

The mill was clattering busily. A cartload of empty barrels was rumbling up the road, pulled by two big Clydesdales. Boxer Sam and Nellie Jean were coming out of one of the sheds and obligingly went to open the goods gate to let the horses through. Nellie Jean was giggling in her full-throated way because Boxer Sam was shadow punching and generally fooling around.

Roderick saw them from the office window and glowered. 'Damn that buggering show-off,' he muttered dourly. 'All muscle and no brains.'

Nellie Jean waved and shouted, 'Mornin', Mr McIntyre.'

'Mornin', Mr McIntyre,' mimicked Boxer Sam in a high voice and the pair went on up Stable Lane together, stifling their laughter.

Roderick's frown deepened, he sat back and brooded over Boxer

Sam. Some day he would rid the mill of the swaggering lout, whatever William Jordan thought! By God and he would!

William Jordan was coming out of the little gate at the bottom of his garden. The smooth running of the factory owed itself to him; he knew how to handle people and got more out of his employees with his respectful approach than did Roderick with all his snooping and domineering.

William Jordan was a tall, strapping man with sandy brows and a jutting jaw. He was smartly dressed in a dark coat with short tails, a high crowned bowler hat, and dark striped trousers with a matching waistcoat. Normally he wore his knickerbocker suit but this morning his wife had insisted he wear the more formal outfit since he was going up to the big house to discuss business affairs with Sir Malaroy. Sir Malaroy himself would most likely be in knickerbockers but anything for peace! Victoria was a woman who liked to get her own way and she nagged at everyone till she did.

God! She was a nag alright! If she and Roderick got together to run the mill there would be no workers left!

Jordan smiled at the thought and paused to take a deep breath of air. A few late roses blazed red against their dark foliage and stooping he plucked one, fixing it to his buttonhole with a flourish.

'There,' he smiled at Anna waiting at the gate. 'The finishing touch, very important that, my dear.' He glanced at the lace nestling at her throat. 'But I see you know that little trick already.'

'Ay, Mr Jordan, it makes me feel good. I was wondering – is Beth coming do you know? Fat Ja– Mrs Higgins – said Beth would be going to school this morning. Usually we meet at the foot of the drive but she isn't there.'

Jordan knitted his sandy brows. 'She went out some time ago. She wasn't in her usual talkative mood this morning. Normally she and my wife gab their heads off at the breakfast table but today it was – um – reasonably peaceful with only one voice going on. Probably the child has got some foolish notion into her head, because she did a good bit of flouncing around before she went off to school.' He smiled again at Anna but he couldn't hide his annoyance at his daughter. 'She's a little madam at times. She ought to have waited for you since it's your last morning at school.'

104

'Maybe she still thinks she's a witch like last week,' Adam chimed in, showing his teeth in a grimacing sort of smile. 'Beth plays witches better than any person I know.'

'Quite,' returned Jordan dryly, his mind on his daughter's sulks of the morning, his wife's indulgence on the matter. Sometimes he felt that a good sound spanking would do the child a world of good but Victoria wouldn't hear of such a thing.

He looked at Anna with her intelligent face and her hair filling the morning with sunshine. Her coarse brown dress hung around her skinny body in shapeless folds, her stout leather boots would have been more fitting on a boy, yet for all that she had grace and dignity and the kind of manners that were inborn.

The boy was more tastefully clad: his grey suit was of Mrs McCrae's 'good thick material' but it fitted well with the knee breeches meeting long boots of quality leather. A cloth cap was jammed over his mop of tight brown curls and altogether he was extremely well turned out. Yet for all that he looked rough and braggish, truly Iron Rod's son and possibly the reason why he was the more favoured of the children.

'Beth can't be far away,' Jordan told Anna. 'She'll be waiting for you along the road somewhere.'

He began to move off but remembered something. 'Oh, by the way, Anna, Mrs Higgins wants you to pop in for a minute. She says she won't keep you.'

Anna went hurrying through the gate, leaving Adam searching for chestnuts at the roadside.

No sooner was she inside the kitchen door than Fat Jane enveloped her in an affectionate hug. It was like being smothered in a vast feather bolster that smelt of nutmeg and cooking sherry but Anna didn't mind, in fact she clung on to the delicious rolls of fat for as long as she could, enjoying that lovely 'mother' feel that she so missed in her life.

'I've got something for you, my little lovely,' the cook said beamingly. 'I wanted to give it to you last week on your birthday but with Beth being laid up I never got the chance.'

She waddled away to a drawer to withdraw a tissue-covered parcel which she handed to Anna, at the same time bestowing a kiss on her cheek and wishing her an ''appy birthday.'

'Made it myself, I did,' she said proudly, standing back, hands folded across her fluffy doughball of a stomach, grinning broadly.

Anna gazed speechlessly at the blue satin-covered handkerchief case embroidered with pink rosebuds, with the initials A. M. fashioned in dark blue silk in one of the corners.

'Oh, Fa– Mrs Higgins! It's perfect! It's beautiful! I'll keep all my treasures in it. Thank you a million, trillion times.' Standing on tiptoe she put her arms round Fat Jane's shoulders to give her an almighty cuddle. The cook chortled. Straightening up she rearranged her white mutch cap and shooed Anna to the door. 'Off you go now or you'll be late, and Miss Priscilla wouldn't like that.'

A massive shadow darkened the door. Maggie May had arrived for her morning cuppa, a brew that might include 'wee droppies' of whisky, gin, or rum. If these weren't forthcoming from the roomy pockets of Maggie May's apron, there was always the cooking sherry to fall back on, and never mind if the half-depleted bottle had to be topped up with cider vinegar.

The two women greeted one another with the enthusiasm of long lost friends, even though they had both partaken of supper in the kitchen only the night before.

Anna held her breath. It was quite an experience to hear two rich, plummy voices talking at the one time. They reminded her of clouty Christmas dumplings straight from the stove, warm and spicy, full of richness and goodness, crammed with fruity delights, containing just the right amount of sherry to tickle the palate.

Clutching her parcel Anna ran down the driveway to find Adam still hanging about waiting for her.

'What's that you've got?' was his inquisitive greeting.

'A present, for my birthday, from Fat Jane, a hanky holder with my initials on it.'

'Everybody gives you things.' He spoke in a surly voice. 'They all like you, Anna. Jordan always talks to you but hardly ever to me.'

'Not everyone likes me, Father doesn't but he likes you, he lets you off with everything.'

Something was niggling at her. She looked into her brother's face. 'How did you know that Beth was a witch on Hallowe'en? She wasn't wearing her costume at the bonfire on Paddy Stool Hill.'

He gave a triumphant leap in the air, trying to catch a horse chestnut branch laden with green spiky fruit. 'I know *everyone's* secrets, I know *your* secrets. You were dressed as a ghost last week and went to the party at The House of Noble.' He pounced on an enormous chestnut nestling in the dead leaves at the roadside, proceeding to split it with a squat fingernail. His preoccupation with the chestnut was deliberate, a play for time that was calculated to make his sister squirm.

'Look, Anna.' He held out a square, sweaty palm in which reposed a large red chestnut. 'Wait till Danny Black sees this, he'll try and knock me out at conkers but he won't crack this one.'

Anna's face had turned white. 'How did you know I was a ghost last week – and why have you waited all this time to mention it?'

He danced along in front of her, throwing the conker in the air, giggling devilishly, showing off in his swaggering way. 'Cos I'm magic, that's how! Ghostie, ghostie Annie! Greetin' for her mammy!'

'You listen at keyholes, that's what you do, Adam McIntyre! You're nothing but a little sneak!'

'Let me coorie in bed wi' you tonight and I'll no' tell Father on you,' he said in wheedling tones.

'No!' cried Anna sharply.

'You let Magnus! Is it because he's got a bigger willy than me? Do you like big willies, Anna? I bet Father might get really angry if he knew about last week and about Magnus getting into bed wi' you. All week I've been waiting my chance to get in beside you but he's always beaten me to it. What does he do when he's under the blankets, Anna? Does he play wi' you? Do you play wi' him? Does his willy go big and hard the way mine does whenever I think about you touching it . . .'

'Shut up! Just shut up! Your head's full o' dirt, Adam McIntyre, and I'm not going to listen to any more!'

She had spied Beth's sandy head in the distance, walking with Bunty Walters who, with her fat little legs, could barely keep up with the other's long strides.

'Beth!' Gladly Anna broke away from her brother to catch up with her friend but Beth didn't acknowledge her, instead she began to walk even harder, making Bunty pant noisily in her efforts to keep up.

'Hallo, Anna, I haveny seen you for a whilie,' cried the red-faced Bunty, 'I've been off all week wi' the cold – just like Beth. Did you know I won first prize for my guiser costume at Lady Pandora's Hallowe'en party? I got a fine pair o' new boots all stuffed up wi' stockings and sweeties. My mammy let me wear them today because I've had the cold but then I've to keep them till the weather gets really bad.'

'*SHE* should know all about *THAT*,' Beth butted in, her tones heavy with implication. 'About the boots, and the sweets, and everything.'

Bunty shook her head. 'No she shouldn't, Anna wasn't there, she . . .'

'Shut up, fatty!' stormed a tight-lipped Beth.

Bunty's chubby face quivered with hurt and she began to run, as fast as her sturdy legs and her new boots would carry her, on up the road to school.

'You didn't have to shout at poor wee Bunty like that,' Anna said in dismay. 'What ails you anyway? Have you got a headache?'

Beth tossed her head. 'I've got a best friend ache, that's what. A best friend who calls me selfish! There I was, ill in bed all week, and all I could think about were the names you called me after the party. It just rankled and rankled. Sometimes I think you must be mad like your mother, Anna McIntyre.'

Anna gasped with horror. 'You are selfish, Beth Jordan — and cruel into the bargain! And fancy brooding your time away over nothing. I'm just getting a wee bit fed up with all these tantrums o' yours!'

Adam caught up with them, in nice time to hear his sister's words. 'I don't think you're selfish, Beth,' he said ingratiatingly, 'or soft like these other stupid girls in the glen.'

So engrossed were the three in their argument they were totally unprepared for the cacophony of bovine bellows that suddenly erupted from a thicket of bushes, nor were they prepared for the unexpected appearance of Sally McDonald as she rushed out to dance in front of them, the most realistic impersonations of cows and cockerels issuing from her grinning lips.

At thirty Sally was the eldest of the family. Unlike her brothers she was gypsy dark and so beautiful at times it was hard to believe she was anything else but sane. But just then she appeared to be wholly mad, with her raven hair matted with grass, her black eyes glazed, and her oddly sensitive mouth twisted.

'You stupid, daft fool!' fumed Beth, 'You should be locked up!'

'Crazy bastard bitch!' Adam cursed. He had suffered a genuine fright: his heart was pounding, he felt weak at the knees. 'I'll pay you back, silly old Sally! You wait and see if I don't!'

Daft Donal was marching purposefully through the fields towards the road but this morning he wasn't chanting out any of his usual rhymes. When he drew nearer, the children saw that he was scrubbing his eyes in an effort to stifle the dirty rivers of tears pouring down his face.

'Davie hit me,' he sobbed pitifully. 'Last night he hit Sally wi' stick! Him drinking!'

'Drinking,' repeated Sally, 'Sally like whisky but Davie drink it all.'

Sorrowfully Donal rubbed his stomach, 'Donal hungry. No breakfast.'

'Breakfast,' Beth corrected scornfully.

Kneeling on the grass Anna rummaged in the lap bag she had made to carry her books. Withdrawing the packet that contained her mid-morning play piece she carefully divided it, giving half each to Sally and Donal.

'It isn't much, but it will keep you going till dinner time,' she told them. 'Go you away now, Donal, they'll be waiting to hear the time down at the mill.'

Donal beamed. 'Ay,' he agreed importantly and strode away, wolfing down the food Anna had given him.

Extricating a box of matches and a clay pipe from her filthy apron, Sally proceeded to stuff the pipe with a mixture of dry leaves and grass. After lighting it she sat herself down on the verge to alternate her attentions between her pipe and her piece, a look of supreme content-ment settling over her features.

Beth sniffed haughtily. 'My, my, Anna, you certainly know how to handle people like that. You'll go hungry at playtime now for I shan't share my sandwiches with you nor my madeira cake. Fat Jane gave me two big slices and two apples.'

'I don't care,' returned Anna with dignity. 'It's only this once, they go hungry quite often, especially if Davie's been drinking.'

'Ach, you're soft,' sneered Adam. He held out the hand that contained the big chestnut. 'Look, Beth, I'll give you this if you play wi' me at break and I'll give you a buttered bannock.'

The school bell tinkled, Beth looked at Anna but couldn't hold her friend's unwavering gaze. Tossing her hair back from her shoulders she patted her ribbon into place and said condescendingly, 'Come on then, Adam, don't just stand there, later I'll give you a game of conkers and I'll share my cake with you – if you promise not to show off like a baby.'

Adam was momentarily ashamed of himself. Glancing at Anna he saw the mist of tears in her eyes. She looked so pale and delicate that Adam, in a rare burst of sensitivity, felt that a puff of wind could blow her away, as easily as if she was made of thistledown.

'*ADAM!*' Beth's tone was authoritative. 'Are you coming or not?'

'Ay,' he said gruffly and scampered after Beth without another look at his sister.

'Anna, stay behind for a moment please,' bade Miss Priscilla.

Anna waited while the room emptied and the door of the classroom squealed shut. 'Really,' said Miss Priscilla in annoyance, 'I keep forgetting to oil those hinges.'

She opened the lid of her desk. When she closed it she held a neat little case in her hand which she carried over to Anna. 'I want you to have this, Anna. It belonged to my father, he used to take it into the country and paint whatever took his fancy. Open it, child, I've replaced everything.'

Slowly Anna released the tiny snecks that held the lid in place. There before her were tubes and tubes of oil paints, pencils, charcoal sticks, two containers for paint thinners, and several brushes of different sizes.

For quite a few moments Anna said nothing, then she got up and put her arms round her teacher's neck. Miss Priscilla felt bony, she smelt of chalk and lavender. She also felt strong and solid; the smell of her was redolent of all those lovely school years that Anna had known and loved. This tiny school in Glen Tarsa had been an orderly world – and homely for all that, with the fire burning in the grate and the clock ticking busily on the wall.

Anna would always remember the smell of the dinnertime toast, the heat prickling her face and hands as she held the fork to the fire, watching the bread growing golden and crispy. Miss Priscilla had begun the little ritual some years ago. She hated to see hungry children, and there were a few of those in her keeping. Just minutes ago the last slice had been eaten, the last crumb dusted away; the smell of hot toast lingered in the room.

Anna knew she would remember the fire and the clock, the chalk and the lavender, for the rest of her days. She kissed Miss Priscilla's faded cheek.

'Dear me,' the teacher sniffed and pretended to have a speck of dust in her eye. She searched for her hanky. Anna handed her one made of snow-white linen with the initial A embroidered in one corner.

Miss Priscilla was a lady, she deserved the best, even old Grace would have admitted that – though she might not have approved of Anna handing over her birthday present for someone else to blow their nose on.

CHAPTER FOURTEEN

Dark Deeds

RODERICK WAS IN AN unusually benevolent mood. It was Friday evening, soon the weekend would be here to do with as he liked.

He stood in front of his wardrobe mirror and looked appreciatively at his appearance. He had spent ten minutes grooming his thick iron-grey thatch, and there wasn't a hair out of place. His side whiskers were still quite dark, worn well below his ears so that they framed his face and made his strong, square jaw seem finer than it was. The fashion of the day was for big bushy whiskers but he preferred to be clean shaven. He didn't need all that hair to make him look like a man. Beards were for weak chins and pimply faces, a form of disguise and an unhygienic one at that.

Picking up a fine-toothed comb he ran it through his wiry eyebrows, stuck out his heavy chin, and gazed reflectively into the mirror.

'Very distinguished, my lad,' he told himself approvingly.

Turning his attention to his clothes he wet a thumb and forefinger and ran them down the seams of his grey-striped trousers even though Anna had already pressed them to perfection.

'Very distinguished,' he murmured again and smiled with satisfaction, wishing that Lady Pandora could see him looking so immaculate.

Musingly he rocked on his heels, wondering if she had meant those veiled hints and half promises. He would carry out his side of the bargain and see what happened from there. The prospects were very exciting! Ay, very exciting indeed!

But he'd have to watch out for Sir Malaroy. It would never do for him to find out what was going on though the poor bugger had almost certainly been through it all before. Mallard too would have to be watched, no telling what a hot-blooded lad like that might do if he thought someone else was trying to muscle in on his territory. He had brawn and brains but he was only the boys' tutor after all and had no rights to exert when it came to the bit.

Gleefully Roderick rubbed his hands together and glanced at the spacious double bed with its elegant drapes. Tonight Nellie Jean would cavort in it, big breasts bouncing, her well-rounded bum wiggling about in his face.

Touching the blue chenille coverlet he tried to imagine Lady Pandora lying there, her hair cascading around her creamy shoulders, her violet eyes fascinating him with their promises, her pink tongue travelling slowly between those luscious lips of hers. The very thought of her in his bed made beads of sweat pop out on his brow and he sat down heavily, conscious of a desperate need to have possession of the beautiful creature who had avoided him for so long. Now the possibility of having her floated temptingly on the horizon though he knew he would have to wait awhile yet. Anna was his passport to paradise but first he'd have to spend some money on the little madam.

He couldn't send her up to The House of Noble looking like a peasant, some finery was a must but it would be money well spent, very well spent indeed if Lady Pandora one day filled his arms with her enchantment. Meantime he'd have to make do with Nellie Jean who wasn't such a bad compromise. Tonight he was throwing caution to the winds by meeting her in the Coach House Inn where he wouldn't have the irritating presence of Boxer Sam to contend with.

The man was a buggering nuisance! Roderick's mouth twisted. He much preferred the Munkirk Inn where he could let his hair down a bit, indulge in a few outrageous subtleties like pinching the barmaid's bum and having a tussle with her in the snug. Cuddles was his pet name for her, it made her go all coy and giggly and push out her breasts at him. Once he had managed to get his hand up her skirt to discover that she wasn't wearing bloomers. The surprise had taken his breath away and the things he had done to her had made her gasp with pleasure till some sod had rattled the snug door.

Opportunities like that were no doubt available at the Coach House Inn but he made it his business to shut his eyes to them. Mustn't set the gossips' tongues a' wagging, it would never do to jeopardize his reputation . . .

His thoughts were interrupted by a short little tap on the door followed by a voice saying, 'It's Magnus, Father, can I speak to you?'

113

'Enter,' bade Roderick pompously.

Magnus came in, carrying an iron bowat lantern. His skin looked golden in the soft light, bronze highlights shone in his hair, and he carried himself proudly erect as he addressed his father.

'Davie has just brought down a note from Jeemie. Beauty is foaling, he hasn't anybody to help except Davie who isn't all that good wi' animals. Jeemie wants me to go over to the stables.'

'And where is Calum? It's his job to tend the horses.'

'He went away wi' the mail coach this afternoon to see about buying a mare from Hamish Watt.'

'Ay, of course,' grunted Roderick. He had no interest in the horses and ponies who pulled the little goods wagons through the mill. He dealt with people, not animals, and he only listened to Magnus with half an ear. 'Alright, boy, on you go.'

'I might be there all night, the old lass always has a bad time foaling.'

'Well, I'll see Jordan about it and make sure you get paid for your time. I won't have my children working for nothing.'

Magnus regarded him with contempt. 'If Beauty delivers her foal safely that will be payment enough for me.'

'Ay indeed,' agreed Roderick with sarcastic affability. He put his big florid face close to that of his son. 'Quite the little romantic, aren't you? But notions like that don't put the clothes on your back or the food in your belly. When you're out in the world you can give all your money to charity for all I care, right now it's time you got your priorities right, my lad!' Roughly he brushed Magnus aside. 'Out o' my way now, it's time I got going . . . you've kept me long enough as it is.'

Davie was waiting for Magnus in the kitchen, standing in the middle of it, staring with apparent fascination at the fire, seemingly oblivious to the antics of Adam who, for the last few minutes, had danced round him, uttering every kind of insult he could think of.

Anna had warned him to stop his nonsense but he had paid no heed. 'The deaf old sod can't hear a word I'm saying,' he had told her and had gone on with his teasing.

After a while the man's lack of response had frustrated Adam, so much so he had finally resorted to standing in front of him to pull faces and make all sorts of animal impersonations in the hope it would get through to him that he was mocking Sally. Still Davie kept staring unwaveringly at the fire, an odd lack of expression in his pale blue eyes.

He was a young man of small stature, gauntness in every line of him, the flickering firelight emphasizing hollows in a face that wouldn't have looked out of place on a middle-aged man. Already his hair was thin and greying with a distinct bald patch at the crown; the flesh at his neck sagged; his brow was deeply furrowed; his skin was dry and ingrained with dirt.

But despite his thin frame he had the strength of an ox and could hoist up barrelloads of gunpowder as if it were cork. He rarely spoke to anyone and carried with him a continual air of grievance, bottling up his suppressed feelings till his temper would finally explode with Sally and Donal bearing the brunt of it.

'How's your silly old sister then? Still as mad as ever?' Adam went on relentlessly. 'I'll tell you something you daft, deaf sod. One o' these days I'm going to frighten the daylights out o' Silly Sally, pay her back for scaring me like she does. I'll get all my pals together and we'll get Sally in a shed and take her knickers down! I'll get . . .'

Davie's hand shot out, and in one swift movement he cracked Adam across the face, so hard the boy staggered backwards, mouth agape, eyes wide with shock, the marks of Davie's fingers lying red and angry on his skin. The impact of the blow was such that Adam's teeth tore his inner cheek; his hand went up to mop away a froth of blood and saliva. Davie had very effectively stilled his devilish tongue.

Davie showed no sign of emotion. He had resumed his former stance, hands still and peaceful at his sides, his expressionless eyes gazing unseeingly at the flames in the grate.

'*FATHER!*' Adam found his voice. '*FATHER!* Davie hit me!'

Roderick strode into the room, taking in the scene at one glance: the marks on his son's face, the quiet, trancelike pose of Davie.

'Adam was tormenting Davie,' Anna spoke, her voice tense. 'Calling him names and saying things about Sally.'

A muscle began to twitch spasmodically in Davie's cheek, his fingers curled ever so slightly.

'Wheesht, madam,' Roderick barked at Anna. 'I'll have no tales from you!' He turned to Adam who was holding his hand to his stinging face and biting his lip in an effort to keep back the tears. 'Well, son,' Roderick's voice had grown softer. 'Is it true? Were you teasing the daft

115

bugger? I warn you, I want no lies or it's a warmed arse you'll get to match your face.'

Adam was trembling with apprehension. 'No, Father, it isn't true,' he lied quickly. 'Anna's making it up. I was only having a bit o' fun wi' him but I wasn't swearing at him or tormenting him. He's mad, Father, he enjoys hitting people, he hits Donal and Sally all the time for nothing.'

Very deliberately Roderick turned to Davie and leered into his face. 'A child beater above all else, eh, you useless messin? Well – maybe this will teach you never to molest my son again . . .'

His big meaty fist smashed into Davie's face in a sledgehammer blow. Davie's head jerked violently back; his lower teeth pierced his upper lip, splitting it open; blood spurted, dripping down over his chin, soaking into the soiled collar of his serge shirt.

He made no sound but his fists curled at his sides and a look of hatred replaced the vacancy in his eyes.

Roderick straightened. 'Well, that's that. Fair's fair. Get along now or you'll find the toe o' my boot up your arse as well!'

Magnus took Davie's arm and led him gently away. A chilly silence pervaded the room.

Roderick took a deep breath and flicked an imaginary speck of fluff from his jacket. 'Must be off now,' he said calmly, though his face was suffused with blood and his heartbeat pounded in his ears. 'Stop sniffing, Adam!' he warned. 'I want no son o' mine to shed gutless tears! Get along down to the well wi' your sister and help her to fetch up water for the morning.'

He stormed out of the house, his brief mood of benevolence totally consumed by rage. He knew he shouldn't have let go like that over such a trivial matter but that buggering Davie always brought out the worst in him. It was that accusing air and vacant expression that he couldn't stand, nor had he ever felt at ease in the company of a simpleton whose puny appearance so contrasted with his disturbing physical strength . . .

The glen was dark and deserted except for a lone figure striding purpose-fully along. Donal was abroad, swishing his feet through the long road-side grasses, stirring up the dead leaves because he liked the crackle they made.

When he saw Roderick's unmistakable form coming towards him his fine features twisted into a grin even while fear invaded the innocent depths of his eyes. Hurriedly he fumbled for his watch and blurted out anxiously, 'Nearly eight, be at the gate. Nearly eight be at the gate.'

His light, hollow voice echoed inside Roderick's head. He felt that he could take no more McDonalds: first Davie, now this stupid bastard with his watch and his pitiful voice going on and on . . . And he had stopped walking, as if waiting for the next move on the board, waiting in the darkness with trepidation in his heart and hope in his mind for a farthing, or a lump of tobacco, or maybe just a few kind words to set him happily on his way.

Roderick was in no mood to give away any of these things; the fire of his temper still burned within him . . . and there was no knowing what he would do if Donal didn't stop that irritating chanting . . .

A pain shot through Roderick's head and he looked this way and that as if seeking escape. Nellie Jean's unlit house was nearby, one of three cottages built into the boundary wall of the mill. No refuge there. Nellie Jean would be at the Coach House Inn, waiting for him . . . waiting . . . He had to escape Donal . . . madness, it was all around him, too much of it for one night . . . The gate leading down from the cottages, the steps joining up with the grassy track that ran to the stables . . . He would evade Donal if he went that way . . .

A long, low whinnying cry split the night. He stiffened, it was the Clydesdale mare, Beauty, in the throes of her labour pains . . .

The sound did something to Roderick, it was a sound of great suffering yet so resigned and patient it reminded him of another time . . . Lillian giving birth to Adam. It had been a hellish nightmare for her, the midwife, and for him. God! He could remember it all as if it had happened yesterday. Lillian had refused to cooperate. She had actually tried not to give birth to his son!

Writhing in torture, sweat pouring from her, her belly almost bursting apart, she had kept her legs squeezed tightly shut, and all the time she had cried repeatedly, 'No, it mustn't be born. It's wicked to give life to a child who will grow up to be mad – like him – like its father!'

If the midwife hadn't been there he would have hit Lillian for those dreadful ravings; as it was he'd had to help in the actual delivery, if such a word could be applied to the terrible struggle he and the midwife had endured with Lillian.

She had fought them like a wildcat and in the end they had been

117

forced to resort to drastic measures, tying her hands to the bed-head, taking her legs and pulling them apart to allow the child to come slithering out. Despite all the trauma he had endured he was very much alive and kicking with 'lungs on him like an elephant' to quote the midwife.

'Let it die!' Roderick could hear that accursed scream yet, issuing from Lillian's twisted mouth. 'Let it die! Let it die! Let it die! The de'il is in it! Poor, poor mite! Not its fault! Let it die! Let it die!'

But Adam had lived and had grown big and strong. Throughout his infancy Lillian had cared for him and had cuddled him because the mothering instinct was strong within her. Even so she had never loved him, not in the way she loved Magnus and Anna, and Roderick had known, he had always known, that she was afraid of his son, afraid of an innocent boy whose only fault, if it could be called that, lay in the fact that he had ever been conceived at all. But that was why Adam was so special to him, why he had to protect him . . .

Beauty's cries mingled with Donal's whining voice and something snapped inside Roderick's head. Taking Donal's arm he began to lead him back up the road to where another gate led down into the mill.

'C'mon, Donal,' he coaxed, as gently as his harsh voice would allow, 'How would you like to see the guns in the testing shed? A lot o' fine guns they are too. Boxer Sam works in there. It's his job to make sure the powder is working alright by testing it out on the guns.'

At the mention of Boxer Sam Donal smiled. He was very fond of the big Munkirk man who fooled around and made him laugh. Boxer Sam was also kind, always ready to share his lunchbox with Donal and give him an occasional puff of his pipe which made Donal cough but want more.

It would be nice to see Boxer Sam. Nevertheless, he didn't want to go with Iron Rod who terrified him, so he hung back, looking nervously over his shoulder, but Roderick's grip on his arm grew tighter, forcing him to go through the gate and down onto the grassy track.

To the left of them was the boilerhouse; opposite that were the changing sheds; further along, the gable wall of The Gatehouse rose up, darker than the surrounding blackness.

The shadows that were Anna and Adam flitted about nearby, moving among the trees as they drew water from the well. They were engrossed in their task, but they were also arguing, the sound of their raised voices filtering through the damp darkness. Neither of them saw Roderick pull Donal away, back into the greenery that grew thickly under the wall.

'Now, Donal, you must be very quiet,' Roderick whispered. 'We're going to play a wee game. You like games, don't you?'

'Ay,' Donal said eagerly.

'We're going to play at statues . . . you like that game, I've seen you playing it wi' the bairns in the village. First we'll creep across the track, quieter than mice, then we'll hide behind the trees and be as still as statues till it's safe to go on. Do you understand?'

'Ay,' choked Donal, saliva oozing from his mouth with excitement.

They had left the track behind and were soon lost amongst the trees surrounding the mill buildings. It was very quiet, very dark. Donal stumbled and fell his length in a tangle of bramble bushes.

'Silly sod,' muttered Roderick as he pulled the young man to his feet and dusted him down. 'You'd best stay here while I fetch a lantern – and stop girning about those wee scratches, Boxer Sam will put some oil on them and make them better.'

Taking a bunch of keys from his pocket he inserted one into the lock of a store shed where he hastily lit a safety lamp . . .

Beauty's cries echoed through the woods, Roderick stiffened, his heartbeat accelerated . . . He felt touched by a presence and he knew that the devil stalked the night, the evil was all around him, touching him . . . he couldn't help himself, he couldn't . . .

'Donal,' he hissed urgently, 'Come in here a minute. I'll show you the gun store another time.'

'Boxer Sam,' Donal's voice filtered eagerly through the darkness. 'Want to see him.'

Roderick cursed. Moving out of the shed he held up the lantern to look at Donal's slobbering young face. 'God, you're no' much o' a catch, are you? But you can be a stubborn bugger when you want. Alright, just you follow the lantern.'

The murmur of the River Cree was nearer now; the gun shed was situated on the opposite bank of a deep lade spanned by a rough plank bridge. A row of crudely-built latrines loomed up, basic affairs with holes cut into the flooring, built over the water courses. The men made jokes about them and used them only when it was strictly necessary as it was a frightening experience to squat over the holes when the courses were swollen with rain and the water was churning below.

Roderick led Donal towards the bridge, but by now the young man was growing more frightened with every passing minute.

'Donal need to pee,' he whimpered and stumbled off towards the latrines.

But Roderick caught his arm. He sensed the terror in Donal; it made him feel elated, excitement coursed through his veins. 'Ach, use the bushes, man, be quick now or Boxer Sam might go away home.'

The gun shed was silent and deserted. 'Sam no here,' whined Donal.

'Ach, he will be another time. I'll show you the guns myself.' As Roderick spoke he was leading Donal further into the shed. 'Look, Donal, see these holes in the walls? That's where Sam aims the guns at the butts to try them out. C'mon, bend down and see for yourself.'

Obediently Donal leaned towards the openings in the walls. An owl screeched in the woods, the River Cree thundered – and a whinnying cry of pain reverberated amongst the trees.

Roderick gave vent to a fiendish laugh and from a shelf he grabbed a bottle of lubricating oil. 'Drop your trousers, Donal,' he ordered softly. 'Don't turn round, just do as I say or I'll knock the living daylights out o' you.'

Tears coursed down Donal's cheeks. He was too petrified to do anything other than obey the other man's demands. Pain shot through him, he sobbed quietly as Roderick's grunts filled his head.

'There you are, Donal, that wasn't so bad, was it?' Roderick gasped some minutes later. 'Be grateful for it, you daft sod, for it's about the only thrill you're ever likely to get. Say a word to anyone and you won't live to breathe another.'

Donal was propped against the wall, crying helplessly, but he was shown no mercy. Roughly he was seized and bundled outside; the key grated in the lock; without another word Roderick walked quickly away, towards the path that wound its way through the mill to the Clachan of Corran.

He felt no twinge of compunction about the deed he had committed, nor did he feel uneasy. Donal was far too inarticulate to convey to anyone the events of that night, events that had, in a short space of time, snatched him harshly from his innocent world into one so ugly that all he could do after those dreadful moments was to cringe on the ground like a terrified animal.

CHAPTER FIFTEEN

Betrayals

DAVIE STOOD LISTENING TO Roderick's retreat, waiting till the snapping of twigs was far enough distant for him to step out of the shadows.

He had heard everything for he could hear as well as a fox, his pretensions of deafness having started as a childhood defence against the grim reality of his existence, growing into a habit which he either couldn't or wouldn't break.

Glaring malevolently in the direction taken by Roderick, his muscles tensed in his jaw. 'Swine,' he muttered softly. 'Filthy swine.'

He had come out of the stable to have a puff at his pipe and to nurse his aching mouth in silent misery, all his thoughts centred on Roderick and those ready fists of his. A gleam of light, moving through the woods had attracted his attention and, making some excuse to Jeemie, he had set out to investigate, following the wavering glow made by the safety lamp. It had led him to the testing shed and though he wasn't fully aware of what was happening in there he had soon put two and two together when Roderick had come out, doing up his trouser buttons, bulldozing Donal in front of him, speaking to him as if he were no better than a dog . . .

Hatred for the man had churned afresh in Davie's stomach, but the moment of revenge would have to wait. First he had to see to his brother, find out exactly what that dirty pig had done to him.

Donal, crouched sobbing on the damp ground outside the shed, started up in renewed terror as Davie's figure loomed. 'No, no, Mr McIntyre,' he whimpered, 'don't hurt Donal again, please, Mr McIntyre, I'll no tell on you, I'll no tell what you did to Donal.'

Davie took his brother's shoulders in a grip that was both gentle and reassuring for despite his bouts of sadism he was extremely protective towards Donal and Sally. What happened between the three of them was in the family and was nobody's business, what happened outside the family was his business and woe betide anyone who touched a hair of Donal's or Sally's head.

'It's no Iron Rod, Donal,' he said soothingly, 'it's Davie. Dinna fash anymore, I'm here, I'll look to you.'

'Davie!' Donal gasped in relief, falling into his brother's arms like a trusting baby. 'Iron Rod a dirty man. He – he hurt Donal.'

'Where did he hurt you, Donal?'

Donal shook his head, as if to try and rid his mind of the horror of the night. For several minutes he couldn't speak then he whispered, 'Trousers – he made Donal take trousers off – Donal couldn't see – something hard and big – pain – bad pain, Donal feel sick, a bad thing, dirty thing to do.'

It was all Davie needed to know. He put Donal's head on his shoulder and stroked his soft hair reflectively. 'Ay, Donal, but he'll no do it again for I'll be watching out for the de'il every minute o' the day and night from now on.'

Anna missed Magnus about the house. She needed him badly that night because her last day at school had been very disappointing with Beth acting so contrarily and Adam being very sneaky and threatening.

But Beauty needed Magnus more than she did. He was so good with the horses, good with any animal, be they sick or well.

Setting the bowat down on the low, broad shelf of the washhouse, she half filled one of the deep wooden sinks with water she had heated in the boiler.

Adam had rather grudgingly helped her to fetch the water from the well, and now a row of full pails sat on top of the wooden slats under the double washtubs. The fire beneath the boiler made the washhouse cosy and after she had put shirts and woollen combinations to steep in the steaming water she leaned her arms on the edge of the sink, cupped her chin in her hands, and stared out of the window.

The black mass of Coir an Ban rose up against the sky; the River Cree swished into The Cauldron; the mournful screech of an owl rang through the trees . . . and faintly in the distance came the sounds of a horse in distress.

'Poor Beauty,' whispered Anna. She half thought of putting on her shawl to go to the stables but decided against it, knowing she couldn't be of much help there. She would only get in the road and Jeemie would get cantankerous because he loved his horses and wouldn't rest till Beauty delivered her foal.

Clover stamped in the byre and rattled her chain. Taking down an armful of clothes from the pulley Anna put them into a basket then went out to make her way to the byre.

'Wheesht, girlie,' she soothed the cow. 'Is it Beauty you're hearing? Don't fret, come morning there will be a bonny wee foal and I'll be one o' the first to see it.'

After putting a few handfuls of hay into the manger she left the byre to check that the hen houses were secure, collected the linen basket and carried it into the house to air the clothes on the brass drying rail above the range.

The room was very quiet and peaceful. Adam had gone meekly through to bed half an hour ago which had surprised her as he could easily have taken advantage of Magnus's absence by staying up as late as he dared.

Anna deliberately let another half hour elapse, filling the time with all the usual nightly chores and a few more besides. Tomorrow she was going bramble picking and was looking forward to getting away from the house. It had been a good summer for soft fruits; preserves of all kinds already sat in comfortable abundance on pantry shelves throughout the glen.

Anna loved the mellower days. If the weather was good Saturday after Saturday could be spent picking brambles, rowanberries, apples, and sloes. It also meant hours stirring jellies and jams over a hot fire but to see the jars filling with the bubbling juices made all the labour worthwhile.

The thought of tomorrow, with Maggie May's ponderous good humour, Kate McLeod popping more berries into her mouth than she gathered, Miss Priscilla intriguing everyone with her knowledge of wild flowers, made Anna hum a joyful little tune.

She remembered the artist's case that Miss Priscilla had given her and she went to the lobby to take it out of its hiding place, a small crofter's kist filled to the brim with Roderick's cast off coats and hats that he couldn't bear to part with, even though he would never wear them again. Later she would put the case under her bed to join the rest of her treasures but for now it was safe to open it, to lovingly touch the tubes of paint, to lift up the sable brushes and glide them over her skin, to test out the charcoal sticks on the back of her hand, and best of all – to imagine herself out in the country, painting pictures as Miss Priscilla's father had done, capturing the beauty of nature with her brushes and paints . . .

A thought struck her, why not take the case with her tomorrow? Miss Priscilla had given her a small canvas to start her off; they could both sit and draw and paint in between picking berries. She could just see it in her mind: the children spread out, looking for the best bushes, tramping barefoot through the grass, singing as they went along, forgetting the little trials and tribulations of daily life.

Her heart began to sing, she danced round the table, laying it for the morning, pausing every now and then to rattle the spoons against the crockery in a tinkling cascade of sound.

She stopped suddenly, holding a spoon in mid-air. Beth wouldn't be at the berry picking! Something had huffed her so badly she had told Anna she wasn't going.

'It's not for the likes of me,' she had said with a toss of her head. 'Mother never liked me doing it. She says it will ruin my hands and anyway, Fat Jane makes all the jams and jellies we need.'

Giving Anna a glowering look she had gone on, 'It's alright for the likes of you. I mean, you *have* to make ends meet somehow, I suppose.'

Off she had flounced without another word and some of Anna's happiness left her as she remembered the scene. At times she was at a loss to understand her best friend. Beth had everything, good looks, nice clothes, a fine house, wonderful parents – *two* parents all to herself – and doting grandparents who lavished her with presents and took her for long holidays to their seaside home in Torquay. Yet nothing seemed to make Beth really happy.

Anna fingered the necklet nestling inside her dress and felt that a little part of her mother was close to her. Somewhere in her young mind she knew that these were the kind of things that really mattered, that small personal belongings were more precious than all the riches put together – even so, it would be lovely to have some of the things that were so abundant in Beth's life . . .

Her heart quickened, her father had promised to buy her some new clothes, which was a beginning . . .

'But I mustn't let my spirit fly too high,' she murmured, 'Or I might miss getting into heaven.'

At that moment Tibby leapt high in the air which meant she was getting ready for her nightly performance of spirited antics. Anna forgot all about Beth, as hugging the cat to her breast, she danced with her all round the kitchen before depositing her outside.

It was past her bedtime now, but even so Anna occupied herself for another ten minutes, winding the clock, damping the fire, washing the grate, straightening things, delaying going through to the bedroom for as long as possible.

In the end she crept through in bare feet, holding her boots in one hand, her artist's case in the other. All was quiet. The room was inky black, though after a while her eyes adjusted and she could just make out Adam's bulk huddled under the bedclothes.

She gave a sigh of relief. All day he had plagued her relentlessly, asking if he could go to bed with her, threatening to tell Roderick about the Hallowe'en party if she refused. The thought of her father finding out about that made her feel sick but she consoled herself with the thought that not even Adam could stoop so low as to clipe on her. He was bluffing, Adam did that quite a lot, just to see how far he could go with people.

She thought of Magnus, and of how lonely and incomplete everything seemed without him. He always made her feel safe and protected and she stood with her back to the door, wishing that he was here now. The room felt creepy and strange . . . and sort of . . . waiting.

She shuddered and half thought of lighting the candle which sat on a shelf just inside the door. Roderick had instructed that it wasn't to be lit unless strictly necessary, maintaining that artificial light of any kind was just a waste in the bedroom.

This was one rule that Anna was glad enough to abide by. Every new day made her more conscious of her maturing body and she was aware that Adam tried to watch her as she undressed for bed each night.

But it was very dark tonight and perhaps if she lit the candle, just for a moment, she could reassure herself that those black shadows in the corners were harmless enough and that Adam really was as peacefully asleep as his stillness suggested.

Her fingers curled round the candleholder, she half lifted it then put it quickly back on the shelf. She wouldn't light it. If Adam was still awake she wouldn't give him the satisfaction of seeing her undress – particularly now, with Magnus absent and unable to exert his control over his brother.

With a sudden decisive movement she slipped hastily out of her clothes and into her nightdress. Shivering slightly she pulled back the blankets. Safe, safe now, Adam hadn't seen anything, he hadn't said anything, he was asleep . . .

'Got you!' Adam's triumphant shout pierced her eardrums, shock spurred her heart to a breathless gallop. He was in her bed, had lain there waiting to pounce on her. His strong arms slid round her waist, pulling her down, down, till she lay sprawled across him, her nightdress at her thighs, her legs in mid air in those first helpless moments.

'I fooled you, Anna,' he chanted. 'I put my bolster under the covers to make you think it was me. And you did! You did, Anna!'

'You let me go this minute!' she cried, struggling to break the vicious hold he had on her.

His hands slid to her belly, interlocking his fingers together he held her in a vice-like grip. 'Only if you say you'll coorie into me the way you do wi' Magnus. Please, Anna! I get lonely sometimes and I wish – I wish Mother was here. Remember, Anna, how she used to love us and knock goodnight to us through the wall?'

Anna stopped struggling, hot tears pricked her eyelids. Adam had never before spoken so forlornly. He was more prone to mocking her when she spoke longingly of their mother and she had thought that he didn't miss her at all.

In those moments she wondered if his lack of visible emotion owed itself to an inability to voice his deeper thoughts. He wasn't always a bad brother. At times he could be very funny and he often made her laugh. He was charming too in a braggish sort of way, but he always spoiled it by showing off which made him popular with his friends but despised by his elders who saw him as just a cheeky young upstart.

The room was cold. Anna felt the goose pimples rising on her bare flesh. She was aware of Adam's body relaxing beneath her, his hold on her had slackened, she too allowed her limbs to loosen a little . . . only to stiffen up almost immediately. His hand was on her thigh, moving up ever so gently towards her buttocks.

If it had been any other twelve-year-old boy it might not have meant much, but lately there was something about Adam that made her feel uneasy. Beth's words came to her, 'He's like your father already. He'll grow up to like anything with a skirt on . . .'

She began to struggle and kick like a wildcat. 'Get out o' my bed, Adam McIntyre! I'll *never* lie with you. You're wicked and cruel and you tell lies all the time. You made Father hit Davie because you're a liar – and – and a coward!'

'I'll tell Father you were at the Hallowe'en party.' Adam's voice was full of menace.

'I don't care! You're a tell-tale as well as a coward. You're always telling tales! Why don't you get up and wait for Father to come home? That way you can tell on me the minute he gets in. The sooner the better.'

'That's just what I *am* going to do – and I'll watch through the keyhole while he's beating you!'

In the dark both children trembled, one with shame, the other with trepidation. The bed springs creaked, the next moment Adam was at the door, letting in a faint shaft of light from the kitchen.

'You asked for it, Anna,' he quavered weakly.

Shutting the door he stood leaning against it, his brain whirling wildly. Should he forget all about it? Just go back into the bedroom and apologize to his sister? Anna, his Anna. Brave and spirited, beautiful and kind. He had always admired her, always, and he couldn't do this to her, he couldn't.

But she had called him a liar and a coward. A coward! He who was the most daring boy in the whole glen! The one his friends looked up to and relied upon to lead the way. He did things that made them laugh even when they were scared out of their wits and looking over their shoulders in case they might be caught in the act of some mischief.

No, he wasn't a coward, and Anna was wicked to call him that. She deserved to be punished so that in future she might not be so ready with her tongue.

He straightened and crept away from the door, into the kitchen to sit in the inglenook near the fire, his legs drawn up to his chin, his baggy nightshirt tucked all around him.

Despite the warmth from the fire he shivered – but not with the cold.

CHAPTER SIXTEEN

Punishments

RODERICK WALKED OUT OF the smoky atmosphere of the Coach House Inn to lean against the whitewashed wall and take a deep breath of cool night air while he tried to contain his seething emotions.

Nellie Jean had been there to meet him alright, all done up in a tight-waisted dress that had pushed her breasts so high up it had really seemed that they might pop out of her bodice at any moment.

Beside her had sat Boxer Sam, his muscles bulging under his coat, his ruggedly handsome face aglow with laughter at some joke he had been sharing with Nellie Jean. He had greeted Roderick affably and had gone to see about drinks, his jaunty steps suggesting supreme confidence.

Roderick had seated himself at a discreet distance from Nellie Jean, courteously greeting acquaintances and generally behaving in the manner of a refined gentleman.

Nellie Jean had found this extremely funny. She had consumed enough liquor to make her throw caution to the winds and leaning towards him, her breasts straining against her frock, she had pouted her lips at him and had talked to him as if he was a baby. 'Och, c'mon now, Rod, you're no going to act like a bairn just because I asked Sam to join us – are you now?'

'Hold your tongue, woman,' he had warned in a furious aside.

Maggie May had waddled over with the drinks, her treble chins curling into the swathes of fat at her neck as she bent to put the tray on the table.

She had looked from Roderick to Nellie Jean then at Boxer Sam coming back from the bar, and her eyes had twinkled mischievously. 'All together then, dears? Same table?'

Stretching her lips wide to show thin, empty gums she had addressed herself to Nellie Jean: 'Ach well, lassie, safety in numbers I always say. Three might be a crowd but if the going gets too hot you can always lock your door while they're fighting over you. Mind you, when you get to my age you'll maybe be glad to keep your doors *and* windows open, just in case a stray man might chance along.'

Roderick's eyes had bulged with chagrin at this while Maggie May's stomach had wobbled like a jelly, so heartily had she laughed at her own humour. She had gone off chuckling, feeling well pleased with herself, for there was nothing she liked better than to 'ca' the horns from Iron Rod.'

Roderick had suffered the situation for almost an hour, during which time Nellie Jean had become more inebriated and giggly, encouraging Boxer Sam to flirt with her and make improper suggestions that were more for Roderick's benefit than hers.

In the end he could take no more. Very regally he had bade everyone a reserved good evening and with a twirl of his silver-handled cane he had walked unhurriedly outside, though every fibre in him had urged him to run from the place.

Now, leaning against the wall, he tried to calm himself, half expecting that Nellie Jean would follow him outside, but the minutes went by and there was no sign of her.

'Bitch,' he muttered fiercely, 'Faithless bitch!'

'Why, Mr McIntyre – Roderick McIntyre!' He was startled out of his angry musings and was hardly able to take in the fact that Lady Pandora's coach had stopped beside him and that her face was at the window. Somehow he managed to compose himself sufficiently to doff his hat to her and to say most civilly, 'My lady, how nice to see you. I trust you are well.'

'Indeed I am and all the better for seeing you for you are just the man I want. I haven't seen you since our little chat at the Hallowe'en dance and I have been wondering if you have given any more thought to my proposals.'

'Proposals, dear lady?'

'Silly man! Don't you remember?' She sounded impatient. 'About Anna of course. Surely you haven't forgotten that we talked about the possibility of your daughter becoming my companion.'

'Ah, yes, that. Of course I haven't forgotten, it's just that I'm a very busy man, my dear, and of course, there's the question of presentation. First I have to take my little girl shopping, bits and bobs, you know, everything right and proper for the sort o' thing you suggest. The initial outlay will be expensive but worth it in the end, I'm sure o' that.'

'If it's a question of money we can surely come to some arrangement.' A cold note had crept into Lady Pandora's voice. 'You needn't be out of pocket, I can assure you.'

There was a short silence. Neil Black huddled on the box, wishing that her ladyship would hurry up, it was chilly sitting here, and besides, Roderick McIntyre wasn't the sort of man that a person of her standing should be hobnobbing with. As usual he was counting everything in terms of sillar . . . something to do with his daughter . . . Neil had a head cold, so he sniffed and blew his nose and strained his ears to hear better what was being said.

Roderick glowered suspiciously at the hunched figure on the box. He coughed, pulled back his shoulders, and said in a low voice, 'Money doesn't have to come into it at all, my dear, you know that as well as I do. You said things to me, implied that certain favours would be granted if . . .'

Andrew Mallard's face appeared beside Lady Pandora's. The steamy windows of the inn didn't give out much light but it was sufficient for Roderick to see the dangerous glint in Mallard's eyes. He said nothing but he didn't have to: his clenched jaw, his lowering brows said it all and unconsciously Roderick backed off a step or two. 'My lady,' graciously he lifted his hat once more, 'I think what we have to discuss would be better done in private, meantime I wish you a pleasant goodnight and a safe journey.'

Lady Pandora made only a cursory response. The whip cracked, the wheels turned. Roderick stood watching the coach disappearing.

'Bugger that hot-arsed sod,' he muttered darkly. 'Pushing his nose in, interfering – as if he owned her . . .'

Two horses came spanking along, pulling a trap containing people that Roderick knew but had no wish to acknowledge in his present frame of mind. The hoofbeats slowed and stopped at the inn and Roderick melted into the shadows, setting his footsteps homewards.

He was in no mood to be trifled with further and he certainly wasn't ready to face another upset that evening. When he saw Adam huddled by the fire he snapped out, 'What ails you, boy? You should have been in bed long ago!'

Tears welled up in Adam's eyes, springing from the fear that flooded his being as he sensed the blackness of his father's mood. He dug his knuckles into his eyes. He mustn't cry. His father hated to see a boy crying.

'Tears, Adam!' snarled Roderick. 'Do you want me to knock them out o' you?'

Adam's heart pounded; hastily he gasped, 'Please, Father, it's Anna, she wouldn't let me sleep. She asked me to come into bed wi' her, all she wants is to talk about that silly Hallowe'en party at The House of Noble. She . . .'

'*Party*, boy, are you havering?'

Adam regarded his father with round-eyed innocence. 'But – I thought you knew about it, Father, Anna says you told her she could go. She went as a ghost and Beth Jordan was a witch.'

For a long moment Roderick said nothing. He stared down at Adam, whose face was just a white blur in the dim light. 'Is this true, Adam?' he said with ominous calm. 'I warn you, if you are lying you won't be able to sit down for a week. I've never had cause to thrash you yet but if I ever found out a son o' mine was deceiving me . . .'

'It's the truth, Father! Cross my heart and hope to die.'

'Be careful, boy, don't use the sign o' Christ so lightly, if you're being untruthful He will smite you down as sure as I stand here.'

'I'm not lying, I'm not!' Adam cried desperately, crossing his fingers behind his back in the childish belief that such a gesture would absolve him. It was alright to do that, all his friends did it to get away with fibbing and nothing very terrible had happened to them.

'Fetch me my shaving strop, son . . . then go and bring your sister ben here.'

Adam scurried to obey though his heart twisted with guilt when Anna came through without a murmur of protest.

She stood in front of her father, her hands folded behind her back, her hair gleaming like a halo in the firelight.

Roderick ran his hand over the smooth leather of the strop and licked his dry lips. He had thrashed Anna many times in the past but things were different now. If she had been to the big house without his consent then a good walloping was indeed called for – but he would have to be careful – many things had to be considered. Lady Pandora had fired his curiosity as well as his passions, there was no turning back now. Very soon Anna would be going to old Grace to be fitted for new clothes . . . and she couldn't very well go with her body covered in weals. The old woman adored the girl and that wagging tongue of hers would quickly spread it around that Roderick McIntyre beat his daughter.

'Go to bed, Adam,' Roderick ordered and Adam scampered gladly back to his room. Now it was just the two of them in the kitchen, father and daughter, the silence of the house all around them, waiting, waiting, one for the pain and the hell yet to come, the other for the right moment to begin inflicting the punishment.

Roderick pushed a big fist under Anna's chin and pulled her head up roughly. Her eyes looked up at him, big and blue and unwavering.

'Is this true, girl? This business about you being up at the big house without my knowledge – without my permission?'

The ticking of the clock invaded the hush of the room.

'Answer me, girl!'

'Ay, Father, it's true.'

The proud defiance in her voice puzzled Roderick as much as it enraged him. There was no remorse here, no pleas for mercy, no feeble excuses, just a simple admittance of the truth – in that tone that never failed to make him feel inferior . . . and uneasy . . .

'Anna,' he barked, 'I don't want to hurt you – there are things you should know – Lady Pandora has spoken to me; she has taken a shine to you and it is her desire that you should be her companion. It would be a chance for you, girl, a chance for you to do something wi' your life. Climb the ladder, who knows where it could lead.'

Anna said nothing and he glanced at her sharply. 'Struck dumb, eh? Can't believe your luck? Well it's fact right enough and the reason why you have to have some decent clothes on your back. Lady Pandora and myself have had some nice cosy wee chats together and I'm sure we'll all benefit from this bee she has in her bonnet about you.'

There was something in those last words, something about his tone that got to Anna. Smug, like a cat anticipating the cream, waiting for the right moment to pounce on the goodies.

Magnus's words came back to her, 'Take care, the old man's up to no good.' So, that was the reason for the new clothes, not because he wanted her to better herself but because he had his eye on Lady Pandora, and he had no qualms about using his daughter to further his lustful desires . . .

Anna lifted her chin and looked him straight in the eye. 'I don't want your clothes, Father – and – and I don't want to be Lady Pandora's companion. I'm not cut out for that sort o' thing – as you yourself have told me often enough. I'd rather go about in rags than try and be something I'm not meant to be.'

Her words incited him to fresh rage; his rising fury almost choked him. 'Why you – you little brat!' he screamed. 'How dare you talk to me like that! You're right, you never were anything and you never will be anything!

'There is no future for the likes o' you! Mad! Mad like *her!* The mother who deserted you! Deserted us all!'

Grabbing her by the throat he shook her like a dog. Her head spun, she felt the chain of her necklet snapping. His grip relaxed and she made a desperate lunge to grab at the piece of jewellery before it slipped to the floor.

'Bend over, girl!'

Without a word she obeyed. With a disdainful flick he lifted her nightdress till it was bunched round her shoulders in rough folds. Her thin little buttocks gleamed white in the half darkness. The very vulnerability of her, waiting wordlessly for the first lash of the belt, gave him a momentary pang of pity. The purple marks of previous beatings crisscrossed her back and her thighs. Poor little bum, he thought, yet she never cries. Why doesn't the little bitch cry?

But he already knew the answer to that. Her strength lay in her very stillness, she was only a child yet for all that she was stronger in her way than he was in his – and he couldn't take that – he never could take that . . .

She would never get her new clothes now – and he wouldn't get Pandora . . .

The strop came down, the crack of it on the girl's bare flesh lashed through the silence.

Roderick staggered as a wave of dizziness washed over him. Careful, lad, he warned himself, You've had a buggering hard night of it! God, what a night! First Davie, then Donal, then that degrading interlude with Nellie Jean and that swaggering pig, Boxer Sam! Now this business with Anna. It was too much, far too much for a decent man to take.

The strop came down again. Anna pushed a fist into her mouth, clamping her teeth against her fingers to stop herself from crying out. She wouldn't give him that satisfaction. She wouldn't. With her other hand she clung grimly to her necklet and said to herself over and over, Mother. Mother. Mother.

Roderick was taking his time with the belt, pausing between each swing, prolonging the agony. Anna only wanted it over and done with but he seemed in no hurry and she wondered if this was a cruel new tactic.

'Are you ready to say you're sorry, girl?' he questioned harshly, unwilling to go on with the punishment because he was afraid that if he really got going he would never stop.

The feelings he had experienced in the woods with Donal were mounting in him. Elation! Exhilaration! Marvellous sensations of power that were so pleasurable they were almost on the same par as a sexual tussle with Nellie Jean.

That bitch! That faithless hoor! He'd show her who was boss! She would never laugh at him again! Never!

He raised the strop high above his head in order to get a good swing at that poor bloody white little bum of Anna's . . . There was a mist in front of his eyes . . . Anna's bum – or Nellie Jean's? It didn't matter, they both deserved to be punished, to have the living daylights thrashed out of them.

Adam was at the bedroom door, his eye to the keyhole. The kitchen was poorly lit. Roderick had taken no time to light the lamp but the glow from the fire was sufficient for Adam to see his sister's defenceless figure bent over the couch; the menacing figure of their father above her, the strop in his hands; the evil black phantom that was his shadow, dancing on the ceiling.

Adam sniffed, he wondered if the pact he had made with Beth Jordan was worth his sister's agony. He could hear Beth's words ringing in his ears. 'Listen, Adam, I want you to tell your father about Anna going to that party. If you do I'll share my cake with you every playtime *and* I'll let you kiss me in the shed.'

He had wanted to know why Beth was so mad at Anna and with a toss of her head she had said huffily, 'Because she accused me of being selfish and cruel, *that's* why. After all I've done for her – besides – she's leaving school and won't be my best friend anymore – not my *real* friend anyway.'

Adam knew it was a very unreasonable argument. He also knew that Beth was just using him to get her own back on Anna, but that hadn't mattered. He liked Beth, she was hard-hearted but she was exciting – he had always sensed that there was something very exciting about Beth . . .

The strop made a whining sound as it cut through the air before meeting flesh – Anna's flesh. Pain, such pain. Adam's legs wobbled, terror released the contents of his bladder, the warm trickle ran down his legs to the floor. In panic he rushed for the chamber pot but it was too late, only a miserable dribble ran into the pot.

Grabbing at his shirt he scuttled hastily to mop the floor just as the ugly cracking of leather on flesh beat into his ears again . . . and again.

Tears coursed down his cheeks, mingling with bubbles of mucus flowing from his nose. He put out his tongue to lick away the froth and muttered weakly, 'I'm sorry, Anna, I'm sorry.'

PART TWO

1891–92

CHAPTER SEVENTEEN

An Invitation

IT WAS ALMOST CHRISTMAS. Outside the schoolroom window the snow was whirling down, blotting out the fields and hills, swirling amongst the trees, plastering itself against walls and hedges.

Master Peter Noble was sprawled over his desk, seemingly engrossed in his books, but his thoughts were elsewhere. He was thinking about Anna; he had thought about her a lot since that night of the Hallowe'en party. More than two years had passed since then but he had only ever glimpsed her from a distance, going about the village, walking in the glen, once or twice talking to Magnus at the home farm.

Then last week he had met her face to face, quite by chance, outside the gates of Knock Farm. In silence they had stared at one another as if mesmerized, till he found his voice and had said softly, 'Little ghostie, we meet at last, after all this time.'

Her brow had furrowed. In some surprise she had said, 'I thought you would have forgotten all that, it was such a long time ago – and how did you know who I was anyway? I was draped from head to foot in a sheet.'

'I heard your name mentioned, there's only one Anna in the village, it was that simple – and I never forgot you. How could anyone forget such a spectacular escape? A small ghost figure, flapping away down the drive, like a white bat.'

At that she had reddened and had hurried away from him, but since then, thoughts of her had haunted him, keeping him awake at night as he had wondered how he could meet her again, unwilling to go to The Gatehouse because he knew her brothers would be there and might start asking awkward questions, particularly the one called Adam whom Peter knew to be loud and impertinent.

Normally Roderick would have been the biggest stumbling block of all, but six months ago Sir Malaroy had called Roderick into his office. There had been some sort of row; everyone in the house had heard their raised voices and when Roderick finally emerged he had been red-faced and furious looking.

Shortly afterwards he had gone away to the artillery unit at Canon Point some fifty miles away, to stand in for the manager who was ill, and there was no knowing when he would be back.

Word of his banishment had soon spread.

'Stand in for the manager indeed!' Janet McCrae had snorted. 'A likely story. Sent packing more like. I've been hearing things about him from Molly the cook who hears a lot from Daisy the housemaid. It's said that the rascal pesters Sir Malaroy for money – been doing it for years. Blackmail Molly thinks, but then she aye was a mite fanciful. Whatever it was he went too far and his lordship just parcelled him up and sent him away, as quick as you like.'

'About time too!' Moira O'Brady said, her face having gone as red as a beetroot at Janet's mention of blackmail. 'I for one wouldn't miss him if he never came back and that's a fact.'

Everyone agreed with Moira and as the weeks passed with no sign of Roderick returning he soon became just a memory, albeit a bad one for those who had suffered at his hands in one way or another.

After a time Peter raised his head, propped his chin in his hands and gazed thoughtfully at his brother.

'I've been thinking,' he said suddenly. 'I'm going to apologize to that McIntyre girl. It was rotten, to humiliate her at that party and I want to say I'm sorry for what I did to her – what we both did.'

Master Lucas Noble was even less interested in his books than his brother and he was glad of any excuse to ignore them for a while.

'Apologize!' he said bitingly. 'But all that happened more than two years ago! And besides, you don't even know her, she's just one of the villagers, another of Aunt Dora's charity cases, one who very nearly ended up enjoying the comforts of home – *our* home. If Aunt Dora had her way they would all be here, eating us into poverty.'

Peter ran his fingers through his fair thatch and looked defiant. 'I don't care. I've seen Anna McIntyre going about, she's different from the others, sort of regal and dignified and . . . different – as if – as if she was born to know better things.'

142

'Different?' scoffed Lucas. 'Oh, she's different alright, she's Roderick McIntyre's daughter. He's a cunning beggar if ever there was one. I mistrusted him from the moment I saw him and she'll be tarred with the same brush. She's beautiful, I will admit that, but she's still a McIntyre, and all the McIntyre's are mad, everyone says so. Her mother's in the asylum, been there for years and never likely to get out. One of the brothers is certainly unbalanced, does things that no one in their right mind would do.'

'Not any worse than the things we've done,' laughed Peter. 'Come on, brother, don't tell me you think you're sane. One of these days you'll break your neck at the end of a rope.'

'That's thanks to Quack Quack and all his ideas as regards toughening us up to face the big bad world.'

'Well anyway, Magnus McIntyre's alright. He might not like us swooping about the farm the way we do but he's too good mannered to say anything.'

Lucas was growing bored with the subject. Restlessly he flicked through the pages of a book and glanced towards the window. 'I wish Quack Quack would hurry up, he promised he'd take us out before lunch.'

'When he's with Aunt Dora he always forgets the time.' Peter was silent for a moment then he went on. 'I wonder if there's anything really going on between him and her. I often feel sorry for Uncle Malaroy, hanging about, waiting for her, never knowing what she's getting up to from one minute to the next.'

'Of course there's something going on!' hooted Lucas. 'There will always be something going on with Aunt Dora. She can't help herself, it's just the way she's made.'

'You sound as if you know a lot about women.'

Lucas's face darkened. 'I wish I did but I'll never find out cooped up in this pile. I'm glad we're going off to school soon.'

Peter gazed round the room, at the fire burning warmly in the grate, the pastel-coloured walls hung with paintings of sailing ships, the tall, elegantly draped windows, beyond them the view of the moors and the hills. 'You speak for yourself,' he said quietly. 'I like it here at dear old Noble House. And you don't have to wait till you go to school to have a bit of excitement in your life. You're a snob, that's what. If you were more like Aunt Dora you'd mix with the folk of the glen – you'd

143

apologize to people like Anna McIntyre and get to know what life's like on the other side.'

Lucas's mouth twisted. 'Hark at Father Time. All wisdom and no brains! For your information, brother dear, I have no wish to mix with the peasants, nor do I particularly want to ingratiate myself with Mad Miss McIntyre.'

The light of anger flashed in Peter's blue eyes. 'Suit yourself. I will seek her out and say I'm sorry. I've wanted to speak to her for a long time and an apology is as good a way as any of getting to know someone that looks worth getting to know.'

'Sir Galahad,' Lucas said mockingly. 'Do you desire a white charger to go on your errand of goodwill? If so I'll see Black and order him to have ready your faithful steed.'

Both boys looked at one another and burst out laughing. Harmony was restored, but when Peter pretended to get back to his books he didn't see a word, all his thoughts were concentrated on one thing. He had made up his mind. He would find Anna and he would most certainly make amends to her, even if it was all so long ago she might have forgotten what it was he had to be sorry about.

Anna hadn't forgotten, though when she went to answer the soft little knock on Miss Priscilla's door and saw Peter standing there, she certainly didn't think he had made his way through the snowy night just to see her. In fact, she was so confused at the sight of him, she was unable to think too clearly for a moment and could only stammer, 'Oh, it's you! Who was it you wanted to see? All the McLeods are in – but perhaps I'd better get Ben.'

Despite this, she made no movement and they both stood staring at one another while the wind blustered its way through the open door, bringing in eddies of snowflakes.

Peter was like a snowman: his coat and trousers were white; his eyebrows were speckled; his nose was red; flakes of snow clung to his eyelashes; the lick of hair that escaped his hat was sodden wet against his brow.

'I've come to see you,' he said bluntly. 'I knew you would be here, you come every Monday and Friday evening and I wanted to . . .'

'Shut that door!' came a roar from the kitchen. 'You're letting all the heat out o' the house.'

144

'You'd better come in,' Anna said, standing aside to allow him access. But first he stamped his feet to remove the caked snow on his boots and took off his coat to give it a good shake. Only then did he step inside, allowing Anna to take his coat and hang it on the stand beside a motley collection of outerwear.

Then she thought she'd better try and dry it and taking it down she threw it over her arm before leading the way to the kitchen, hesitating at the door as she wondered how she should introduce a visitor from the big house. Ben took the matter out of her hands in his genial, down-to-earth way.

'Come away in, lad,' he invited hospitably. 'Just in time to take over here for a while. Kate roped me into holding this damned yarn for her and my arms are aching out o' their sockets.'

Peter looked a little surprised at this unusual reception but obediently he went to sit in the rocking chair that Ben had willingly vacated and held out his arms to receive the yarn that Kate was busily winding into a big blue woolly ball.

He had walked into a very homely and festive-looking scene. Between them Miss Priscilla and her sister, Kate, had gathered a variety of greenery to weave into Christmas garlands. Sprigs of holly decorated the picture rails and the mantelshelf. Sprays of spruce and fir hung from the pictures; a variety of evergreen leaves had been woven into a rope which had been arranged in loops on one wall; another was coiled round the brass drying rail above the fire and altogether the atmosphere was one of welcoming cheer. With Christmas so near Miss Priscilla and Anna had abandoned books and learning in favour of more seasonal pastimes. The table was littered with bits of material and ribbon and everything else pertaining to gift making.

Miss Priscilla hadn't stirred at Peter's entrance but sat stolidly where she was, her specs on the end of her nose, her fingers busy with a fluffy soft toy she was making for a neighbour's new baby.

Anna arranged Peter's coat on the guard then stood for a moment, not quite knowing if she should rejoin her teacher or entertain the visitor in some way, but seeing that everyone else was going unconcernedly about their business, she went back to the table to resume where she had left off.

Peter glanced round the room; it was a great novelty for him to be here, in this house, this night, and he sat there, not saying anything, drinking it all in, the homely faces surrounding him, serene and contented in the lamplight, and something of that peace touched him too.

For a long time there was a companionable silence in the room, broken only by the clock ticking on the mantelpiece, the contented snoring of an old sheepdog called Puddle, and the crackle of yule logs in the grate. At least, Kate had said they were yule logs, even though they looked no different from any of the others that normally fuelled the fire. 'They had snow on them when I brought them in,' she had explained to Ben and though he had told her that her head was full of fanciful notions he had soon been referring to them as yule logs himself because it sounded good when you said it to visitors.

And Peter, whatever his station in life, was just another visitor to Ben and, bending to the fuel box, one eye on the boy in the rocking chair, he said carelessly, ''Tis a chilly night, I'll just put on another yule log.'

'We have them too,' Peter said eagerly, twisting round to look at Ben, in the process slackening the yarn on his arms till a click from Kate's tongue made him hasten to restore the required tension.

Turning again to Ben he went on, 'Aunt Dora ordered a big pile to be cut and brought in. Me and Lucas went with old Duncan into the woods and helped him saw up pine branches. It was great fun though Duncan got a bit annoyed when we started throwing snow about. Daisy the housemaid wasn't too pleased either when she saw the logs stacked on the hearth. She clicked her tongue . . .' Here he grinned disarmingly at Kate. '. . . and complained about the mess but Aunt Dora just said it was Christmas and to hell with a few stains on the tiles!'

'Right enough, lad, right enough.' Ben lit his pipe and blew a cloud of smoke in the air. 'It only comes but once a year and we have to make the most of it.'

At this Kate snorted and Anna hid her smiles, amused at many things that evening but most of all at the sight of Master Peter Noble, sitting there in the firelight, holding Kate's yarn, afraid to move a muscle for fear of earning more of her disapproval.

Peter, however, wasn't as engrossed in his task as he appeared to be. Surreptitiously he was observing Anna, sitting there at the table, seemingly absorbed in what she was doing till, glancing up, she caught his eye and smiled at him. It was a strange little smile, something elusive and mysterious about it, reminding him somehow of that portrait of Aunt Dora in the hall above the fireplace.

146

Peter held his breath. Anna's head was down-bent once more, there was a stillness about her that struck him forcibly – yet – he sensed the tremendous life forces that beat and flowed within her and he wanted just to look and look at her forever.

She had changed a lot in the last two years. Now fifteen she was no longer a child; she was slim rather than thin; there was promise of great beauty in her fine-featured face; her breasts were young and firm, her waist slender and well defined, her hair a mane of pale gold in the light from the oil lamp that sat in the middle of the table.

The dress that she wore was obviously home made – the material was plain and uninteresting – but Peter saw only the bits of pure white lace, the tiny cameo brooch nestling at her throat, and that night he fell in love with Anna McIntyre of The Gatehouse and wondered how soon he could get her alone so that he could talk to her.

'You'll be here for a reason, lad?' Ben said suddenly, catching Peter unawares, making him loosen his hold on the few strands of yarn that remained on his outstretched wrists.

'It doesn't matter.' With a flourish Kate finished winding her wool, holding up the enormous woolly ball for everyone to see. 'Now, will I get it finished in time for Christmas,' she wondered, reaching down to extract a pair of needles from her knitting bag.

'Get what finished, woman?' asked Ben in surprise. 'You've just done that, I saw you wi' my very own eyes and me and this lad have got aching arms to prove it.'

Kate tutted. 'Not the wool, the pullover I'm knitting, a present for someone – I'm no saying who. A fortnight, only a fortnight. Be quiet, Ben, and let me concentrate.'

Ben raised his eyes to the ceiling, muttered 'women,' then winking at Peter he said, 'Well, lad? You haven't answered my question. Is everything alright wi' her ladyship? Did someone want to send a message down to one o' us?'

'No, sir, nothing like that, I – well, it was Miss McIntyre I came to see really – though of course – now that I'm here it's wonderful to see you all, it's just . . . well, it's a private matter between her and me – though I've no doubt she doesn't know what I'm talking about,' he added, seeing the look of bemusement on Anna's face.

Ben knocked his pipe out on the bars of the fire and leaned back in

147

his chair. 'That's fair enough by me, son, and now that you've made the break you're aye welcome here at Knock Farm.'

Miss Priscilla stood up. 'Supper time,' she said in her no-nonsense voice. 'We must get you home, Anna, before the weather gets too bad.'

Seizing the toasting fork from its hook, she handed it to Peter who, despite his privileged position, was, to her, no different from any boy she had ever taught, except perhaps that he wore boots and had a well-fed look about him. 'Right then, Peter, since you're here we might as well make further use of you. Have you ever made toast?'

She was looking down her nose at him. He reddened and nodded. 'Me and Lucas make it all the time in the schoolroom – piping hot, piled thick with butter and bramble jelly when we can get it.'

'Good, plenty of that here; my sister and I picked the berries ourselves and there's always more than enough butter – though mind, too much of that isn't good for anyone, is it?'

Feeling that he needed some support Anna jumped to her feet, 'I'll help,' she offered readily. 'I know where everything is.' She was back in a few moments with pots of honey and jam, a large pat of butter and a plate piled high with crusty home-baked bread.

Peter was already seated on a long, low, padded stool in front of the fire and she settled herself beside him, spreading the toast as it became ready, laying the buttered bits on one side of an enormous plate, the honey and jam on the other.

There was something rather special about sitting there with Peter, both of them bathed in firelight, surrounded by the peace and the comparative darkness of the room. She felt as if they were locked into a little world of their own, warm and safe, in harmony though not a word passed between them.

Peter looked very handsome. His skin was golden; she could feel his arm brushing against hers every time he moved. Turning his head, he looked at her. There was an expression in his eyes that made her heart beat a little faster and in confusion she stood up with the plate and set it on the table.

As soon as supper was eaten Anna got to her feet. 'I have to go, Magnus will come out looking for me if I'm late.'

Peter jumped up also. 'I'll have to go too,' he said quickly.

'I'll walk the pair o' you home.' Ben looked from one young face to the other. 'I'll just get on my boots.'

'No, no,' Peter sounded anxious. 'It's very kind of you but please don't bother, I'm sixteen and quite well able to look after myself – Quack Quack – Mr Mallard has seen to that.'

Ben stretched and yawned. 'Ach well then, right enough, you're a big laddie and you should be able to fend for yourself. But it's Anna I'm thinking of, she'll need an arm along that road, it will be gey treacherous on a night like this.'

'She can have mine,' Peter blurted out the words, not looking at Anna.

'Right, that's settled.' Kate handed him his coat which, though still damp, was warm and steamy.

He stuck his arms into it, wound his scarf round his neck and jammed his hat on his fair head. 'Goodnight and thanks, everybody, it's been great,' his infectious smile lit his face. It had been a most unusual evening for him, one that he would never forget for its simplicity and warmth.

'Come back for your tea one night,' Miss Priscilla invited off-handedly. 'Anna comes quite often and later you can both make supper – I've never tasted such good toast as I had tonight, Kate always burns it and Ben's is underdone.'

'I'd *love* that!' Peter's blue eyes were shining, the words were out of his mouth almost before she had finished speaking. A giggle escaped Anna at the look of indignation on Kate's face and the sheepish grin on Ben's.

'Oh yes, I'd love that,' Peter repeated. 'Only thing is, when Lucas hears about it he might want to come too.'

'Well, why not?' Kate threw her sister a mischievous look. 'The more the merrier – he probably makes better toast than any o' us.'

'Good idea,' Miss Priscilla said dryly, though her eyes were twinkling behind her glasses. 'It's Christmas after all. Anna, you might want to bring Beth, that would make it a nice foursome.'

'Great idea, Priss,' Ben said heartily. 'It's nice to have young people about the place.'

'Ay, it is a great idea!' Kate clapped her hands like an eager child, her large mouth smiling its approval. 'I'll get everything ready and I'll start tomorrow. I always set a marvellous table.'

'That's settled then,' Miss Priscilla said in her brisk fashion. 'Friday, six o'clock, if that's suitable to everyone.'

Anna and Peter looked at one another. They said nothing but their eyes were sparkling.

CHAPTER EIGHTEEN

An Apology

BEN ESCORTED ANNA and Peter to the door and, grabbing the shovel that was propped conveniently against the wall, he quickly cleared a rough path to the gate.

The snow had stopped and the clouds had dispersed. It was a frosty clear night; the sky was littered with countless stars, winking and sparkling in the blue-black heavens. A brilliant moon was peeping above the hills, rising higher with every passing minute till soon the glen was illuminated as if by a great lantern, exposing an enchanting landscape of snow-covered dykes and tracts of virgin fields with little white cottages dotted here and there.

Anna and Peter waved their farewells to Ben and he watched till they had shut the gate before turning back to the warmth of the farmhouse.

Once out on the road the way was slippery and Peter took Anna's arm, glad of an excuse to get close to her.

He glanced back at the farm, sitting there atop the hillock, cosy looking amidst the white world, the soft lights glowing in the windows, smoke drifting lazily from the chimneys. 'I'm looking forward to going back,' he said softly. 'They made me feel so at home.'

'I know. The McLeods are like that, every one o' them, even Miss Priscilla for all her glowers and her clipped tongue. In fact, I'd go as far as to say she's the most soft-hearted of them all, she just hides it better than most.'

'You really like her, don't you?'

'I love her,' Anna said decidedly. 'She gave me hope when I most needed it and she has taught me so much. I'm never happier than when I'm at Knock Farm; there's always something going on. If it isn't the animals it's Ben with his interesting talk or Kate with her funny stories

151

and of course Miss Priscilla with her skills and her teaching and her knowledge. Sometimes old Grace drops in to make girdle scones and we all eat them round the fire, piping hot with jam or butter.'

Her foot slipped, his hold on her arm tightened. Anna felt herself growing hot. He was very close to her. She could smell the dampness of his coat and the freshness of his skin, she could hear his breathing, she could see his profile in the moonlight, young, beautiful – innocent . . . and most disturbing of all, she could feel his warmth beating into her and it was as if one half of her was on fire – while the other half – the side that was away from him – seemed to cry out to be touched by him . . .

It was too much. Somehow she had to escape his nearness . . . Tearing her arm out of his, she dashed away and, seizing a lump of snow, she faced him with it, holding it up like a trophy, her face glowing, laughter catching in her throat.

'Don't you dare!' he cried, but it was too late. The snowball hit him fair and square, bits of it slithered down his collar. He let out a yell and, without further ado, he gathered up a handful of snow, scrunched it into a large ball and took aim.

It was a wonderful snowfight. They danced about, there in the middle of Glen Tarsa, laughing, breathless, plastering one another, forgetting everything in the fun, the excitement of the moment.

Moira O'Brady, the postmistress, on her way home from visiting a neighbour, was most astonished to hear the shouts of merriment ringing in the still air. She had only walked a short distance, but already she was frozen to the marrow and looking forward to getting her feet up at the fire. Unfortunately for her she landed plunk in the middle of the battlefield. Rounding a bend, she received the full benefit of a large snow missile that had been meant for Peter. It was a bullseye, hitting her full in the face and she let out a shriek, stretching out her hands as if to ward off further attack.

'Master Peter!' she cried in outrage as soon as she had recovered her dignity. 'Just what do you think you're playing at? And you a young man who should know better . . . but of course . . .' She turned her attention to Anna. 'I might have known, Anna – Anna McIntyre.'

She had no need to say more. The tone of her voice said it all. Her dislike of Roderick extended to his children although none of them, not even Adam, had ever given her cause for such prejudice. They were McIntyres and in Moira's book that was explanation enough. Every one of them was mad and bad, in Adam's case wild and unruly . . . and now it seemed, Anna had joined the ranks with her disorderly conduct.

She discounted Master Peter. He was a Noble, he was different . . . and besides . . . she needed the custom of the big house. Sir Malaroy and Lady Pandora had never been too above themselves to turn up their noses at her tiny establishment; they came in person for their little requirements and they came regularly. For this accolade Moira O'Brady was grateful, she felt herself to be a person of some esteem . . .

And then would come Roderick McIntyre, knocking all the confidence out of her with just a few words from that boorish tongue of his, nosying into her affairs, making her life a misery, a constant reminder of that tiny lapse from grace . . . never letting her forget . . .

She was therefore not at all kindly disposed to being 'set upon' by Anna McIntyre and she might have waxed eloquent on the subject had not Peter seized Anna's hand and made her run with him till they were nearing The Gatehouse. Only then did he allow her to stop so that they could both regain their breath.

'What was that all about?' he panted. 'She seems to have it in for you.'

Anna shrugged. 'I really don't know, she used to be alright but now she looks upon me and my family as some sort o' ogres.' She omitted to mention Roderick; somehow she knew that Moira's attitude owed itself to him, as did so many of the resentments that had built up in their neighbours over the years.

'Oh, well, it was a great fight anyway.' He took her hands and held them tightly. 'In fact, the whole evening was wonderful . . . Too bad me and Lucas are going off to school when Christmas is over – to a military academy in England. Just when I was – getting to know you, Anna.'

A strange disappointment swept through her. 'School?' she murmured, unable to keep a note of dismay from her voice.

'I know, I feel the same. I want to stay here but Aunt Dora thinks the time has come for us to broaden our horizons as well as our education. Mr Mallard won't be leaving – Aunt Dora has managed to dig up a couple of young protégés that were lurking somewhere in the family, so that should keep him occupied for a while.'

153

He moved closer to her. She could feel his breath fanning her face, his mouth was very near hers. 'Anna,' he said softly. 'I don't want to let you go now that I've found you. Let's get to know one another better. I have at least a month before I have to leave and we could see each other a lot in that time. There's our date with the McLeods to start us off and afterwards you could come to Noble House to visit us – we could have more fights in the snow and sledge rides and all sorts of marvellous things. It could be the best Christmas we've ever had.'

His enthusiasm was infectious. Anna felt herself being swept along on a tide of euphoria. Her emotions were in a turmoil: the wonder of the night, the moon, the stars, the glistening white countryside, made her feel lightheaded and abandoned.

'I want to do it, Peter, everything you suggest. Let's go up to the hills and sledge down side by side, feeling the wind rushing past us and . . . and let's be together as much as we can . . .'

He gave a great shout of joy, 'Anna, you *are* mad and I love you for it! I love you, Anna McIntyre!'

He seized her and kissed her full on the mouth. For a fleeting moment she felt the warmth of his lips, she knew the wonder of his nearness, before they broke apart to gaze at one another wordlessly.

'Anna,' he murmured, 'Don't be angry, I couldn't help myself, it just – happened.'

'I know,' she said softly. 'And I'm not angry – in fact – I feel so good I want you to dance with me.'

'Dance?'

'Ay.'

'Now?'

'Here and now.'

He held out his arms; she went into them, and there, in the middle of the road, by the light of the moon and the stars, they held one another and they floated, as if they were made of thistledown, weightless and as one.

'I must go,' reluctantly she broke away from him. 'I'll remember this night, Peter, for the rest o' my life I'll remember it.'

'Me too.'

Taking her hand he kissed it, he moved away from her.

154

At the door she turned. He was still standing where she had left him, watching her, just watching.

Her voice came to him lightly. 'What did you mean? When you said you had a private matter you wanted to see me about?'

'To apologize, Anna, about the things Lucas and me did to you at that Hallowe'en party.'

'And you came to Knock Farm, two years later, to tell me that?'

'I wanted to say sorry a long time ago but somehow I never got the chance. Had you forgotten? The little white ghost? Fleeing from the party because you were afraid we would discover who you were?'

His words brought everything vividly back to her, the delight of that night, the anxiety of it . . . the beating she had received at Roderick's hands when he had found out about it . . .

'No, Peter, I hadn't forgotten – I never shall.'

The door opened and closed on her and Peter wondered why she had sounded the way she had, forlorn somehow – and lost – as if she had stepped back in time and hadn't liked what she had remembered.

As soon as Magnus saw Anna's face he knew that something momentous had happened in her life. He also knew that things were never going to be quite the same for him again. Anna, his lovely, fiery, gentle Anna, was growing up, she was spreading her wings.

Her heart, her soul, her mind, had known wonderful things since he had helped her along the snowy road to Knock Farm earlier in the evening. It was all there, in the pink flush of her frost-stung cheeks, in the brightness of her eyes, in the secretive little smile that lurked at the corners of her mouth.

But more than these she radiated life and light, those tremendous forces that pulsed inside her and which were only released when she was particularly happy and excited.

'Anna,' he took her hands in his and rubbed them briskly, 'you're cold.'

'But my heart is warm, Magnus, and I feel wonderful.'

His eyes swept over her. 'You look wonderful, all glowy and sparkly. Has something happened?'

'Master Peter Noble happened, he came to Knock Farm tonight and helped Kate wind her wool. Afterwards he and me made toast in front

155

o' the fire and he walked me home. We had a snowball fight and then we danced, out there on the road – in the snow.'

'Danced?'

'Ay, we danced, and it was like floating on a cloud. And then he said he was sorry for something he and Lucas did at that Hallowe'en party two years ago. They tried to take off my ghost sheet and I was so scared I ran away from The House of Noble.'

'He apologized! After two years!'

'It was an excuse, Magnus, just to see me.'

A disquieting emotion seized Magnus. His knuckles tightened, he felt jealousy boiling up into his throat. He knew he oughtn't to feel like this, not about his own sister, but it wasn't a new feeling for him, he had experienced it before, many times, and no matter how hard he tried to push it down it always came back, just when he thought he had conquered it.

He couldn't understand it and made excuses for himself. He had looked after Anna since her infancy; he had protected her all through her childhood; it was only right that he should feel the way he did – a big brother looking out for a little sister who had suffered so much at the hands of a bullying father.

But there was more to it than that and Magnus knew it. Those feelings he had about her, urges to touch her and kiss her and love her in a way that wasn't natural for a brother. He had long ago stopped getting into bed with her to cuddle her asleep – if he hadn't there was no knowing what might have happened . . . that lovely young body, that perfect sweet mouth, moist, pink, desirable . . . It was bad enough having to sleep in the same room as her; just thinking about her lying across from him was enough to bring him out in a sweat . . .

And then he would think – Roderick was right – they would go mad like their mother – they would all go mad – except perhaps Anna. She would be spared. Pray God, she would be spared!

He shook himself out of his bitter thoughts. Anna was watching him, and there was an odd expression in her eyes. 'I said, Magnus, are you alright? I was telling you about Peter.'

'Peter, ay, Peter.' Magnus forced himself to smile at her. 'Never mind him just now. I've made cocoa, I wanted us to be together to drink it at the fire.'

Anna bent to pick up Tibby, burying her face into the cat's soft fur, kissing her ears, cuddling her. The kitchen was warm and bright; Magnus had heaped logs on the fire; two oil lamps and three candles illuminated the room. The atmosphere in the house was happy and carefree, as if a great shadow had been lifted, allowing air to get inside and life to breathe and flourish. Roderick's shadow, enveloping every-thing it touched, smothering everyone with its evil.

None of them knew how long he would be gone – no one cared if he ever came back. They hardly dared voice their thoughts, but in their hearts they prayed for deliverance from him for as long as possible.

Adam came through from the bedroom in his nightshirt and all three of them sat by the fire, sipping their cocoa. Anna and Magnus relaxed as never before in their young brother's company. He was still Adam, a daredevil, a boy who would take a long time to become a man, but the wickedness had gone from his mischief, the cunning had gone from his deeds. With his father away there wasn't the same need to impress everyone with his strength and his false bravery. Anxiety and fear had departed from his life and he had never been more likeable, more touchable.

'I'm making a snowman tomorrow,' he announced, clasping his fingers round his cup, his boyish face alight. 'As big as a house, as fat as a hilltop. I'll make it so big that everyone will see it, whether on the road passing by or riding along in a carriage. Tell Tale Todd will get the biggest fright o' his life. He'll rush around, telling the whole glen and they'll all come to look at it and maybe throw coppers into the bucket I'll put at its feet.'

Magnus and Anna looked at one another and laughed. 'We'll all make a snowman,' said Magnus. 'And when we've decided whose is the biggest, we'll pay homage to the winner and do their share o' the chores right up till Christmas Day.'

'And then,' Anna laughed, 'we'll see which o' us can eat the biggest Christmas dinner without actually bursting.'

'Och, I'll do that easily,' Adam said with assurance.

'What? Burst?'

'That too, I'm good at everything I try.'

The three of them exploded – with mirth – and all around them the heartbeat of the house throbbed in a pleasant, easy rhythm.

*   *   *

157

Magnus wasn't the only one to feel that change was about to come into his life. Lucas felt it too, that very same night, the minute his brother put his face round the drawing room door.

Lucas wasn't in a very good mood. The evening had been long and lonely for him without Peter's good-natured company. The brothers were seldom apart from one another and Lucas had displayed a good deal of surprise when it became apparent that Peter had actually meant what he had said about trying to see Anna.

'You're as mad as the McIntyres,' Lucas had stated warningly. 'And besides that you could be starting up something you might not be able to stop.'

'Who says I'll want to stop it?' Peter had returned ably. 'I'm going and that's final – whatever you say.'

And he had gone, into the snowy night, leaving his brother to fume and fret and in the end, wish that he had gone also.

Now here was Peter, his blue eyes shining, his face all frosty fresh, bubbling over with enthusiasm. 'You should have come, Lucas,' he said, dumping himself down on the couch. 'The McLeods are great people – and Anna – well, she's unbelievable, lovely as a flower, full of life and humour. We danced in the snow and had a marvellous snowball fight . . .'

'You *are* mad!' cried Lucas, his face darkening.

'You're right, madly in love with Miss McIntyre. It's a wonderful feeling, Lucas, you should try it, get rid of some of these emotions you bottle up. I'm going back to the farm – I've been invited to tea next Friday, so have you.'

Lucas's thunderous expression grew blacker. 'You can leave me out! I won't go and listen to those two batty sisters squeaking on about nothing nor will I listen to that boring Ben rattling on about cows and cockerels!'

'Suit yourself. You can stay here and have a wonderfully bracing evening of boredom. Anna's going – so is Elizabeth Jordan,' he added slyly.

'That little snob . . . Peter, stop sniggering, she is a little snob and a madam into the bargain . . .'

'And you consider yourself to be anything but a snob?'

'Not that sort.'

'So, there are different kinds of snobs?'

'Oh, what's the use of trying to talk to you when you're like this? I'm going to bed, are you coming?'

Together they ascended the stairs. 'She's quite good looking,' Lucas said thoughtfully. 'I mean Beth Jordan. Long legs, long hair, a good figure for a girl of her age. Big . . .' he pushed out his chest, '. . . breasts. She always tries to rub them up against me whenever she comes here with her father. She's had her eye on me for ages, tries to seduce me with everything she's got.'

'I thought you said you didn't know anything about women?'

'I don't, but I do know a bit about girls. Quite a few of them ogle me whenever they get the chance. Girls like that are ten a penny and Beth Jordan's no exception. She's the sort that would let you do anything to her if she thought it might lead to a bed of roses.'

'You're a cynic.'

'Honest, dear brother, just honest.'

'So, you'll come to Knock Farm then? All honesty and charm.'

'I didn't say so.'

'You will just the same, I can tell by your voice . . .'

'Thought I heard voices.' Mr Mallard came out of his room, tying the cord of his dressing gown, a look of disapproval on his ruggedly handsome face. 'Where have you been, Peter? Your aunt was worried about you going off on your own like that on a night like this.'

'I told you, sir,' Lucas said quickly, 'he promised to lend a book to Ben McLeod of Knock Farm.'

A wry grin touched the tutor's face, 'And you picked a night like this to do it in – and Ben McLeod's house so full of books as it is he could make a bonfire out of them.'

'He's asked us to tea next Friday, Mr Mallard,' Peter got in while the going was good. 'Lucas and me.'

'And that girl you were talking about as you came up the stairs?'

Peter also grinned. 'Her too – and Anna McIntyre of The Gatehouse, we've all been invited.'

'Anna McIntyre.' Mallard frowned. Roderick's daughter, the one Pandora had been so keen to have as a companion some time ago.

'You'd best talk to your aunt about it,' Mallard began when Sir Malaroy appeared from his room, also tying his dressing gown.

'Don't I have a say in anything that goes on here?' he began, somewhat

159

testily, his keen blue eyes regarding Mallard accusingly. 'Ask Pandora about what?'

'Explain, boys,' ordered Mallard.

Peter hadn't bargained on any of this. The entire household seemed to be up and about and showing an intense interest in his affairs and with a stifled sigh he plunged into an account of his evening at Knock Farm.

By the time he had finished talking, a look of disapproval had settled on Sir Malaroy's features. 'Anna McIntyre, so you've been seeing her, have you? Remember, Peter, you're only sixteen and you're going away to school soon. It's a bit late to start making friends with the villagers, should have thought about that a long time ago. Anna McIntyre isn't for the likes of you . . .'

'Why, Malaroy,' Lady Pandora appeared at that moment, wrapping the folds of a blue satin *peignoir* round her slender figure. Her honey-gold hair flowed down her back in rich tresses; her skin was radiant; the delicate perfume of roses wafted from her newly-bathed body.

Mallard stared at her, openly appreciative, but it was to her husband she went, curling one hand into the crook of his arm to give it a little shake of gentle reproof as she went on. 'It isn't like you to talk like that, darling, you've never been class-conscious and you never will be. What's wrong with Anna McIntyre, I'd like to know? She's never done you any harm. I don't see why the boys can't go to Knock Farm for tea. They'll be off to school soon enough and will forget all about the McIntyres and the McLeods and anyone else they care not to remember. Don't you agree? For me?'

He was like putty in her hands. With a brief nod of acquiescence he turned on his heel and went back into his room, pointedly leaving the door open for his wife.

Placing a hand on each of the boys' shoulders she smiled at them and gave them a little push along the corridor. Left alone with Mallard she gazed at him for a long moment. He took a step towards her but she evaded him and he was left, a muscle twitching in his cheek as her door closed on him, softly but firmly.

CHAPTER NINETEEN

Tea Parties

ANNA WAS HAVING SATURDAY afternoon tea with the Jordans. At one time she had considered this event to be a rare treat, but that had been when she was too young to know any better.

The Ordeal was how she described it to herself now, something to be got through as quickly as possible without yawning openly and fiddling too much with her spoon. She only came because of Beth, knowing how impolite it would be to refuse since her friend declared that she couldn't get through these afternoons either without some youthful support.

For a start there were Mrs Victoria Jordan's friends to contend with, sanctimonious ladies who waxed long and loudly about their woes and ills but who soon loosened up after a glass or two of sherry when the talk then turned to common or garden gossip of a spicy variety.

These overdressed ladies weren't Mrs Jordan's more exclusive friends, the ones she saved for Sabbath afternoons, social climbers who gathered together because they felt comfortable with one another since they were all of the same mind and shared the same shallow ambitions. These middle class members of The Victoria Jordan Sunday Club as Beth had wickedly christened the gatherings, talked much of church affairs, the high hopes they harboured for the future of their daughters and sons, the things that Colonel so and so or Lady such and such had said to them in passing – 'such delightful people' – and the latest fashions of the day.

They stuck out their pinkies whilst partaking of tea, never burped, gulped, or choked, or indulged in any of the other things that they considered to be 'shockingly rude' in others. The word 'fart' had never passed their lips, far less from their posteriors. They never spoke about such vulgarities, and never, never, did they perform such abominable acts of nature, leave all that to lesser mortals who didn't know any better! They never sat in any other pose but ramrod straight; they read passages from the bible; they vied with one another as to which of them had experienced the most significant brush with the gentry since last they had met, and all the while they scrutinized one another critically and none of them liked each other very much.

Compared to this, The Saturday Ladies Social Club – another of Beth's little titles – was much more relaxed and informal. It was true that these ladies also stuck out their pinkies whilst drinking their tea but usually they were so busy gossiping they sometimes forgot these small social graces. Sometimes they dribbled and had to mop themselves up, occasionally they choked on a crumb of cake, very often they had to smother a wayward burp since Fat Jane's cake was 'so awfully good' but rich enough in content to induce the odd ball of wind.

Whatever the day, whichever the class of people, Mrs Victoria Jordan, a tall, angular woman with a large mouth and a discontented face, always talked too loudly and too long, and since Mr Jordan was required to attend tea on both days, he was wont to frequently raise his eyes to the ceiling while desperately racking his mind for an excuse to escape. Anna supposed that the long-suffering look on William Jordan's face had always been there only she hadn't recognized it for what it was in her earlier childhood.

Miss Primrose Pym, Beth's home tuition teacher for the past two years, was also expected to be present at both the Saturday and Sunday meetings. Miss Pym was a woman of indeterminate age; she had buck teeth, scrubby hair tied back in a bun, a poor skin, and a somewhat solid figure.

Beth hadn't wanted Miss Pym to be her teacher. 'I think a young man would be better, Mother,' she had said after her first sighting of the unfortunate lady. 'The Noble boys have Mr Mallard, he gives them plenty of scope but still manages to keep them under control.'

Victoria Jordan's nostrils had flared at this but she hadn't been as eloquent on the subject as she might otherwise have been, the Nobles were Nobles when all was said and done, though privately she was of the opinion that Lady Pandora was sometimes just a wee bit flippant over certain matters, education being one.

'Women for girls, Elizabeth, men for boys,' she had stressed firmly. 'I certainly don't want someone teaching my daughter how to swing from trees or to dive naked into pools of icy water. You're a young lady, Elizabeth, and it's high time you learned to behave like one. Miss Pym has excellent references and she speaks French, which is something you must learn if you want to get on in the world.'

But despite her good references Miss Pym wasn't one of Victoria Jordan's favourite persons. Her looks left a lot to be desired, she was too self-opinionated, she was prudish even by Mrs Jordan's standards, and she talked too much and too loudly!

But she had many points in her favour: she was patient and she was kind. She was God fearing, a trifle too fervently perhaps; she was respectful of her employers and she didn't talk about men. Most importantly she was possessed of the great strength of perseverance which, as Mrs Jordan knew only too well, was a great asset when it came to dealing with her daughter.

So Miss Pym stayed and settled herself into the household, a trifle uncomfortably, owing to her awareness of her pupil's precocious character. Beth was smart and she let it be known to Miss Prim Pym, as she had quickly been christened, that she was not only smart but devious with it. Miss Pym soon realized that she had taken on quite a challenge with Miss Jordan but she told herself that she wasn't a minister's daughter for nothing, she was a match for Beth any day of the week.

And so the battle of wits began, sometimes enjoyable, sometimes not. Whichever way, Miss Pym was always on her mettle and always ready to air her opinions. Whether they were listened to or not didn't matter very much to her; she liked to hear her own tongue and it was quite interesting when she was in Mrs Jordan's company to see which of them could out talk and outwit the other.

So, Miss Pym was reasonably happy in her position, even though she was aware that Beth put up with her under sufferance and that Mrs Jordan's tolerance of her was borne out of necessity. And she wasn't the only one to feel like that. Anna knew Mrs Jordan only tolerated her visits to Corran House because of her friendship with Beth. She was only Anna McIntyre of The Gatehouse after all, and as such was considered to be on a much lower social scale than the Jordans of Corran House.

All things considered, Anna never felt comfortable at The Saturday Ladies Social Club and today she was very relieved to see Beth beckoning to her from the doorway.

With more than a touch of dignity, Anna got to her feet, made her excuses and went out to the hall where she and Beth immediately collapsed in a state of the giggles.

'Did you see Mrs McDuff's hat!' exploded Beth. 'Like a bird's nest sitting on top of a haystack!'

'And she was so proud o' it,' choked Anna. 'Patting her hair and gazing about her to make sure that everyone was noticing her.'

'And old Fanny McWhirter's frock,' went on the incorrigible Beth. 'Those poppies! As red and as garish as her rouge!'

'Mrs Simpson couldn't keep her eyes off it!'

'Did you hear our Miss Prim?' gasped Beth. '"Further education really is so important for young ladies these days. I myself, as you all know, have benefited greatly from learning, thanks to my far-sighted father, God rest him. He was a minister you know, a man of great integrity till the day he died, God rest him. He believed that everyone has brains of some sort, even the poor and mentally flawed in our midst – yes – even those!"' Beth pranced about in front of Anna, mimicking her teacher's high grating voice and mincing walk to perfection.

'Poor Mrs Simpson didn't know where to look!' Anna clutched her stomach in an agony of mirth. 'Every time Miss Prim said "God rest him," Fanny McWhirter looked as if she expected a dead body to materialize from nowhere and gazed anxiously at Mrs Simpson as if hoping that she might wave a magic wand and spirit *our* minister in to perform a funeral ceremony!'

'And Father! Raising his eyes to the ceiling as if wishing he could grow wings and fly right out of that room!'

'We shouldn't really laugh,' said Anna, whereupon she and Beth once more erupted into helpless giggles.

'Come on,' Beth wiped her eyes and took Anna's hand. 'Let's go and see Fat Jane, it's much more fun listening to all her chat. She's made jam doughnuts for tea, we'll grab some before they disappear down the greedy throats of the Saturday Ladies. Don't worry, later on I'll tell Mother we simply had to leave the room because we had a headache – or something.'

Fat Jane wasn't in the least put out when the girls appeared in her kitchen. 'Can't say as I blame you, me dears,' she greeted them with a plump, good-natured smile. 'I'd 'ave done the same in your shoes. 'Ow those ladies can sit there roasting themselves at the fire and drinking sherry while their tongues run ahead of their minds beats me.' So saying she took a large swig of cooking sherry reposing innocently in a dessert dish and went to fetch a plate from the stove piled high with hot doughnuts.

'There you are, me dears, just you tuck in and don't mind your manners for me.' Digging into a bowl of sugar she sprinkled generous amounts over the doughnuts and the girls needed no second bidding to feast on the delicious sweetmeats.

'Any room for me?' William Jordan popped his head round the door. 'Another minute in there and I'll grow wings and depart this earthly coil.'

Anna and Beth looked at one another and exploded afresh while Fat Jane pulled a chair out from the table and bade her employer to 'sit down and tuck in.'

Rather sheepishly he did as he was told. Beth pushed the piled plate towards him, he picked up a large doughnut and dug his teeth into it, releasing a jet of hot jam onto his face, his hair, and the front of his immaculate shirt.

'Really, sir!'

Fat Jane rushed for a cloth. She mopped him up. He looked at her, she looked at him, the girls looked at one another and all four of them burst into riotous fits of laughter.

When they had a moment alone together Anna told Beth about the invitation to tea at Knock Farm.

'The McLeods.' Beth made a face. 'Um – I don't know, Anna, I've never socialized with them very much – only when I was very little.'

'Lucas and Peter Noble have been invited too. Peter came to see me there on Friday – and it was wonderful, Beth. He walked me home, I like him a lot.'

'Peter and Lucas,' Beth's tone changed. 'Why didn't you say so in the first place, Anna. I'd be delighted to come – but – why did Peter want to see you?'

'To apologize – for teasing me at that party two years ago.'

'Apologize! After two years! How peculiar.'

Anna's head went up. 'Not so peculiar. He's wanted to speak to me for ages and on Friday he decided the time was right.'

Beth slipped her arm through Anna's. They wandered into the hall. At the door Beth said abruptly, 'Anna, I'm sorry too.'

165

'For what?'

'Oh, just this and that. You know how it is?' She sounded strange – and she had reddened – which in itself was also strange since Beth seldom blushed for anything or anybody.

'Can't you tell me what you mean, Beth?' Anna said slowly.

'No, not now or ever, I just wanted you to know I appreciate – you being my friend and everything – even though sometimes I haven't been very nice to you.'

'Is that all?'

Beth said nothing and Anna made her way to the gate, lost in thought, wondering, wondering what Beth had meant by saying she was sorry and why she had sounded so odd when she had said it.

Mrs Jordan was in the parlour, having a rest after her day's labours, when Beth came in to see her.

'I've been invited to tea, Mother.'

'Oh, where?'

'Knock Farm.'

'Knock Farm.' Mrs Jordan's voice fell two octaves.

'Lucas and Peter Noble have also been invited.'

'Oh!' Mrs Jordan had a habit of saying 'oh' in her loud voice, the inflection she put into the expression depending on her mood of the moment. On this occasion she put everything she had into it, followed with, 'Lucas *and* Peter. Oh! How lovely, Elizabeth . . .'

Wait till she told her Sunday ladies about this, she thought, before continuing excitedly, 'We must go down to the seamstress at Larchwood and see about getting you a new dress. You haven't had anything new in a long time and you simply can't go to the McLeods' looking like a tramp.'

Beth was bored with new clothes. A 'long time' in her mother's book spanned anything from a week to a month and the novelty of 'seeing the seamstress at Larchwood' was wearing thin for Beth.

'Mother, it isn't a fancy affair. I don't need a new dress or anything else new for that matter. My wardrobes are filled to the brim as it is.'

'Then we'll just have to give some things away to the Relief Centre for the Parish Poor. They're always delighted with my donations since nothing I hand in is in any way shoddy. Tomorrow is Sunday, a day of rest and worship, but on Monday, Elizabeth, we will look through your things and decide what has to go. Waste not want not my own mother used to say and anything that goes to charity is never wasted.'

Beth said no more, knowing from experience that she would be wasting her breath.

There could have been no greater contrast between Mrs Victoria Jordan's stiff little tea parties and the one that the McLeods of Knock Farm gave to their young guests.

Kate, as good as her word, had set a 'beautiful table'. Bowls of holly and fir cones made festive centrepieces; a garland of variegated leaves with berries had been pinned all round the edges of the table; bunches of black and green grapes, rosy red apples, nuts, and pears had been placed willy-nilly on the sparkling white tablecloth and looked most effective in the candlelight, so much so that Beth determined to tell her mother that fruit needn't be confined to dishes in order to look good. At each placing was a tiny parcel, wrapped in red crêpe paper, each bearing the name of the intended recipient in carefully scrolled green lettering.

The atmosphere of the house was warm and welcoming. An enormous log fire leapt in the grate; Puddle had been joined by another retired sheepdog called Puck. Neither were asleep, each being too alert to the delicious smells filling the kitchen to spare a thought for anything else, not even the mischievous attentions of a black and white cat who was playing with their wagging tails and boxing their flicking ears.

A pan of broth was simmering on the hob, a clouty dumpling sat cooling on the sideboard, beside it reposed a turkey with a breast so large it had burst apart its own skin. The smells of roast potatoes, boiled potatoes, and baked potatoes mingled with one another and with everything else that was savoury and wholesome in the room.

Ben's only concession to dressing for the visitors was to don his best cap; Kate was enveloped in a roomy white apron; Miss Priscilla still wore her classroom 'uniform', a black dress with a large brooch pinned at the neck, but she had attached a single white Christmas rose to her bosom which she considered was decoration enough for the occasion.

Lucas had deigned to come after all, arriving with his brother in a somewhat surly and critical frame of mind. The savoury smells that met him were the first steps in the softening process. The warm welcome

167

he received from the McLeods added to the glow that was rapidly thawing his reservations.

The girls had come with the boys, having met at the end of the drive of The House of Noble. Beth was overdressed, she knew it the second she stepped over the threshold. Her green velvet dress, her diamante clasps, her upswept hair, were much more suited to an evening of grandeur than a simple, homely supper.

'I'll simply roast in this,' she muttered crossly to Anna as she tried to struggle out of her fur-trimmed velvet cape. 'Mother really is the limit telling me what I should and shouldn't wear and she never gets it right!'

'Here, let me.' Peter was there, gallantly helping her out of the cape.

Lucas was there too, watching everything with half-closed eyes, a habit of his when he was being particularly critical. They were also glittering a bit, something in them that might have been appreciation as the removal of Beth's cape revealed her in all her glory.

'Thank you, Peter.' Pointedly she acknowledged his mannerly gesture, but it wasn't Peter she was looking at when she spoke, it was Lucas – and her pale blue eyes were glittering as much as his.

'You look – very charming tonight, Beth,' drawled Lucas. 'In fact, I'd go as far as to say you look wonderful.'

Beth immediately blossomed, like a crumpled flower opening to the sun. She turned to him, she smiled, they gazed into one another's eyes, an immediate spark of attraction flashing between them.

Peter turned to Anna. He said nothing for a moment, so lost was he in the wonder of being near her again. Her flaxen hair was tied back with a blue ribbon, the colour of it matching her only good dress, a garment of utmost simplicity, its chaste folds only serving to emphasize her youthful curves: the cameo at the neck, the white lace, giving it that touch that was so essentially hers. Her grey eyes were big and dark in the pale loveliness of her face; she was looking at him a trifle nervously and, slipping his arm through hers, he whispered, 'I don't want you to get away, you look so – so ethereal tonight, Anna.'

At that she laughed. 'Oh, I'm real alright – and I'm starving – all those lovely smells, my mouth is watering already.'

A hearty roar came from the kitchen. 'C'mon ben! The lot o' you! Unless you want to eat your food out there in the lobby!'

There were no pretensions during the meal. Ben dunked his bread in his soup, Kate said 'bugger it!' when she burned her throat on a

168

mouthful of hot potato, Miss Priscilla kept everyone entertained with incidents from her years of teaching. The young visitors soon relaxed and joined in the banter and fun.

Lucas forgot that he was a Noble mixing with 'the peasants', Beth forgot her discomfiture with her clothes, Peter and Anna almost forgot everything so taken up were they with one another.

The parcels contained lace handkerchiefs for the womenfolk and larger ones for the men. Ben looked at his pure white square and said in bemusement, 'I can't see myself out on the hill wi' this, the back o' my hand is good enough for me.'

'Ben!' scolded Kate. 'You shouldn't say things like that in front o' people!'

'Who am I to say them to, if no people?' he grinned. 'The sheep wouldn't understand, nor would the cows, and just you try wiping your nose on a hanky in a blizzard or while pulling milk from a cow's udder . . . Speaking o' which . . .' he turned to the boys, '. . . Bluebell is calving, how would you two like to come and give me a hand wi' her?'

Lucas made a face at his brother but followed him willingly enough outside.

Kate and Miss Priscilla did the dishes between them, Anna and Beth put them away in their respective cupboards.

'I never do this at home,' Beth confided to Anna, as if she didn't know that already. 'But somehow it's fun here – and I love the dresser and all the little drawers and everything neatly in its place. Fat Jane's a great cook but a bit untidy in the kitchen. She says it's all to do with method, her method, because she knows where everything is even if no one else does.'

When the menfolk returned and had washed themselves everyone gathered round the piano to sing Christmas carols. Kate had thrown pine cones in the fire, they expanded and opened and sent showers of sparks up the lum; the mellow glow of oil lamps lit the room; the atmosphere was one of peace and goodwill.

Miss Priscilla's hands flowed over the keys, Still the Night, Holy the Night . . . Peter's fingers curled into Anna's, Lucas's arm rested lightly on Beth's shoulders. No one failed to appreciate the unity of that special evening with the music and songs of Christmas filling the room.

Supper consisted of toast and hot pancakes dripping with butter and jam, washed down with mugs of piping hot tea and afterwards, just a 'teensy tot o' sherry for the road.'

No one wanted the night to end but there was no stopping the hands of the clock. The last goodnight, the final thank you echoed in the hall, the youngsters tramped out into the snowy night.

Beth and Lucas walked in front, Anna and Peter came behind, their hands warmly entwined.

'Anna,' his lips brushed her ear. 'You were all I thought about the whole week. I couldn't wait for tonight, now it's over.'

'Don't talk,' she urged, her face burning in the freezing air. 'Just enjoy, it's ours, all o' it. Look at it, Peter, the white world, the quietness, this wonderful feeling of being alive.'

His hand tightened on hers, they trudged along, their awareness of one another quickening their hearts, keeping them warm.

They didn't stop when they reached the Noble House driveway. 'We'll walk you home,' Lucas threw over his shoulder and he and Beth kept on going, talking quietly, their heads very close together . . .

'There you are, Anna!' The door of Nellie Jean's cottage opened and she came stumbling out, bumping against Lucas who deliberately moved away from her. Her dark hair was an unruly mop, her clothes were crumpled and smelt of sweaty scent, the whisky fumes on her breath invaded the air. 'I thought I heard your voice,' she continued in slurred tones. 'When is that father o' yours coming home? I never thought I would say this but I miss the old bugger. He and I were good pals, eh, Anna, we had some wild times wi' one another, him and me.'

Anna shivered. In just a few sentences Nellie Jean had brought it all flooding back, the things she had tried so hard to forget these last few perfect months. Nellie Jean and her father, lying lusting together in her mother's bed, the feeling of unease in the house, everything that was restricted and terrible in her life.

'I don't know when he'll be back,' her voice seemed to come from a long distance. 'And to be quite honest, Mrs Anderson, I don't care.'

Nellie Jean gave vent to a high pitched giggle, 'Quite the little madam, now, eh, Anna, hob nobbing wi' the gentry, ashamed o' your own kind, even your own father . . .'

'Come on.' Peter took Anna's arm and hurried her away, Nellie Jean's drunken cackle echoing in their wake.

'Come and see us tomorrow, Anna.' Peter could feel her tension, sense the anxiety that had suddenly robbed her of her happiness. 'We'll go sledging, glide along together over the slopes and the fields.'

'Ay, oh, yes, I'd love that.' Anna sounded desperate, as if she were trying to cling to the last remnants of a freedom that had been so precious to her lately.

'Great idea,' approved Lucas. 'The snow should last for a while yet. You'll come too, won't you, Beth?'

Without hesitation Beth accepted the invitation, aware that Lucas was watching her and that there was more than a hint of assurance in his voice. More than anything in the whole world she wanted to meet him again, they had a lot in common, she and he . . . and what a feather in her cap! Lucas Noble of The House of Noble, desiring her company, desiring her, if his whispers in her ear just minutes ago were anything to go by. Wait till she told her mother that she was seeing him again! Of course, she wouldn't mention that they were going sledging, that would certainly be met with disapproval, though there were times that Beth felt her mother would put up with anything if it meant getting on the right side of the gentry.

Beth made her farewells, her hand lingering in that of Lucas as he said softly, 'Tomorrow morning, Beth, ten-ish, best to get out as early as possible.'

'I'll be there,' she injected a husky note into her voice. In the darkness he smiled and his eyes glittered. She'd be there alright, all wrapped up in furs, dimpled and demure, sweetness and light, showing everyone what a proper young lady she was – and all the while she'd be burning, underneath the coolness she'd burn and ache and yearn for a word, a touch from him to kindle the fires that smouldered in her breast. It was all there in her eyes, those big pale blue eyes of hers, trying so hard to look innocent but unable to mask the vixen that lay within. She was a sly one was Beth, wily and manipulative – and mature for a girl of her age – physically at any rate. She was ripe and ready for womanly experiences and he was ready and able for her!

'I'll see you all tomorrow,' she said with a nod and swept regally away.

'Anna,' Lucas held out his hand, 'it's been a pleasure.'

'For me too, Lucas, it was nice to meet you properly at last.'

'All forgiven and forgotten?'

'Not forgotten, never that, but forgiven, ages and ages ago.'

She and Peter eyed one another. Reluctantly she said her goodnights and walked the short distance to The Gatehouse.

Peter smiled at his brother. 'What a performance you gave! All honesty and charm.'

'Don't rub it in!' growled Lucas.

He grinned and threw his arm round his brother's shoulder. They walked home through the sparkling white night, silently, one thinking about Anna McIntyre of The Gatehouse, the other thinking of Beth Jordan of Corran House, a little gold digger if ever there was one – but fun just the same – and available – very available.

CHAPTER TWENTY

Confessions

THE SNOW LASTED FOR two weeks. During that time Anna knew true joy. The world seemed to have opened and expanded for her, her life took on new meaning. She didn't know how long it would last but while it did she held it to her heart and wished that it would go on forever.

'Be careful, Anna,' Magnus warned when it became apparent how attached she was becoming to Peter. 'The Nobles aren't for you, these lads will go away and forget all about you and you'll only get hurt in the end.'

'Och, Magnus,' she chafed gently. 'I know fine it's only a passing thing. I don't expect it to last forever.'

A muscle pulsed in his jaw. 'Yes you do. You're so starry eyed you can't even think straight these days. Peter's a nice lad, much nicer than his brother who's a fox if ever there was one, but they're Nobles, the gentry, they live in a different world from us. There's one set o' rules for them and quite another for the likes o' us. Peter will just love you and leave you in the end.'

'Magnus,' she took his arm. 'He isn't like that, he's warm and generous and loving. He knows when I'm happy and when I'm sad but I'm grown up enough not to believe in fairy tales. I know Peter will go away into a bigger world than this. He'll meet other people, other girls. In the meantime he wants to be wi' me and I love being wi' him, so don't try and take this lovely time away from me. It will all end soon enough.'

'Anna.' His voice was husky. 'I want you to be happy, it's what I've always wanted for you but I can't help being . . .'

'Jealous, Magnus,' the words were out before she could stop them. 'Because you are jealous, aren't you? I've sensed it for a long time now and it's getting worse as we both get older. I'm your sister, Magnus, only your sister . . .'

'Are you!' With a swift movement he pulled her towards him, crushing her to him, his mouth coming down on hers in a kiss of fierce and uncontrollable passion.

She was too taken aback to struggle, too shocked to even try and break away from him. Then something strange and inexplicable happened to her, a feeling of terrible weakness took possession of her. Without being able to help herself she found herself responding to him. She moulded herself to his warm, hard-muscled body, she held his face in her hands and thrilled to the demanding pressure of his lips. She had never known anything like it, she never wanted it to end – then the realization hit her. This was Magnus! Her brother! How could she? How could he?

Tearing herself away from him she stood staring at him, panting, stunned by the ferocity of her feelings.

He too was panting, dazed looking. His broad chest was heaving, his eyes, when he at last struggled out of his emotional abyss, dark and wild and desperate looking.

'Anna!' he spread his hands, his voice rasped in his throat, 'What can I say . . . ?'

'What can we both say?' she threw at him. 'Can we pretend to each other that it's alright for a brother and sister to express their love for one another in the way we've just done! Can we, Magnus?'

'No, no, it isn't alright,' he replied shakily. 'I must never touch you again – but – listen, Anna, I . . . only know I love you, in a way that a brother would never love a sister.'

She was barely listening, so incensed was she with shame and anger. She kept her eyes averted from him as she straightened her clothes and tidied her hair.

'Don't talk, Magnus, just don't say anything else about it. I hate myself and I hate you more! And to think you had the cheek to warn me about Peter! At least he isn't my brother or my cousin, or anything else that might make a mockery of how we feel about one another.'

'Stranger things have happened, Anna,' Magnus spoke gruffly, his tone a mixture of love and shame.

'What do you mean?' But she sounded exhausted, as if all the fire and fight had gone out of her. 'Not to me, Magnus, I'm Anna McIntyre o' The Gatehouse, plain and simple, and you're my brother . . . and I'm going to enjoy my life while I can, where I can, and with whom I can. Right now it's Peter Noble and I promised I would meet him fifteen minutes ago!'

'Anna,' he stood there, crushed looking, his voice breaking with emotion. 'Don't leave me like this, angry and resentful. You don't hate me, you'll never hate me, will you? Will you, Anna?'

At last she looked at him. His hazel eyes were full of misery, his strong, beautiful young body was as taut as a bowstring.

Her breath caught on a sob. 'Oh, no, Magnus, I'll never hate you, but we both know that things will never be the same between us again. I'll have to leave. Lady Pandora once wanted me as a companion. If she asks me again I'll say yes and I'll move my things up to The House of Noble. That way we'll be separate from one another and out o' the way o' temptation.'

She left him standing alone and lonely in the middle of the room, and she didn't see the mist of pain in his eyes nor hear his voice brokenly whispering her name.

Peter was waiting for her halfway along the drive and she ran straight into his arms, wanting to feel his nearness, wanting everything that was normal in those traumatic minutes.

'Hey!' he laughed and swung her high, his blue eyes gazing up at her, filled with light and happiness. Exuberantly he swung her round and round till the sky spun and the hills danced, then he lowered his arms till her face was touching his and their mouths met in a kiss of sweetness and delight.

'Peter.' She clung to him. 'I've missed you! Oh, I've missed you so much!'

'But you saw me yesterday.'

'That was in another time, a lot o' things can happen in twenty-four hours.'

'Eighteen hours to be precise.'

'Have you been counting?'

'Every tick of the clock, every chime of the hour. My life doesn't exist without you. Quack Quack looks at me because I don't answer him, brother talks to me and I don't hear, Uncle Malaroy frowns at me for not clearing my plate at dinner and Aunt Dora clucks mildly and thinks I'm coming down with something.'

'Oh, Peter, you're daft!,' she cried, kissing his ears. 'Even dafter than I am and I love you for it!'

He was suddenly serious, his eyes very blue and intense in his frost-stung face. 'Do you, Anna? Do you love me enough to wait for me? Be here when I come home on holiday? Never look at anyone else while I'm away?'

'Peter, I'm only fifteen and you're just a year older. We have to grow up a bit before we know how we really feel about each other.'

'I know how I feel, here and now, ever and always. I love you, Anna. From the moment I saw you standing at the door of Knock Farm I knew that I loved you. When I used to see you going about the glen I was mesmerized by you and longed to meet you face to face. Now I have and I'll never let you go.'

'Come on.' She put her hand into his, hiding her confusion in flip-pant words. 'Let's enjoy ourselves while there's time. Today I want to go faster than I've ever done before, I want to swoosh and fly through the snow like a bird, like a cloud scudding before the wind. I want . . .'

'To be an elephant like Beth!' he grinned. 'Falling off your sledge and skidding about in helpless circles so that you can cry out for me the way she does for Lucas.'

Anna's dimples showed. 'I know, she doesn't try very hard, does she? But she enjoys herself in her own way and if that means falling flat on her face in the snow, then so be it!'

Laughing, they walked hand in hand up the driveway to a hayshed near the stables where the sledges were kept.

Beth and Lucas were just emerging from it, flushed and dishevelled, Beth fastening the buttons of her fur cape, Lucas brushing bits of hay from his trousers.

'You're late,' was his greeting to his brother. 'Beth and I were getting things ready. Let's get the sledges out.'

He and Peter disappeared into the shed. Beth turned to Anna, her eyes sparkling in triumph. 'He can't keep his hands off me, Anna, I've been keeping him hanging on, making him wait, but today . . . I'm just glad you were late – that's all.'

She folded her lips meaningfully. She didn't have to say more; a faint animal odour emanated from her. Anna could smell it and she recog-nized it for what it was. She had smelt it often enough before – when she'd had to change the sheets in her father's bed after he and Nellie Jean had lain in it.

The boys reappeared, dragging the sledges. Beth pouted a little. 'Let's not spend too long sledging today, I'd like to go for a walk along the river bank, it's a nice day for it.'

She was staring at Lucas as she spoke. He hesitated, his mouth twisting into a sardonic smile. 'Sounds like a good idea to me, I'm getting a bit bored with playing in the snow anyway, after all, we're not children anymore.'

Peter looked as if he could have expanded on that, instead he contented himself saying, 'You two go your own way then, me and Anna will do likewise.'

Lucas and Beth needed no second bidding. They went off, his arm round her waist, her head on his shoulder. Peter glanced at Anna, 'Do you really want to float like a cloud and fly like a bird?'

Her eyes shone, she nodded. 'I'd like nothing better – just as long as you're there to catch me when I fall down to earth.'

They laughed and, grabbing the sledge, they hauled it along, their feet scrunching in the snow, their breath puffing out into the frosty air. Somehow they still managed to hold hands and when they reached their desired destination at the foot of Coir an Ban he pulled her towards him and brushed her lips with his. 'I wanted us to go into that shed, Anna,' he whispered into her hair. 'I dream about touching you and making love to you, I go mad thinking about us lying together – but –' He pulled away to gaze into her eyes, '–you're so precious to me, I don't want to spoil the lovely thing we have between us. That's why I try not to be alone with you because then I couldn't trust myself not to go wild. That will come, in time it will come, right now it's wonderful, getting to know you, being with you, seeing you every day like this.'

She caressed his cheek with her thumb, 'I feel the same,' her voice was hushed, filled with tenderness. 'You're so good, Peter, you make me feel like a lady.'

'You are a lady, Anna, there's something in you that gives you a special quality, very, very special.'

She giggled. 'Today I don't want to be ladylike. I want to shout out loud when I'm flying downhill like a bird, I want to sing at the top o' my voice when I'm floating along like a cloud.'

He kissed her again. 'Very well, m'lady, today we'll be very noisy birds and very musical clouds. Let's go!'

Together they flew down the slopes, they sang as they whooshed along. The sky was blue above them, the hills were white around them, the world was big and wide and wonderful below and beneath them and they revelled in every fun-filled moment.

When they grew tired of hauling the sledge uphill they abandoned it for a while and trudged along, talking and laughing, throwing snowballs at one another till their clothes were soaked.

'Let's go up to the house,' he suggested. 'We'll dry off in the kitchen. Molly's a good sort . . .' he grinned, '. . . she will give us succour and rest and hopefully not cuff our ears when we drip all over her floor. We can leave the sledge at the back door and I'll put it away later.'

Molly was a good sort, but before she provided them with succour she gave them a thorough scolding for leaving wet footprints all over her newly-washed floor.

'But, Molly,' protested Peter, 'we took our boots off at the door. How can we leave dirty footprints?'

'Your stockings must be wet then,' she persisted, her pleasant face with its upturned mouth managing to look severe. 'Take them off this minute and put them and your boots near the fire – and here's hoping the master doesn't smell them and think he's getting sweaty socks for dinner . . .' At that she burst into uproarious laughter, holding her sides, her mouth opened so wide Peter later swore that he could see right down to her tonsils.

Baird the butler appeared. Rather sourly he acknowledged Peter, glowered at Anna, and settled himself at the table for his midday repast.

One by one the rest of the servants appeared. Anna gave Peter a nudge and hissed, 'You didn't tell me about this. I thought it would just be Molly.'

'Sorry, I lost all track of time out there and forgot it was lunchtime. Don't worry, they won't eat you, just remember you're a lady – even if you are a musical cloud with little noisy birds carolling away inside of you.'

She clapped her hand over her mouth to stifle a nervous giggle. Daisy the housemaid was staring at her curiously; the kitchenmaid was wriggling in her seat and looking as if she too was getting ready to burst into giggles; Baird had picked up his spoon and was frowning at it disapprovingly.

'Mary,' he addressed the kitchenmaid. 'This spoon has not been cleaned properly. Take it away and get me another one.'

'Really, Mr Baird,' Molly said heavily. 'I examined all the cutlery myself before Mary laid it. You would need a magnifying glass to see dirt on any o' it.'

'Not on the floor though.' Daisy glanced at the socks and boots steaming at the fire. 'You've been enjoying yourself, Master Noble.'

'Ay, he has that, he and Anna both,' Molly sprang to Peter's defence. 'It's that sort o' house, Daisy, in case you haven't noticed, Master Lucas and Master Peter often come to see me in my kitchens, as does Sir Malaroy and her ladyship. Now then, Mary, just you slide along the table a bit and make room for our guests, there's a good girl.'

Molly was a plain but competent cook. Her steak and kidney pie was delicious, her tangy apple tart a delight.

Peter ate ravenously, Anna less so, conscious as she was of Baird's unsmiling face, Daisy's covert glances, Mary's shy smiles.

After lunch the servants took themselves off and Anna relaxed, but not for long. Lady Pandora herself appeared in the kitchen, not a new event by any means as quite often she enjoyed rolling her sleeves to her elbows to make jam or toffee or anything else that took her fancy. Today she wanted to see Molly to discuss a recipe for seed cake. When she saw Anna and Peter she stopped in her tracks and her face broke into smiles of pleasure.

'Anna! Anna McIntyre! What brings you here? But of course, you and Peter were out in the snow. How I'd love to do that myself, fly down the slopes, my hair loose, streaming behind me, the wind in my face, my cheeks frozen yet burning. I remember it so well from child-hood but what would everyone say if I did that now? I'm tempted mind you, quite often I think, to hell with convention, let yourself go, Pandora, and never mind what anyone thinks!'

Her gay laugh rang out and, going over to Anna she gave her a hug. 'I've thought so much about you and hoped that you'd come back to see us one day . . .' She stood back, her head to one side. 'You're all wet and bedraggled . . . Come on,' she took the girl's hand, 'we'll go upstairs and get you some dry things.'

Taking Anna upstairs to her dressing room she invited her to pick what she liked.

'Oh, no, I couldn't,' protested the girl, shaking her head, overcome with shyness.

'Don't be silly!' Lady Pandora began rummaging through the vast array of clothes hanging in the wardrobe. 'Here.' Lifting out a moss green day dress of fine wool she held it against Anna. 'Perfect. So lovely with your hair. Put it on, and, while you're doing that, talk to me about yourself. Miss Priscilla tells me you're coming along with your art. Why don't you come and paint my portrait?'

'Och, I'm not nearly good enough for that yet,' Anna said evasively.

'Come on, Anna,' Lady Pandora spoke in her most persuasive tones. 'You're a natural. I've kept up with your progress. Miss Priscilla showed me some of your work. You have a rare gift, it's time you put it to good use . . . and . . .' she added with a devilish smile, '. . . it would be an excuse for you to come and see me.'

Anna held her breath, how she would love that, to come to Noble House to visit Lady Pandora and to be near Peter . . .

'But why should we resort to excuses for you coming here?' Lady Pandora's eyes flashed. 'If you were to become my companion you could be here at Noble House all the time. I'll see your father about it as soon as he gets back. That is, of course, if you would like to come and live with me, Anna.'

'Oh, I'd love it.' Anna's eyes were shining, her future stretched before her, bright and beckoning.

Sir Malaroy came into the room and was immediately seized upon by his wife. 'Darling,' she greeted him warmly, twining her arm into his. 'Anna is here, I've told her I'll speak to her father about her coming to live here as my companion. What do you think?'

He turned his keen blue gaze on Anna. 'Young lady, we meet again. I believe you and Peter have been seeing rather a lot of each other recently?'

'Oh, never mind all that,' his wife said before Anna could speak. 'They're just children enjoying themselves. I asked you a question and you haven't answered me.'

'You've already made up your mind, haven't you, Pandy? So why ask?'

Lady Pandora turned to Anna. 'Go downstairs and wait for me, Anna, I'll be down in a moment.'

Anna sensed an atmosphere, and she left the room hastily, shutting the door behind her. Lady Pandora looked at her husband. 'What's wrong, darling? You sounded disapproving just now.'

Sir Malaroy was silent for a few moments, then he said slowly, 'I don't think it's really a good idea – bringing Roderick's daughter to live here.'

'Why ever not?' she cried in dismay.

'I feel that she and Peter aren't really suited to one another, so rather than be encouraged, they ought to be dissuaded from seeing so much of each other.'

His wife stared at him. 'I seem to remember a similar conversation to this – when the boys were invited to Knock Farm to have tea with Anna. Have you got something against her, Malaroy? Something I should know about?'

'Not her personally, the McIntyres as a whole – or rather, their father. If she came here he would see the gesture as one foot in the door – and when he comes back from Canon Point I don't want him coming around here any more than is necessary . . .' He hesitated and when he spoke again he did so quickly, as if he had been bottling it up for a long time and couldn't wait to get it out. 'It isn't just that, it's you and this Mallard chap! It's been going on too long! Everyone's talking and I'm the poor fool who has to stand back and take it. Well, I've had enough, Pandy! If Mallard doesn't go, I will.'

A pink flush diffused her skin. She turned away so that he wouldn't see it. When first Andrew Mallard had come to Noble House, she had been particularly restless and unhappy. Her husband had been away a lot on business, she had felt neglected and lonely and the tutor had arrived when she had been at her most vulnerable. He had provided the excitement, the admiration she needed in her life, but lately his damands on her had been growing more and more. He had wanted her to go away with him but never could she hurt her husband that way. In spite of all her disappointments in him, her earlier frustrations, she still loved him.

Therefore the face she turned back to him was one of innocence when she said softly, 'Darling, darling Malaroy! Stop that at once! It's you I love, you must know that. I'll admit I enjoy Andrew's company, he's interesting and amusing but that's all it is.' Reaching up she kissed him tenderly on the lips. 'My darling, this has worried you a good deal, hasn't it? You mustn't trouble yourself anymore, I know I'm a flirt and a tease, it's just the way I'm made and doesn't mean anything. You've always stood by me, we've had our troubles, right from the beginning, it wasn't always easy for us but through it all I loved you, I always did.'

Somewhat mollified, he put his arms around her waist and drew her close. 'Pandy, Pandy,' he murmured into her hair. 'I'm sorry, it's just that I'm afraid, afraid of losing you, you're so bright and beautiful and I'm so quiet and staid compared to you.'

'You've never been any of these, and you'll never lose me.'

'The McIntyre girl,' he said slowly, 'She means a lot to you, doesn't she?'

'Yes she does, I want to take her out of that dreadful environment she lives in, she doesn't belong there – somehow I feel she was born to know better things.'

'Then bring her here, Pandy,' he conceded. 'You're right, she's too good to run after the likes of Roderick McIntyre.'

'But I thought you and he were friends. You always appeared to have plenty to say to one another.'

'Friends no, never that, the man's a devil! I suppose I'd better tell you, should have done long ago but the time never seemed right. He came to me with a hard luck story. I felt sorry for him, his wife in hospital, a young family to bring up. I gave him money, he put pressure on me, always wanting more. Eventually I had a row with him and packed him off to Canon Point to be rid of him for a while.'

'You could have sacked him.'

A wry smile twisted his fine features. 'You said yourself, Pandy, how sorry you were for the young McIntyres. What would happen to them if their father lost his job and his home? Magnus is a fine lad, he works hard but could never keep the family together on his own; the other is just a poor miserable boy who swaggers around to hide his feelings of insecurity and fear.'

'Malaroy,' she whispered. 'I always knew you cared about others but I never realized how much you knew about their problems.'

He smiled down at her. 'I was born and bred in the glen, Pandy, and I know all that goes on in it. Now . . .' He gave her bottom a playful smack, 'be off with you, woman, I want to lie down after my lunch. Afterwards send Mallard to me. Young Robert and Ralph will be here after Christmas and I want to discuss their curriculum with their tutor. Less acrobatics and more learning, I'm going to insist on that.'

The smile she threw at him was radiant, his spirits lifted. She closed the door softly and went on her way with a singing heart.

CHAPTER TWENTY-ONE

Watersheds

TELL TALE TODD HURRIEDLY fixed an oat-filled nosebag over Firth's face, gave him a pat, and went puffing into the Jenny All shop to regale Janet with all the latest happenings in the district, especially those of his journeyings up Mill Brae.

'Monkeys!' he announced triumphantly. 'More monkeys! Little ones this time! Swinging about in the trees. One wi' ginger hair, the other no' much better!'

He had quite an audience in the shop that day, one of them being Moira O'Brady, a tall attractive woman with a strong, unsmiling face and a mop of flaming hair of her own.

'And what's wrong wi' red hair, Todd Hunter?' she demanded aggressively, eying his thinning sandy dome. 'At least it's a lot better than having practically no hair at all!'

'Ay, ay, you're right there, Moira,' he said apologetically. 'I am not criticizing the lad's hair, just telling you the colour o' it – and he had freckles too, sprinkled over his face like pepper.'

'I had freckles when I was young,' Moira said dryly. 'Besides, how could you see his face when he was swinging from the trees? Maybe it was spots before your eyes you were seeing, no' an unusual occurrence in a body who drinks too much.'

Todd moved to safer ground. 'There were girls too, Beth Jordan and Anna McIntyre, no' swinging from the trees but running around in an unruly sort o' way and shouting at the tops o' their voices, the Noble lads chasing them and grabbing them to tussle wi' them. Girls o' that age shouldn't be doing that sort o' thing – at least they shouldn't be running around screaming and showing off.'

'Some obviously do,' said Janet with a sniff. 'And don't forget, one o' them's a McIntyre, they're mad enough to do anything – even if it is Anna.'

'Ach, you're just an old blether, Todd Hunter! Anna doesn't scream nor does she show off,' old Grace rushed to Anna's defence. 'She's just young and she's enjoying herself.'

'Was that Mr Mallard there, Todd?' asked Janet curiously.

'Ay, he was that, telling the little lads what to do.'

'There was some talk o' him leaving – when Master Peter and Master Lucas went off to school.'

Todd grinned slyly. 'Her leddyship wouldn't part wi' him, oh no, he stayed on to teach the new lads – distant relatives they are – or orphans o' some sort. She'll take them and make them – if that tutor laddie doesn't break them first – their necks I mean. The older boys are home for the Easter holidays so they're all having a fine time o' it – the lassies included.'

Janet folded her lips. 'Hmph! Our Mrs High-and-Mighty Jordan must be slipping up, allowing her lassie to run wild like one o' our more common bairns.'

'Ach! She'll go to any lengths to hook a gentry family!' Moira said scathingly. 'I doubt she wouldn't bat an eye even if she knew her lass was dropping her breeks to Master Lucas. I've heard one or two snippets o' that nature and I must say, it doesn't surprise me. Our Miss Jordan will get herself into trouble one o' these days. She was aye a handful, even when she was little.'

Grace gave Moira one of her deceptively coy smiles, 'Ay, well I hope I'll no hear you saying the same things about Anna. She and Master Peter are just having a good time, and that is all it is. Her life will be back to normal soon enough for there is talk o' her father coming home from Canon Point – if normal is the right word to use for the kind o' life she has to endure at the hands o' Roderick McIntyre, evil creature that he is.'

At the mention of Roderick's name, Moira turned pale. Her air of confidence dropped from her like a cloak, and she glanced over her shoulder, as if expecting the man in question to pounce on her at any moment.

Without a word she left the shop and went hurrying along the road leaving everyone to gaze at one another and shake their heads meaningfully.

*   *   *

The very next day Roderick marched confidently into the Post Office, rubbing his hands, his darting glances taking in the fact that the shop was empty but for him.

Moira, hearing the bell tinkling above the door, emerged from behind a curtain, her expectant expression turning to one of horror when she saw who awaited her.

'Well, well, Miss O'Brady!' Roderick affected great affability. 'I'm back, you'll be pleased to know, and looking forward to collecting my dues. No doubt you'll have missed me all this time but things are back to normal now, eh, my dear lady? No harm done – quite the opposite in fact. I must have amassed quite a nice wee nest egg by now.'

Moira's hands felt suddenly sweaty, beads of it had also popped out on her brow. 'I'm sorry, Mr McIntyre,' she got out with difficulty, 'I can't give you it all at once. I'm not a rich woman as you well know –'

'Come, come, my dear,' he broke in, still genial, still smiling, 'The state o' your financial affairs are no concern o' mine. I'm no' a man to poke my nose into other folks' business – except . . .' He almost burst trying to keep in his amusement, '. . . when it is staring me in the face and I can't very well ignore it – nor, my dear Miss O'Brady – forget it.'

His voice had changed, it had become insidious, oily. 'Now then,' he continued, his eyes burning into hers, 'Are you going to keep me here all day, begging you for what is mine? I haven't even been home yet; my family don't know I'm back; of all the people in the village you have the honour o' being the first to see me – and what do I get? No welcoming smiles, no word o' greeting . . .'

'Stop it! Stop it!' Moira looked and sounded as if she were at the end of her tether. Her eyes were wild and staring, her chest was heaving, she seemed to be having great difficulty in breathing.

'Why, Miss O'Brady,' He sounded surprised. 'Not throwing a tantrum I hope – at your age!'

'Get out o' my premises, this minute!' she raged, tears starting to course down her face.

'*Your* premises?' Roderick spoke softly, threateningly. 'If I had a mind to do so I could easily make them *my* premises, but I'm a fair man and a generous one, I only want what is due me . . .' His fist came down on the counter with a bang, his voice rose to a roar, '. . . And if you don't play fair wi' me I'll make damned sure the whole o' the glen finds out about the sort o' woman you are! I'll blacken your name from here to kingdom come! You'll never hold up your head again, you will lose all your custom and then you might as well close up your damned premises for no one that is decent and God fearing will want to darken your doorstep *EVER AGAIN!*

Anyone that knew Moira as a strong, determined woman, wouldn't have recognized her in those dark and bitter moments of her life. Her face was ashen, her body was shaking uncontrollably, her very chin was trembling, so much so she couldn't speak but just whimpered instead, like a puppy dog who had just received a punishing kick in the ribs.

His fist banged down on the counter for a second time and sobbing, hardly able to function, she fumbled with the till, withdrawing from it a small sum of money which spilled from her nerveless fingers onto the floor.

'*PICK IT UP!*' he ordered furiously.

She fell to her knees, grovelling in the sawdust on the floor. Reaching down he grabbed her by the scruff of the neck and hauled her to her feet. 'Coppers, Miss O'Brady!' he bellowed, glaring into her terrified eyes. 'You know where you can put them, don't you! I want real money and I want it fast. Tomorrow, at dinnertime, you know where the bank is, the mail coach will get you there in the morning and have you back in plenty o' time!'

With that he hurled himself out of the shop, his features contorted and congested with fury.

On the way home he encountered Daft Donal who backed away from him as if he were the devil personified.

'No hurt Donal, please, Mr McIntyre, no hurt Donal,' pleaded the young man, his gaping mouth foaming with fear, his eyes big and petrified.

'Hurt you!' roared Roderick. 'I'll kill you, you bloody simpleton if you don't get out o' my way this minute.' So saying he dealt Donal a resounding blow with his cane and went on his way, his brows black and thunderous.

There was no one in the house when he got in. Magnus was at the farm, Adam was working in the mill, Anna had gone to visit old Grace at Moss Cottage.

Roderick stood staring around him, at the pictures fixed to the walls, the colourful tartan rug thrown over the couch, the tiny ornaments on the mantelshelf, the bowl of daffodils on the windowsill. Everything was sparkling, the brass knobs on the doors, the copper coal scuttle, the martingales hanging by the fireplace.

The house was peaceful and warm, too bloody warm! The fire was piled high with coal, carefully damped with dross. All nice and cosy for later when no doubt they would all drape themselves round it and talk about the nice cosy day they had spent.

He had come back just in time. Things had slipped while he had been away! No discipline, that was the trouble! Well, he would soon sort that, by God and he would!

Roderick smirked. It was good to be home, how he'd hated it at Canon Point: they'd all resented him being the manager and had made life as difficult for him as possible till it had got to a point where his authority meant little.

He wondered if Nellie Jean had missed him at all or if that buggering Boxer Sam had kept her well and truly amused. But Nellie Jean liked money, she liked trinkets, she enjoyed having money spent on her – and Boxer Sam couldn't afford to give her any of those things.

Roderick's thoughts turned to Anna. Rumours concerning her liaisons with The House of Noble had reached his ears at Canon Point. At the time he'd been furious but he'd calmed down since then. One never knew, it could all be to his advantage – his hankerings after Lady Pandora had never left him – and there were also the financial rewards to consider . . . He smiled again and threw himself into a chair . . . to wait . . .

Boxer Sam, going into the Post Office for tobacco, found Moira sitting on a chair, shaking from head to foot as she gazed blankly into space, as if she wasn't aware of anything that existed outside the private hell of her own thoughts.

'What ails you, lass?' Sam asked with kindly concern. He had never seen the postmistress like this. Everyone knew her as a strong determined woman who seemed not to have a nerve in her body. Now here she was, looking like a nervous wreck, a woman whose eyes were black and stark in the pallor of her face.

Sam went to her and gave her a gentle shake. 'Moira, Moira, lass, it's

188

me, Sam, can I get you anything? Is there anything I can do for you?'

She shook herself out of her torpor to gaze up at him and, quite suddenly, she burst into helpless tears that soon turned to great, dry, gasping sobs.

'Moira, come on now, it can't be as bad as all that.' He took her in his arms and talked to her in a soothing voice. 'Tell me, Moira, you can trust me. Speak to me and get it out o' your system – whatever it is I might be able to help. A trouble shared is a trouble halved.'

At first she couldn't speak and then it all came tumbling out. 'It's Roderick McIntyre! Oh, Sam, I shouldn't be telling you this but if I don't tell someone I'll go mad. Some years ago I was treasurer o' the kirk funds. At the time I was going through a bad patch financially – and – and I took money out o' the funds. It wasn't much, just enough to tide me over, but he found out about it. Embezzlement was what he called it. He said if I gave him some o' the money he wouldn't tell anybody – and it's been going on ever since, his demands get heavier all the time. Today he came to see me and wanted a lump sum, the money due to him, he said, for all the months he's been away.'

'Blackmail!' Sam said with a whistling intake of breath. 'The evil bastard! And him wi' all his swaggering and his talk o' being a Christian doing good in the community.' Straightening, he pulled back his shoulders. 'Right, Moira, we're going to sort this out. Tell me exactly what happened.'

Not missing out a single detail she told Sam about her encounter with Roderick. When she had finished speaking, Sam nodded. 'Right, tomorrow at dinner time. We'll get him in his office. You take some money in an envelope, say something pertinent while you're handing it over – and that's when I step in. I'll be witness to his wicked little game and don't worry, he'll never bother you again after he hears what I have to say.'

Moira took a deep, shuddering breath. For the first time in years she felt as if a great weight was being lifted from her shoulders.

Anna walked home with a bounce in her step. Her heart was singing. Spring was in the air, the daffodils were dancing at the roadside, she and old Grace had spent a lovely afternoon making pancakes and girdle scones, and later, after tea – here Anna gave a little skip of joy – she was meeting Peter to walk in the woods with him and look for early primroses. She swung her basket high, she hummed a little tune of joy. Opening the door of The Gatehouse, she went blithely inside only to stop dead. Roderick was sitting in a chair facing the door – like a great bear waiting to pounce on its prey.

'Father!' She could hardly get the word out. 'You're back.'

A leering smile flitted over his face, 'Ay, Anna, I'm back. And that's a fine kind o' welcome to give to your father.'

'I didn't think you'd be here, you never wrote to say you were coming.' Her voice was flat and dull; the euphoria that had bubbled in her minutes ago was replaced by a feeling of dark and bitter dread.

'I thought I would give you a surprise . . .' He glanced round the room, at the pictures, the ornaments, all the little embellishments that made the house bright. 'You've been busy, girl. I can see I've come home in the nick o' time, the place smacks o' cheapness and frivolity.'

Carefully she set down her basket, wondering what was coming next, making an effort to prepare herself for the sneers, the taunts, the criticisms.

'I've been hearing all about you, Anna,' he began slowly, spinning out the suspense, pausing to light his pipe and draw on it for a few minutes before going on. 'The jungle drums have been busy. It appears you have been making a nice cosy wee niche for yourself at Noble House. What is it that attracts you so much to a gentry house, Anna? Is it because you think you're too grand to bide in your own home wi' your own kind? Or could it be something else, something wi' trousers on? Maybe Master Peter Noble, taking his chances wi' you, taking all he can get from you, and you giving it to him, already turning into the little hoor o' my predictions –'

She had turned ashen, it was too much, much too much, her happiness shattered in just a few minutes, all the old terrors flooding back, those dreadful implications spilling from his filthy tongue. 'Stop it!' she cried. 'Don't you dare speak to me like that! We're not all like you, Father! Satisfying your lustful cravings under cover o' darkness! Giving in to your drunken urges wi' a woman who isn't mother! Lying in her bed, giving away her jewellery! Tarnishing her good name . . .'

He rose up, he towered over her, eyes crazed, mouth twisted, fist raised high, ready to strike. But the blow never came. His arm remained suspended in mid-air for a long time before gradually he lowered it. The effort of fighting his fury produced odd effects: saliva oozed from

190

his lips; his bulging eyes were bloodshot; his limbs shook as if he were suffering from palsy.

'No, Anna,' he got out at last, his breath coming in great gulping gasps. 'I'll no' hit you this time, no' this time – but if you ever speak to me like that again I'll kill you – as sure as I'm standing here.'

'That makes two o' us.'

They faced one another and each of them knew that they had reached a watershed. No more was she a frightened silent child; for her he was no more the ogre who had sent her scurrying to his bidding with just a few harsh commands.

'You and I, Father, we don't get on, do we?' she said, and now her voice was even, her trembling stilled. 'Lady Pandora has once again asked me to be her companion and to go and live wi' her at Noble House. She said she would talk to you about it when you returned – and now you have – so she'll be waiting to see you.'

He fell back into his chair, the ebbing of his temper leaving him drained of colour. But his eyes were gleaming and he said thoughtfully, 'Will she now? Well, we mustn't keep the lady waiting – must we? I'll go and see her tomorrow. Meanwhile, I'm needing my tea, girl, and my hot water, I've had a tiring day.'

'You will get your hot water, and your tea – and anything else you need, Father, in that order – when I'm ready and not before.'

There was a new respect in the eyes of Roderick McIntyre when he looked at his daughter – and something else that might have been admiration.

CHAPTER TWENTY-TWO

Retribution

IT WAS DINNERTIME THE next day and Roderick was in a genial mood. Everything was going his way. Nellie Jean had given him a warm welcome home; the promise of future pleasures had all been there, in the flash of her dark eyes, the provocative wriggle of her bum, the beckoning bounce of those bonny big breasts of hers.

He had vowed there and then that tonight he would have her but first things first. In just a few minutes Moira would appear in his office with the money she owed him – and all that before his meeting with Lady Pandora tonight.

He had sent a message to her, telling her he was coming to see her that evening. If he played his cards right there was no knowing what could come of their talk. The possibilities were endless – and utterly exciting. All the time he'd been away at Canon Point he had dreamed of her. The frustrations of being so far away from her had been dreadful but all that was over with. He was back! And he was ready to do business!

His eyes gleamed. He went over to the window, but he wasn't seeing the fuzz of green on the hills, nor the golden rays of the sun streaming through the trees. His thoughts were elsewhere, taking him to realms of fantasy where he wandered with Pandora over the fields and into the dark, mysterious woods. He visualized himself making love to her under a canopy of green, her body white and tempting beneath him, her red lips tantalizing him, her breasts heaving with passion, her arms reaching out to him while she spoke his name over and over.

Beads of perspiration popped out on his brow, he licked his lips and rubbed the bulge in his trousers. Christ! How could he wait for her? He had to have her soon or he would go mad just thinking about her. Swallowing hard he took a deep breath. Tonight! Never mind Nellie

Jean and her brazen ways, she could go to hell for all he cared! It was Pandora he wanted, Pandora he must have. . .

A shadow darkened the door, it opened and Moira stood there, her back to the light, her face in shadow.

'Ah, Miss O'Brady.' Hastily he composed himself, he beamed at her affably. 'Come in, dear lady, come in and shut the door.'

She made no move. 'I'll say what I have to say here, I have no wish to be in the same room as you, nor to breathe the same air that you breathe.'

She sounded confident, too bloody confident for his liking! His temper started to rise. She was watching him and he had the oddest impression that she was deliberately trying to goad him to anger.

'Do you have the money you owe me, Miss O'Brady?' he enquired, making an effort to remain calm.

'Ay, indeed I do, it's all here, in this envelope, only I don't owe it to you. I don't owe you anything, except my eternal curses for all the anguish you have caused me these past few years.'

A sneering grin split his face. 'Come now, dear lady, that's putting it a bit strongly. Of course you owe me, you owe a lot to me, and you'll keep on owing and paying, both financially and spiritually till the day that either you or I drop.'

His voice had taken on an oily note, one that she knew well. 'You robbed the kirk, Miss O'Brady, surely you haven't forgotten that. A sin of such magnitude has to be severely dealt with. One day you might be forgiven, till then you must look upon me as your saviour. By taking your money I relieve you o' the burden o' your guilt, otherwise you would lie in your bed at night, never knowing which way to turn. I have exonerated you, Miss O'Brady, cleansed your soul. By paying me you don't have to pay the devil, look upon it like that and you'll be a happier woman than you are now.'

'You are the devil!' she cried passionately, 'And one o' these days you'll get your comeuppance! Take your money! Take it now so that I can be out o' your sight!'

'Hand it to me, my dear.'

'No, you come and get it. I told you, I won't set foot inside this room!'

He moved away from the window, a smile of triumph spreading over his florid features. In two steps he reached her, his meaty fingers shooting out to grab the envelope, but Boxer Sam was there first, emerging from the sunlight, snatching the envelope out of Moira's hand, pushing past her to stand in front of her and look at Roderick with a dark and burning contempt.

'I heard everything!' he snarled, his muscles flexing under his shirtsleeves. 'You filthy bloody blackmailer! No sooner back but you're wreaking havoc with everything and everybody you touch! Well, listen to this, you evil upstart! Moira is finished wi' you, you'll never get another penny out o' her and I'll be here to make sure you never go near her again. . . .'

'Stay out o' this, McGuire!' Roderick growled. 'This is no buggering business o' yours and I'll thank you to get out o' my office this minute.'

Despite his heavy build Boxer Sam was extremely light on his feet, an asset that had served him well in the many pub brawls he had been involved in during his younger days. Like a streak of lightning he pounced on Roderick to bulldoze him across the room and throw him across his desk as if he were a feather. Roderick lay sprawled and spread-eagled, hardly able to draw breath, so tight was the grip Sam had on his collar.

'Now listen, and listen good, you stupid bastard!' Sam gritted through clenched teeth. 'Blackmail is a serious offence in the eyes o' the law. The police would be very interested to hear how you've been treating Moira. She has agreed to tell them everything if you don't promise here and now to behave yourself. Isn't that right, Moira?'

Moira had agreed to nothing of the sort. The very idea of her misdeeds becoming public property was enough to make her go cold with dread but she was wise enough to realize that bluff was the only way to force Roderick to relinquish the hold he had on her.

'Ay, Sam,' she said, the coolness of her tone surprising even herself. 'I don't care anymore what happens to me. I want that pig to pay for what he did, justice must be done, even if it means telling the police.'

Boxer Sam tightened his hold on Roderick's neck. 'She means it, Roderick, she's at the end o' her rope and can't take any more – so – what do you say? No more harassment for Moira or we bring in the law. A grand story it would make too, Roderick McIntyre, under-manager o' the mill, a fine upstanding member o' the kirk and the community, standing trial for blackmail and God knows what else that might be dug up against you.' He put his face close to Roderick's and, shaking him like a rat, he went on: 'Wee Anna, for instance, her body bearing the scars o' your fatherly love, marks that will never fade or go away for as long as she lives. Oh ay, don't look so surprised, I know about that too, there's a lot I know about you, old Roddy, things that could send you away for a long time.'

Roderick's eyes were almost bulging out of his head; his face was purple; a froth of mucus clogged the hairs in his nostrils. 'Alright,' he gasped. 'Have it your way. I'll do everything you want – only let go o' me before I bloody well choke to death.'

But Boxer Sam wasn't finished yet. 'There's also the question o' your attitude to me, Roddy. I know fine you'd like to be rid o' me and that you've already tried to do so by means of some nasty little tricks that never quite worked. No more o' that, if you know what's good for you – oh, and by the way – a nice wee rise in pay would come in useful. See Jordan about it – and you'd better come up wi' the goods – or else.'

With that he straightened and stepped back, allowing Roderick to get up. He swayed on his feet, rasping, and coughing, but had soon recovered sufficiently to dust himself down and resume a modicum of dignity. 'Get out!' he ordered. 'Out o' my office, the pair o' you, I have work to do.'

At the door, Boxer Sam turned. There was a smile of devilment on his rugged features. 'Don't be forgetting now, Roddy, the boot's on the other foot, your turn to pay up. I'm sure Jordan will be only too willing to swell my pay packet when he hears, straight from the horse's mouth, what a good and conscientious worker I am.'

Adam watched Moira and Boxer Sam emerging from the office and a sly little smile touched his mouth. Creeping away from the window to the shadow of the trees, he stood for a few minutes, lost in thought. Who would have thought it? Miss Sour Puss O'Brady, stealing money from the church like a common thief – and Roderick – blackmailing her for all he was worth – just as he had been blackmailing Sir Malaroy for something that had happened a long long time ago.

Ay, Adam knew all about that – at least he knew enough to make it interesting. Mary, the Noble House kitchenmaid, listened at doors and she was only too eager to tell Adam about the things that she heard. Mary liked Adam, she liked him very much even though he was often surly with her and bossed her about a bit. In other ways Adam more than made up for his shortcomings. He gave her things, small trinkets, the odd copper from his pay packet, once a silk garter for her stockings on the condition that he got to see it when it was on.

He had also taken her out, to a tiny backstreet pub in Dunmor, where an indifferent barmaid hadn't questioned them about their respective ages. They hadn't stayed long enough in the pub for it to matter very much. Adam had wanted to get her outside, 'up a close' to be exact, where he had soon had his way with her.

Mary hadn't minded, in fact, she had enjoyed every minute of it. He had whispered crudely flattering things in her ear and had told her she was beautiful and after that Mary couldn't get enough of him.

But he was besotted with that scheming madam, Beth Jordan, and made no secret of the fact. By this time however, Mary was obsessed with him and would do anything for him.

Her reports about Noble House gossip were often sketchy but enough for Adam to go on. He knew all about the activities of Andrew Mallard and Lady Pandora, and, as for Sir Malaroy and Roderick, Mary had caught snatches of a conversation between them, about some dark and unsavoury secret belonging to the past, something that involved them all, a secret that Roderick was determined to make the most of . . .

It was all too vague at the moment for Adam to make much sense of it – but bit by bit, with Mary's help of course – he might be able to piece it all together and use it to his advantage when the time came. Meantime, here was something that he could use immediately.

He had been happy with his father away at Canon Point, happier than he had ever been in his life before. He had known what it was like to feel peace and freedom from anxiety. Now it was back to square one, the misery, the tension, had returned to blacken his days . . . that is, until now, until hearing with his very own ears the proof that Mr Pillar of the Community Roderick McIntyre was no more than a slimy hypocrite under all that veneer of civility he showed to the world.

A great surge of anger rose in Adam's throat, sickening him, lending him a feeling of power, urging his footsteps forward . . . The old man was about to get his just deserts from more than one source.

*   *   *

Adam was smiling when he made his appearance in his father's office — and he was swaggering — a gesture of confidence that immediately annoyed the irate Roderick.

'What do you want?' he greeted his son irritably. 'I've told you before, I don't like to be disturbed in my office.'

'Sorry, Father,' said Adam meekly enough. 'I just wondered — I'm a bit short o' sillar and thought maybe you could give me a bob or two to tide me over.'

Roderick's face darkened. 'You bloody little spendthrift! Barely fifteen and already drinking and whoring like a man twice your age. If you think I'm going to subsidize that you've another bloody think coming so get out o' here before I throw you out!'

Adam remained stolidly where he was. 'I heard Moira O'Brady talking to you, Father, and Sam. He gave you a buggering rough time o' it — eh, Father?'

Roderick's face turned purple, he made a lunge at his son but Adam sidestepped smartly. 'I don't want to fight you, Father,' he said, his breath starting to quicken as some of his old fear returned at the sight of his father's face. 'I told you I don't want much, just a few bob.'

Taking out his hanky Roderick mopped his sweating brow. 'How dare you?' he growled. 'My very own son, as much as bla . . .'

'Blackmailing you?' Adam felt his confidence draining, he knew that what he had to say had better be said quickly before his audacity failed him. 'Ay well, like father, like son, you taught me well and you needn't worry, I won't tell anybody about this . . .'

He stopped speaking as a thought struck him. While on the subject of blackmail should he mention it in connection with Sir Malaroy? But no! Hastily he decided against it. What he was doing now was sapping his courage, the other thing could wait till he had more evidence to go on — meantime . . .

'I'm on your side, Father,' he continued. 'A dutiful son who only wants to be shown a bit o' appreciation.'

Roderick was feeling ill. He could take no more for one day and with a snarl he dug into his pocket and extracting a ten-shilling note he threw it at his son.

'Not another word from you — do you hear, boy? Let this be an end to the matter.'

'Ay, Father.' Adam picked up the money, and walked out of the office.

His legs were shaking, his insides felt like jelly – but – he had won this round. For the first time in his life he had challenged the old man – and he had come out tops.

A smile touched his mouth. Pocketing the note he went on his way with a bounce in his step.

Lady Pandora was waiting for Roderick in her own private drawing room, an apartment that adjoined her bedroom and one that was filled with elegant paintings, sofas and soft armchairs.

She was wearing a rose-coloured dress of purest silk; her hair was upswept and held in place with gold-studded clasps; she was altogether a vision of light and beauty, but she hadn't dressed up for her meeting with Roderick. Friends from England had arrived for dinner and were at that moment downstairs enjoying cocktails with Sir Malaroy and Andrew Mallard who was treated like one of the family.

It had taken Roderick some time to recover from his encounter with Boxer Sam. For most of the afternoon he had felt shaky and unsure of himself – all due to that buggering lout half strangling him and laying down the law to him. And he had won, a common swine like that, he and Moira O'Brady each, laughing at him, mocking him, making a complete and utter fool out of him.

As if all that hadn't been enough there had been Adam to contend with, listening at windows, trying his hand at a little bit of extortion of his own! Young bugger! He'd better watch his step if he knew what was good for him!

At teatime Roderick had been silent and dour and the atmosphere had been one of unease and watchfulness. Adam hadn't said a word and had kept his eyes strictly on his plate, Magnus had watched his brother, an odd look in his eyes, and Anna had been deep in thought, giving the impression of being locked away in a world of her own.

Roderick had hardly eaten a thing and when Anna had cleared away his untouched plate she had looked at him strangely, as if she were wondering what was in his mind and what he was going to be up to next. Let her wonder! Do her good to be kept in suspense for a while. He still had the upper hand where she was concerned and he wasn't intending to let her go anywhere unless it was to his advantage.

A few stiff drams after tea had soon put him back on his feet and on

198

his mettle. He had felt all his old strength returning, all the fire coming back into his veins. Anna had pressed his best suit and had laid it on the bed. She was prompt with his hot water, she had polished his cane and his shoes to perfection.

'I hope everything will go well tonight, Father,' she had said with a trace of her old uncertainty to which he had made no reply. Better to keep the little bitch hanging, she would appreciate him all the more if – and only if – he managed to procure a place for her at Noble House.

He had dressed himself meticulously, taking his time about it, and when Baird ushered him into Lady Pandora's room he was looking his best and he knew it.

'My dear lady,' he gushed, going forward to take her hand and brush it with his lips. 'I can't tell you what a pleasure it is to see you after all this time. I have to admit you were much in my thoughts during my exile at Canon Point. For exile was what it was to me, away from family and friends, away from you, my dear Pandora.'

Hastily she withdrew her hand and rang for Baird. When he appeared she ordered drinks to be brought. When they arrived, Roderick didn't wait to be asked. Pouring himself a large whisky he retired with it to the sofa beside Pandora, his hand resting lightly in the small space he had left between them.

'Roderick,' she began. 'I have dinner guests so we will have to make this visit short. No doubt you know the reasons for our meeting. Anna will have told you that I want her to come here as my companion, it's as simple as that. I would like her to live with me if that is possible . . .'

'Ah well, my dear lady,' Roderick broke in, downing his whisky in one gulp, 'That is a very tall order, a very tall order indeed. Anna is no longer a child, she is a competent help about the home and indeed, I have every right to expect that she should be. We must all work to earn our keep and if she leaves home I would have to get someone in to take her place . . .'

Lady Pandora moved restlessly. She had heard it all before, the laments, the innuendo, the hints about money.

'I have told you before, Roderick,' she said with as much patience as she could muster, 'if it's money you're worried about, I can assure you that Anna will earn enough to satisfy everyone's needs. We seem to have had this conversation before – if my memory serves me correctly.'

'Indeed it does, my lady,' he said smoothly, his cool manner giving no indication of the fires that were rising within him. The whisky was having its effect, her nearness was driving him crazy. He could smell her perfume, could see the rise and fall of her breasts. His eyes raked her body, undressing it in his mind, the vision of him and her in the woods came to him again . . . his belly churned, his trousers tightened between his legs . . . .

'Pandora,' He spoke her name breathlessly. 'I told you before, the question o' sillar need not come into it. All gifts, I heard these words, that promise, from your very own bonny lips . . .'

She saw the wild beast lurking in his eyes, she smelt the animal smell of him and she too felt her stomach churning, but for different reasons. Carefully she moved away from him but she wasn't quick enough.

He lunged at her; his breath washed over her face, sickening her. 'Pandora,' he rasped. 'I can't wait any longer! Christ, woman! Don't you know you're driving me insane? The bedroom . . . no one will come . . . we can lock the door . . .'

'No! How dare you suggest –!'

'Here then! On the floor! Anywhere . . .' His hands began tearing at her, one kneading her breasts with brutish ardour, the other throwing up her dress to grope at her thighs, sliding upwards . . . upwards . . .

'Pandora.' He hauled himself on top of her, pinning her down, smothering her while he tore at her clothes, fumbled with the buttons of his trousers.

'Let me, Pandora,' he gasped. 'Let me get in there . . . don't play coy wi' me, I know you like them big and hot and bursting and by Christ, I'll give you everything I've got! All for you, Pandora, every last bit o' it! You're no' going to stop me now.'

Sweat poured down his face, his eyes were staring. She heard the ripping of her undergarments, felt the violent movements of his hips, his buttocks, as he tried to force himself into her. Somehow she managed to free her face from the suffocating wall of his chest and she began to scream at the top of her voice.

'Bitch!' he panted, 'Shut up and enjoy it! I can't stop now . . . not now . . .'

The door flew open. Both Sir Malaroy and Mallard came pounding in but it was Mallard who got there first, both hands outstretched to grab Roderick and haul him bodily away from Pandora.

Mallard's fist shot out, and Roderick's head jerked back as if his neck were made of rubber. The blow had been fierce. His brain whirled, he staggered and almost fell. Mallard gave him no time to recover; with an expert flip he spun Roderick round, yanked his hands behind his back and ran him out of the room, down the stairs, and outside.

Left on their own, Sir Malaroy put his arms round his wife and held her tightly.

'Surely you'll sack him now?' she said shakily against his shoulder. 'And be rid of the pest for good. Anna could come and live here, the boys could get one of the smaller cottages for a low rent.'

'That won't solve anything, Pandy,' he said quietly. 'He would come back. His sort will always find a way, and blackguard that he is, he would soon think of some means of getting his own back. Don't worry, I'll be keeping a close eye on him from now on, one slip and he'll have cause to regret it. Meantime, he's learned his lesson, Mallard has seen to that.'

'Malaroy, you aren't keeping anything back from me, are you? Concerning Roderick I mean. You always seem to find a reason for him to stay here and it seems so odd, after what happened just now. And those other times, when you had the row with him, for example, and sent him packing to Canon Point. Why didn't you just get rid of him then – for good? Has he got some sort of hold over you?'

'My darling, whatever next?' Sir Malaroy avoided her eyes, his tone of voice lacked conviction. 'I told you, he wheedled money out of me, I'd had enough and made him cool his heels in the wilds of Canon Point for a while.'

'I see,' Lady Pandora spoke slowly. She knew her husband, she could tell when he was avoiding the issue, he was avoiding it now. It could all have a simple explanation of course, he was a very generous man and could well have been taken in by Roderick and his hard luck stories.

Even so, she felt uneasy, Roderick was such a devil, he could quite easily hurt a man like Sir Malaroy . . . he could quite easily hurt anyone in fact. He could say anything about anybody and think he could get away with it.

She could be next for all she knew, he would want to pay her back for tonight, he might have seen her and Andrew Mallard together, or he might have heard something – and if the notion took him he wouldn't think twice about making life uncomfortable for her.

After what he had tried to do to her, in her own sitting room with her husband and her guests downstairs, she had the feeling that he was capable of anything . . . she shivered . . . and felt sick.

'Now then,' Mallard put his mouth close to Roderick's ear. 'Try doing that once more to her ladyship and I'll fix it so that you'll never be able to pee straight again. As it is, you'd better keep looking over your shoulder; the nights are still dark, you bastard, and there's no telling who might be waiting for you round the next corner!'

'Take your hands off me!' Roderick growled, desperately trying to hold onto some remnants of dignity, no easy matter with Mallard's crushing grip biting into his flesh.

Mallard's eyes blazed. 'Get going, you swine, and keep right on going till you disappear up your own arse in a cloud of dust!'

Roderick flexed his aching shoulders. He lifted his head, with a twirl of his cane he walked steadily down the driveway, conscious all the while that Mallard's eyes were burning into his back.

Anna walked with Peter through the trees. It was an evening of misty sunshine and sweet woodland smells. Despite Roderick's return home, she had never felt so good. Peter's arm was round her waist, her head was on his shoulder, they wandered along slowly, saying little, content just to be with one another. That was one of the things she liked about him, his silence, that aura of peace that emanated from him. When he had something to say he said it, when there was nothing to say he didn't indulge in superfluous chatter. They were two of a kind, he and she, carefree and wild at times, at others quiet and content.

Tonight she had something important to tell him – her father was visiting Lady Pandora. He listened to what she had to say, and when she had finished speaking, his eyes were shining. 'It would be wonderful, Anna, to have you at Noble House all the time. When I'm away at school I could think of you there and imagine you going about all the rooms, in the gardens, at the stables. As it is I can't visualize your life at The Gatehouse, I don't even know what it looks like inside.'

'I'd be waiting for you every time you came home,' she said joyfully. 'I would polish your boots and see to it that everything was right and proper for you.'

'Oh no, none of that,' he protested. 'At Noble House you would be the sort of lady you were always meant to be. I'd polish *your* boots and run after you every time you snapped your fingers.'

They both laughed at their absurdities. 'Don't get carried away, Master Peter, let's just wait and see what happens first.'

'Aunt Dora will make it happen,' he said with conviction. 'She can twist anyone round her little finger. You'll be living with us before you know where you are. Magnus will miss you, though, I've been to the farm several times these holidays and somehow he always brings the talk round to you. I like him, he's got something in him that's special – like you.'

'Ay, Magnus is special, he's looked after me since we were both just bairns.' She paused, thinking about Magnus, how quiet and withdrawn he'd been since Christmas. The thing that had happened between them was never far from her mind and obviously he felt the same. He had changed, at least his earlier points of view had changed, all those convictions and confidences he had shared with her had become less important to him. She knew it was because he was trying to forget, immersing himself more in people and events outside the home.

He had actually allowed Beth to persuade him into taking her to one or two dances in Dunmor. Beth had always liked Magnus, had always had a good word to say about him. Anna remembered Magnus's opinions about Beth and she had come to the conclusion that time changed everything and everybody.

She hoped he wouldn't be hurt. Beth was just using him, amusing herself when Lucas was away at school, amusing herself in any way she could and with anybody she could, surprisingly even with Adam, whom she had purported to dislike so much when they were children.

But even that had changed. Some time ago – she wrinkled her brow, trying to remember – that day, that awful day when she had left Miss Priscilla's school for ever. Adam and Beth, conspiring, making that last day a misery for her. And recently, Beth saying she was sorry. Sorry for what?

Suddenly Anna knew. It was all there, staring her in the face, only she had been too trusting, too foolish to see . . . Adam cliping on her, the beating, Beth's attitude afterwards, guilty, ay, guilty. And Adam, trying to make it up to her, never forgiving himself for what he had done . . .

'Anna,' Peter's voice recalled her to earth. 'Look, see what I've found, primroses, a whole bank of them, growing in the moss.' He held up a single, perfect bloom. 'For you, to remember me by when we're apart.'

She took the little flower and held it in the palm of her hand. 'I'll press it, in the book that Magnus gave me for my thirteenth birthday . . . Oh, Peter.' She put her arms around him, something so poignant stabbing into her heart she felt weak with emotion. Sadness ebbed through her, he was so warm, so dear, she could feel his heart against hers, the rhythmic beat of it throbbing against her breasts.

He took her face in his hands and kissed her until something made them both look up. They had wandered near the road, and Roderick was coming along. His face was like thunder, and Anna knew that Magnus wouldn't be missing her after all.

CHAPTER TWENTY-THREE

Revenge

RODERICK CLOSED THE DOOR of Nellie Jean's house and stood with his back to it, peering into the darkness, listening, waiting, making sure that the coast was clear before he emerged onto the road.

Like a thief in the night he made his way furtively along, keeping as close to the boundary wall as possible, his steps as careful as his heavy feet could make them, cursing under his breath when his foot encountered a stone and sent it rolling onto the road.

He wouldn't feel at ease till he had put as much distance between himself and the widow woman's house as possible. He hadn't wanted to go there in the first place but she had insisted.

'You come to me for a change, why should I always be the one to go creeping away from your bed in the early hours? Of course – maybe you don't think I'm worth the effort or else you feel it's no' worth your while any more. If that's the case we'll call it a day and you can just bugger yourself, Roderick McIntyre!'

Roderick had been desperate for a woman – any woman! All those months away at Canon Point had whetted his sexual appetites and there hadn't been anybody in that place worth bothering about.

His encounter with Lady Pandora had been a frustrating and humiliating experience. For days he had fumed and fretted and had despised everybody who had had a hand in causing him such anguish – especially that swine Mallard with his bulging muscles and his threats. How dare a minion like that treat him as if he were a piece of cow dung! Throwing him out of the house, talking to him in that cocksure, arrogant fashion. The sting of those words had festered in Roderick's mind, he hadn't been able to concentrate on much else – and over and above all there had been this terrible feeling of unease to contend with.

Mallard was as strong as a bull, he also had the advantage of youth on his side and was quite capable of carrying out the threats he had made. He was obviously obsessed with Lady Pandora and would do anything in his power to protect her. Roderick had found himself going warily about his daily affairs, never relaxing – in case – just in case Mallard would be waiting for him round the next corner, behind the next bush.

All of this anxiety hadn't been good for Roderick, nor had it been good for anybody else! He had been surly with the workers, bullying and sneering with his family. Anna had that guarded look about her again, Magnus had been watchful, Adam wary and frightened.

Roderick had felt some of his old power returning. Let them stew in their own juice, it would do them good to know that the boss was back and that nothing had changed as far as he was concerned.

With Roderick's increasing self-confidence also returned his restless animal urges. Ever since his return Nellie Jean had tantalized him with her suggestive wiggles and her flashing eyes. Yet despite her keenness to see him she was having none of the old arrangements. When he had broached the subject she had made her ultimatum and in the end he had capitulated, even though he hated taking the risk of being seen coming and going from her house.

But it had been worth it. By God and it had! His belly still burned with the aftermath of lust. She had cavorted with him, goaded him to frenzy, had made him pant and moan and cry out till it seemed to him that the whole of the glen must surely hear the sounds they both made as they rode with one another to the crests of pleasure.

She had wanted him to stay the night but he was having none of that. He was Roderick McIntyre, a man of position, Nellie Jean, when all was said and done, was just one of his employees, not for him the indignity of sneaking away from her house in the early hours of morning.

An hour or two under cover of darkness was better than nothing and, given time, she would soon agree to the old arrangements, the lure of sillar would see to that. Meantime he had to be satisfied with what he was getting from her.

He smiled to himself as he went along. He was feeling contented and optimistic. Who knew what lay in the future for him? Nellie Jean wasn't the only fish in the sea, something better could easily turn up – he hadn't given up on Lady Pandora. If he played his cards right she could still be his in the end. All that screaming and play of resistance had just been a front, the lovely bitch had enjoyed every minute of his attentions and must by now be regretting her childish behaviour . . .

Huddling into his coat his thoughts turned to the comforts of home. He hoped Anna would have his supper ready and waiting. The little madam had been aloof and cold ever since she had learned that she wouldn't be going to the big house after all.

He had sneered at her and laughed at her in an attempt to shake her out of that mightier-than-thou attitude of hers but none of it had worked. It was as if she had retreated back into her shell and it would be a pity if that happened. He had liked the new Anna, her fire had excited him, he had admired her spirit and had seen it as another challenge, something he could get his teeth into . . .

Perhaps if he went easier on her she would emerge again and he would have a fresh cat and mouse game to play. Amusing, ay, it could be very amusing . . .

Roderick never knew what hit him. One minute he was walking along to The Gatehouse, the next something heavy and hard thudded into him from behind and he found himself hurtling through a gap in the wall, rolling down, down, like a rubber ball, battering his head against stones and branches, tearing himself on snagging bushes, his ribs making a cracking sound against a huge boulder.

Lungs bursting, he hit the leaf-strewn ground in Stable Lane. He tried to get up but a crushing blow to his neck made him collapse to the earth once more, head spinning, senses reeling.

He made another attempt to rise. This time a vicious kick in the ribs robbed him of his remaining wind. For a split second he was aware of a black shape hovering above him before the world spun away from him and he lay where he was, still and silent on the cold earth.

His attacker laughed, a sound that was filled with triumph and contempt. Moving swiftly, he shook Roderick's arms out of his coat and, yanking the empty sleeves across his chest, he secured them behind Roderick's back with a length of rope to make an effective straight-jacket. He then stuffed a filthy hanky into Roderick's mouth, jammed his hat over his face, pulled off his trousers and used them to tie his ankles together.

Then, and only then was Davie McDonald satisfied. Straightening, he gazed down at the dark shape huddled on the ground and he smiled at the sight.

He drew the back of his hand across his mouth. He had waited a long time to wreak his revenge on this worthless scum!

Roderick's months of absence had forced Davie to bide his time, but he had never forgotten his vows to avenge the violation of his brother's innocence. A recent bruise on Donal's shoulders, put there by a violent blow from McIntyre's cane, had set the seal on the under-manager's fate. For the last few days every one of his moves had been observed by Davie. He knew all there was to know about Roderick, from when he came out of the house in the morning to when he went to bed at night.

The visit to Nellie Jean's cottage had been a perfect rendezvous for everyone concerned – including Davie. He had watched Roderick going inside, he had heard the grunts, the moans, the curses . . . the final crazed bayings . . . and the sounds had whipped his blood to frenzy, reminding him as they did of that dark, accursed night when Roderick, on some flimsy pretext, had lured his brother into the gun shed in order to carry out his foul and godless deeds . . .

Delivering a final kick to the inert body lying on the ground Davie crept away, well pleased with himself. He had made a good job of McIntyre – and he had picked a good time to do it in. It was a bitterly cold night: the stars were winking in the cloudless heavens; a freezing vapoury haar was creeping up from the river; the first frost diamonds were forming on the ground.

By midnight the earth would be white and hard and – Davie laughed softly – if all went according to plan, McIntyre of the mill would soon be as stiff and as cold as the ground on which he lay.

Anna stood at the fire, leaning against the mantelpiece, her brow resting on her arm as she gazed into the flames, lost in thought. Peter would be going back to school soon and she was thinking how lonely she would be without him. He had become very dear to her. In the short time they had known one another he had given her true joy, he had shown his love for her in a thousand different ways and most importantly, his was a selfless love, demanding only that she should return his feelings.

'Darling Peter,' she whispered, 'I'll miss you, I'll think o' you every minute when you're away. Everything has changed since we met, I've changed –'

'Isn't Father home yet?'

Magnus's voice at her elbow startled her out of her reverie, she spun round to look at him, her mind still on Peter. 'No, at least I don't think so, I don't know where he went.'

Magnus's hazel eyes flashed. 'I think I do, I'm sure I saw him sneaking into Nellie Jean's house a while back.'

'Oh! Well at least it's better than him bringing her here. I don't think I could bear any more o' that. It was so good when he was away at Canon Point.' Her tones became wistful. 'Everything in the house was different, everybody was different, we were happy together.'

'I know.' He rested his hand lightly on her arm, she didn't draw away from him, instead she regarded him for a long moment, noting the flush on his tanned skin, the tender light in his eyes. 'It won't always be like this, Anna,' he continued softly. 'Time changes everything, nothing stays the same.'

She curled her fingers into his. 'I know that, Magnus, but I hope you will never change –' her breath caught, '– I want you always to be as you are now.'

His hand tightened on hers. 'I will change, Anna, we all will, only time will tell how much. Right now I want you to tell me that you don't hate me any more. I've tried to stay away from you after – after what happened but I can be happy if only I know that you'll – always love me.'

Tears sprang to her eyes, she bit her lip. 'Ay, Magnus, I'll always love you and I never hated you – not really – I was angry, more at myself than anything else. I want you to be as happy as I am wi' Peter, I hope you'll find someone as good as he is.'

A shadow darkened his face, he moved away from her. 'Don't worry about me, Anna, I can take care o' myself. As for happiness . . .' he gave a short little laugh, '. . . it never lasts, does it? Like everything else it fades and dies and grows cold.'

'You shouldn't be thinking like that, Magnus, you have all your life in front o' you.' She sat down on the inglenook and beckoned to him, 'Sit beside me and tell me a story, the way you used to when we were little.'

He had to laugh at that. 'When we were little! A thousand years ago,

Anna Ban. A lifetime away. You're beginning to sound like old Grace. Alright, I'll tell you a story. At least we'll have the place to ourselves for a while. Adam won't be in till late and if Father really is at Nellie Jean's he won't be home at all tonight.'

They sat there by the hearth, the firelight flickering over them while Magnus spun the magical tales that had so entranced her when they had lain together in their innocence, neither of them seeing beyond those precious moments that they had shared so sweetly and with such unquestioning trust.

It was Jeemie the Stableman who found Roderick next morning, his body white with frost, his limbs blue and stiff with cold.

'Jesus God!' Jeemie cried, his eyes bulging with surprise, his nut brown face turning a queer yellow colour. Dropping onto his knees, he prodded Roderick with tentative fingers, expecting the worst, hoping for the best, even though, like many of the mill workers, he had a dozen reasons for wishing the under-manager out of the way. But not like this! Bound and gagged and obviously left to die a harsh and unkindly demise.

For several moments he was too numb with shock to do anything beyond stare at Roderick's death mask of a face, the skin a startling white, lips and eyelids a cold bluish purple.

Frozen to the spot, Jeemie himself appeared to be void of life until he shook himself and began rubbing frantically at Roderick's limbs, feeling all the while that the effort was useless. The man must have lain there all night, no human being could withstand that kind of exposure and still be alive.

Lowering his head, Jeemie planted one hairy lug against Roderick's chest. For what seemed an eternity he listened for a sign of life, then – unbelievably – he heard a dull thud, then another, followed by an almost imperceptible sigh from Roderick's blue lips.

Jeemie sat back on his heels; he drew his hand across his nose, opening his mouth he roared for Calum to come and help him.

Calum, the stable lad, came at a gallop. Between them he and Jeemie half carried, half dragged Roderick along the lane before Calum dropped his half of the burden to run with all speed to The Gatehouse to batter at the door and yell for Magnus and Adam.

*   *   *

210

Roderick was in bed for a fortnight. During that period Anna tended him hand and foot, hardly sleeping or eating herself so constant were the demands on her. Yet, strangely, her hours spent in the sickroom weren't as bad as she had imagined they would be.

At first Roderick could do nothing for himself. His hours of exposure had caused frostbite and it was Anna who spooned food into his mouth, washed him, made him comfortable. She did it all automatically, consciously erecting the barriers around her heart, not wanting to involve herself with emotions that she knew she couldn't cope with.

That mouth, so helpless, opening and shutting to the spoon, like an obedient infant taking its nourishment, the mouth that had so often abused her with harsh words and cruel comments.

Those hands, lying prone and weak on the coverlet, allowing her to lift them and wash them, pare the nails, stroke them occasionally in moments when her heart melted with pity . . . Hands that had wielded the strop to her defenceless body, hands that had crushed and struck and beaten without mercy. Big, strong hands that had never reached out in love or tenderness nor gentle caress.

The face, pale against the pillows, devoid of anger. The head of iron grey hair, submissive to the brush and comb, the eyes, quiet, grateful almost, watching her as she came and went from the room, eyes that had blazed their rage and had seared her with their mockery and hatred.

Gradually strength returned to his limbs, life came back into his eyes. Anna saw it happening, minute by minute, hour by hour. Every new morning she went into the room, expecting to hear the old abuse, the familiar demands, but time went on and they never came.

Roderick seemed to have retreated into himself. He was withdrawn and thoughtful and was quite content to lie in his bed, staring into space, hardly stirring when she appeared with hot water and food and all the other necessities of the sickroom.

Nellie Jean was a regular visitor but not even she could rouse Roderick from his apathy. 'The cold o' that night has done something to his brain,' she told Anna. 'Jeemie said he was half dead when he found him and I'm thinkin' he'll stay half dead for the rest o' his days . . . fancy, our very own Iron Rod . . . only half a man!'

But Roderick was far from being half dead. He was very much alive and thriving and his mind was more active than it had ever been. He was conserving his energies, content to lie back on his pillows and give his thoughts full rein, going over and over in his mind the events that had led up to his attack.

Events – and people! Quite a few of these had had it in for him. Take Boxer Sam for instance. Smug was the word for him, ever since he had got that rise in pay! More than ever he strutted and swaggered and eyed Roderick with a 'you can't fire me now, you bastard!' expression on his face.

Then there was Sir Malaroy, watching him all the time, eyeing him with jealousy and malice and waiting for him to put one foot wrong so that he would have an excuse to send him packing. As if he could! As if any of them could! He still had the upper hand and both Boxer Sam and Malaroy knew it. Besides, Boxer Sam had every good reason to keep him where he wanted him, the bugger was getting his perks, there was no reason for him to try any funny business.

As for Malaroy, he hadn't the strength or the guts to fight his own shadow, never mind try and kill his own under-manager in such a sneaky fashion. He was far too proud to do his own dirty work – but – and here Roderick's thoughts would come full circle – he could get somebody else to do it for him. But no! That wasn't Sir Malaroy's style, he was the reticent sort and would never stoop *that* low just to get his own back.

There were others however who wouldn't think twice about it. Mallard for instance! A man obsessed by another man's wife! So consumed with infatuation for her he would do anything to any other man who dared to try and win her for himself . . .

At this point in his musings Roderick would shudder at the remembrance of the attack. It had come to him like a beast in the night, ruthless, silent, so powerful he hadn't been able to lift one finger to defend himself.

Somebody of great physical strength had done for him . . . somebody like Mallard.

And over and over Roderick would hear the tutor's warnings ringing in his mind: 'The nights are still dark, you bastard, and there's no telling who might be waiting for you round the next corner . . .'

Mallard! Ay, Mallard!

Roderick's mind was made up. Meanwhile he was quite content to let Anna fetch and carry for him. He was enjoying having her around, there was a grace and peace about her that was like a soothing balm to his troubled mind.

The time would come soon enough for her to spread her wings, let her one day fly to Pandora and all the fancy trappings of The House of Noble. He would fly with her, little Anna, his passport to pleasures as yet untapped, waiting, just waiting for him to release them.

But first things first. He had to regain his strength, and what better way to do that than bide in the quiet and safety of his room with Anna tending to his every need. Anna of the fair and lovely face, Anna of the pride and the passion; from the beginning a child whose destiny had been of his making – and which could just as easily be of his breaking – all depending on how well the twists of fate treated him.

CHAPTER TWENTY-FOUR

Reckonings

ANNA RAN AS SHE had never run before, swift and graceful as a deer, her feet barely touching the ground, her breath whispering in her throat, her heart as light as the very air she breathed.

She was wearing a dress of deepest blue; her hair hung down her back, as dazzling in its fairness as the buttercups that danced under her flying feet. It was high summer, the sky was wide and cloudless; the larks were trilling high above; lacy canopies of green swayed lazily in the breeze; the sun glanced through the leaves to pattern the earth, the grass, the myriad of wildflowers growing in shady knolls.

She heard the river before she saw it, splashing over the stones, gurgling into little pools, swishing along the banks.

'Anna!' Peter's joyful cry echoed through the woods. He had seen her coming through the trees, was waiting for her in their favourite meeting place, on the rocks above the wild and wayward waters of The Cauldron.

They ran towards one another. He caught her and lifted her up to spin her round and round till they were both dizzy and laughing. They kissed while their world was still whirling, the mountains, the sky, dancing above them, each of them drunk with the happiness of their reunion.

'Oh, I've missed you, Peter!' she cried, kissing him, standing back to gaze and gaze at him.

'I didn't miss you,' he said, his expression serious.

Her face fell, her mouth trembled. 'You didn't?'

'No, I pined for you instead, from the minute I woke in the morning till I fell asleep at night and even then you were in my dreams. You tormented me, Anna Ban, everywhere I went.'

Tenderly he stroked the hair from her brow, his eyes lit, he smiled, the warm, crinkly smile she knew so well. 'Here, I picked you some flowers while I was waiting, I know how much you like them wild and free.'

She took the bunch of dewy harebells and buried her face in them. 'Like us, Peter, the way we'll be one day,' she murmured.

Taking her in his arms he nuzzled her ear and whispered, 'Like we will always be when we're together, Anna, we'll spend the whole summer being wild and free, just you and me and our love.'

In the days and weeks to come Anna would remember those words, spoken with such delight and enthusiasm.

Andrew Mallard walked slowly along by the river, head bent, hands in pockets, feet idly kicking at stones on the bridle path. It had been raining and trails of misty vapour clung round the dour shoulder of Coir an Ban; the air was fresh and sweet; fish were jumping in the river; dusk was settling over the countryside; it was quiet and peaceful.

But Andrew wasn't feeling very peaceful. His mind was seething, filled as it was with thoughts of Lady Pandora and how she had been avoiding him lately. From the start he had been fascinated by her, a fascination that had grown into something deeper till she had become an obsession with him.

He wanted her to go away with him but he might have known she would refuse. In a way he understood, all he had to offer her was his devotion. A woman like that needed position and power . . . and riches . . . the things she had been used to all her life, things she had been born to. Even so, he had thought her feelings for him were genuine, that she had loved him as he loved her − surely she hadn't just been playing with him, passing her time with him. He couldn't stand it if that were true, he had to know − one way or another . . .

He walked on, his steps taking him down towards the Rumbling Bridge, that place, that spot, where he had walked so often with Pandora, her light laugh ringing out, her perfume in his nostrils, her nearness driving him crazy . . .

The water boomed and roared under the bridge; the lowering sky was bringing early darkness; the trees grew thickly here by the river, and shadows were everywhere . . . Andrew didn't notice one that detached itself from the rest, a thick menacing shape that came at him from behind to knock him senseless with one sledgehammer blow.

It was a good night for fishing. Peter collected his rods and let himself out of the house. It was no use asking Lucas to come along, he had no patience for fishing and would only complain about the midges and the rain and frighten the fish by talking too loudly.

Peter was feeling good as he walked briskly towards his favourite fishing place by the Rumbling Bridge. Thoughts of Anna occupied his mind. Tomorrow they were going on a picnic, to a secluded spot in the glen that they considered to be theirs and theirs alone. If he caught a trout or two they could light a fire and cook them on the hot stones; Mallard had shown him how . . .

It was very still, not a leaf nor a blade of grass moved . . .

Yet something was moving, something swinging from the branches of a tree . . . Peter stopped short, unable to believe the sight that met him as he drew closer to the spot. His blood pumped, there was a roaring in his ears that had nothing to do with the rushing of the river over the stones. That figure, hanging from the tree, he would know it anywhere, he raced forward, panic filling his being.

'Mallard,' he sobbed. 'I'll get you down! I'll get you . . .'

Throwing aside his rods, he scrambled up towards the trees, his feet slipping on the muddy earth. It was a steep slope, wet and treacherous. He was only halfway up when he lost his foothold and down he went, sliding, falling, all the way to the river and the rocks waiting below.

He knew only a moment of consciousness as his head struck an enormous stone.

'Anna,' he whispered before oblivion swept over him like a black cloak, shrouding him in deep and silent darkness.

Tell Tale Todd, on his way up Mill Brae, wasn't sure if his eyes were deceiving him when he saw Andrew Mallard, hanging from a branch that overhung the river, the rope that held him swinging him gently this way and that.

Todd rubbed his eyes, unable to believe what he was seeing. He had drunk more than his usual amount of drams that morning – old Shoris had been celebrating his birthday with Bob the Post when Todd had made his timely arrival into the scene. A bottle of best malt whisky had stood tantalizingly on the table, three quarters full, Shoris and Bob having consumed between them the first generous drams from the newly opened bottle.

Todd had willingly helped them to reduce the level still further and by the time he emerged from Bridge End Cottage he was seeing the world through a decidedly rosy haze.

But Firth, Todd's horse, had been glad to be on his way. He knew the route so well he didn't need the reins to remind him as he plodded up the steep hill, strong shoulders rippling, head bent.

'Whoa!' Todd's sudden commanding roar unnerved Firth. He snickered and tossed his mane, the delivery van rolled back a foot, Firth braced himself and the wheels stopped turning.

Todd jumped down, hardly aware of what he was doing, knowing only that a terrible feeling of nausea churned in his stomach, one that had nothing to do with the amount of malt whisky he had drunk.

He scrambled down the steep bank, his feet slithering on moss and wet leaves, the river thundering below him. Shadows were all around him, the shadows of trees, blotting out the sun, making him shiver, bringing out the goose pimples on his hairy brown arms.

His nose ran, his heart raced. He tripped over something lying on the ground, his heart accelerated faster, his blood gushed in his ears.

'Master Peter!' He stood there, staring down at the boy lying at his feet, his head resting on a huge boulder, his body twisted in an unnatural pose, arms outflung, eyes staring, eyes of blue that would never again see the beauty of a summer sky nor look with joy on the wildflowers upon which his body lay.

Todd didn't want to raise his head to the sight he knew awaited him amongst the waving branches of green. Tears blinding him, he forced his eyes upward and, through a watery mist, he saw what he hadn't wanted to acknowledge from the road: the boy's tutor, still swaying gently on the rope that had broken his neck and killed him.

'Dear God!' Todd, sober suddenly, tried desperately to grasp what had caused such a terrible tragedy. The earth beneath the

217

trees was treacherous with mud and dank leaves, somebody had tried to gain a foothold there recently, the marks of their upward progress could plainly be seen – together with those of their downward plunge.

Todd brought his eyes back to Peter. His hands were bloody and torn, his fingernails broken . . . he had tried to save Andrew Mallard . . . and he had died in the attempt.

Todd removed his jacket and threw it over the boy before he turned away, wishing that he didn't have to be the one to carry this dreadful news abroad. This was one tale that he wouldn't enjoy telling, and his steps dragged as he made his way back to the road and the patiently waiting Firth.

The deaths of Andrew Mallard and Peter Noble were officially put down as tragic accidents, but the people of the glen weren't so easily convinced.

'Somebody had it in for Mr Mallard,' said Janet McCrae with a sad shake of her head. 'Och, I know he was aye swingin' about in yon woods but he was a strong man and he knew what he was doing. He was too canny by far to just go and hang himself at the end o' a rope.'

'It's Master Peter I weep for,' old Grace said with a watery sniff. 'He and Anna both. They were such a lovely pair, just like a couple o' bairns wi' all the world at their feet.'

Miss Priscilla was also very upset by the incident and it was in the homely peace of Knock Farm that Anna found much of her solace though, as yet, she hadn't fully taken in the fact that she would never see Peter again.

Beth Jordan, too, offered Anna her support, in her own practical fashion. 'I'm very sorry, Anna,' Beth had told her. 'I know how much Peter meant to you and it was a dreadful way to die. He'll be remembered as a hero of course, trying to save his tutor the way he did, and it really is quite romantic when you stop to think about it. You'll find somebody else, you're young and you'll forget. I myself don't know how I would feel if the same thing had happened to me, that's why I have to look to my future. One day I'm going to marry Lucas. I've made up my mind about that.'

Anna looked at her friend's determined expression, her tightly set mouth, and fully believed what she said.

*   *   *

218

After the funeral of his brother, Lucas was strange and quiet. Anna tried to break through the barriers; they had both loved Peter, they could comfort one another by talking about him.

'He was always too soft,' was all Lucas would say. 'People like him ask for everything they get, it just came to him sooner, that's all.'

Anna wasn't deceived by his cynicism. She saw the tortured look in his eyes, the pain on his face. He and Peter had been inseparable – she knew he would suffer the heartache and the emptiness of his loss for the rest of his days.

Lady Pandora was stunned by events. Peter had been her favourite nephew, kind, thoughtful, never harsh like Lucas; a boy who had considered others and one whose heart had been as romantic and as loving as her own. As for Andrew, she ached with grief for him. Her feelings for him had never been as strong as his for her but she had become attached to him and had loved him for his passion and his fierce loyalty to her. She would never get over the tragedy of it all! Never!

At first she refused to see anybody, go anywhere, until one day Anna came to her and they cried in one another's arms for their beloved Peter.

'You'll come to me now, Anna,' Lady Pandora said, her lovely face pale with anguish. 'You're growing up fast, losing Peter has turned you from a girl into a woman; no one can stop you living your own life now.'

'Ay, you're right, I have grown up and I will come to you,' Anna said huskily. 'Peter gave me so much joy when we were together, we were just children, running wild and free. He's so far away now – yet so near. He wanted nothing more for me than my happiness, he wanted me at Noble House and that is where my future must lie.'

Adam, his crudely handsome face serious, found it difficult to put his feelings into words. 'Too bad about Peter, Anna,' he said awkwardly. 'It was a terrible thing to happen. I never knew him very well. I always felt he and that brother o' his were snobs but you seem to get on well wi' that sort. I don't know what it's like to love anybody the way you do so I don't really know what you're feeling – except – if anything happened to you I don't know what I'd do.'

'Then you *can* love, Adam,' she said quietly. 'You just don't know how to show it, that's all.'

'I don't know about that, I do bad things all the time. Something in me makes me do them, everybody says it's because I'm mad as well as bad.'

'You're neither o' these things, Adam, you're just unhappy, that's all.'

'I was mad enough to try and get money out o' Father because I heard something I shouldn't.'

She had smiled a little at that. 'We all do things we aren't supposed to do, it doesn't mean we're mad – just human, Adam.'

'Do you think so, Anna, really and truly?'

'Really and truly, Adam, so don't worry about it anymore.'

In her days and nights of terrible grief that followed Anna turned to many people for comfort but most of all she turned to Magnus, he who had protected her all through her infancy and whose arms were waiting to take her and hold her and murmur soothing words in her ear.

'There, there, my babby,' he whispered, his hazel eyes oddly bright. 'I'm here, I'll never leave you, I'll always be here to look after you. When all this is over, I'm going to take you to see our mother and to hell with what *he* says. She knows things, Anna, things about you and me that we ought to know about too. Together we'll find out about the past, but for now I'll be here whenever you need me.'

But the one thing he couldn't do was heal her broken heart, nobody could do that. She would walk alone, through the valley of shadows, never knowing when the brightness would come again, living, existing, one day at a time.

Roderick was the only one who seemed unaffected by the tragic deaths. He was his old self again, as strong as a bull, full of self-confidence, striding about the glen, twirling his cane, lifting his hat to the ladies.

He had never mentioned either Mallard or Peter since the accident but one morning he said to Anna, 'I'm sorry about the lad, Anna, I know he meant a lot to you. He shouldn't have died, it wasn't meant for him.'

Strange words, full of hidden meaning – and no mention of Andrew Mallard – as if he hadn't existed – as if . . .

Anna recoiled in horror. Could he have hated Mallard so much? There had been talk about the enmity that had existed between the two men; rumours had spread about Mallard's rough handling of Roderick the night he had visited Lady Pandora at The House of Noble . . . And afterwards, Roderick, found bound and beaten and left to die in the woods. Nobody treated Roderick like that and got away with it . . . no one . . .

It could have been any one of a number of people who despised him and wished him out of the way . . . but had he laid the blame at the tutor's door . . . ? Surely not even Roderick would be capable of such cruelty.

Anna knew that she must find out. With a stab of pain, she thought of her darling Peter, and knew that she must not let her grief destroy her. She must be strong, for she owed it to him to discover the truth – someday . . .

It was a glorious summer, the sun shone, the birds sang, but for Anna it was already over. Amongst her treasures there was a book, the diary she had kept since that snowy night last Christmas when she and Peter had fallen in love. Inside its covers she had written her deepest feelings, her innermost thoughts.

Although it was almost too painful for her to dip into that happy, golden past, one morning she awoke when the dawn of day was as yet only a promise and the beasts of the fields still slumbered on the dewy earth. Sitting up, the book on her lap, she slowly turned the pages and, as she read the words that she had written, all the laughter, the delight, the joy and the love that she and Peter had known, seemed to come tumbling out, filling her heart and her soul with their innocent beauty.

With reverent fingers she touched the little flowers that he had picked for her, the buttercups and the primroses, the celandines and the harebells, still as colourful as the day he had given them to her: the gold of the sunshine locked into the buttercups, the blue of a summer sky reflected in the fragile harebells . . . wild and free . . . She could hear him saying that, his voice filled with the warmth and the tenderness of his love for her.

Turning her head she looked towards the window. Morning had broken, filling the world with light and the ecstatic music of birdsong.

The future seemed to be beckoning to her in the fingers of sunlight poking through the trees. There were so many things she had yet to learn, mysteries to solve. Yet there was so much still to live for, so many people to love . . .

Somewhere in the shadowy past lay the answers to all her questions. Only time would tell all, for now she had to pause for a while and allow her bruised heart to heal.

'Thank you for giving me your love, Peter,' she whispered and gently she closed her book of memories.